WHAT HAVE I DONE?

ALSO BY
TERESA DRISCOLL

WHAT HAVE I DONE?

TERESA DRISCOLL

THOMAS & MERCER

Published by Thomas & Mercer, Seattle

www.apub.com

Amazon, the Amazon logo, and Thomas & Mercer are trademarks of Amazon.com, Inc., or its affiliates.

EU Product Safety contact:
Amazon Media EU S. à r.l.
38, avenue John F. Kennedy, L-1855 Luxembourg
amazonpublishing-gpsr@amazon.com

ISBN-13: 9781662523151
eISBN: 9781662523168

Cover design by Dan Mogford
Cover image: © IndustryAndTravel / Shutterstock; © icarmen13 / Adobe Stock; © Karina Vegas / Arcangle Images

Printed in the United States of America

WHAT HAVE I DONE?

PROLOGUE

The problem is I only had a split second to decide.

I saw her – this young stranger, heading back towards the hotel door. Towards the dark. Her head was bowed. She looked afraid. About to cry.

It made me think of my two daughters. And so – yes. I offered to share my hotel room with a complete stranger. A simple favour from a worried mother for a stranded traveller which you will either think was completely bonkers of me.

Or terribly kind.

I know the story splits the crowd, because for a while it became my best anecdote. A story I told on a loop at drinks and dinners and parties. A story to draw a crowd. And yes, to divide that crowd.

You need to come over here. You'll never guess what Laura did in France.

Back then I genuinely thought the story harmless. Had no idea of the dark place it would lead to. Back then I enjoyed trying to guess who would say I did the right thing. And who would widen their eyes in horror.

Are you completely mad, Laura? Anything could have happened.

I shook my head at the naysayers because I could not see the danger. And I felt proud that somewhere in the world was the girl's mother, who would hear the story from the *other* side and be glad that I did what I did. Am who I am.

My tale travelled so well that some people even tried to tell it back to me . . . not knowing it was mine.

Here's a good one for you. I heard about this woman at an airport in France . . .

I can't remember when the story changed. At first there were just small and puzzling things happening around me that I did not realise were in any way connected.

But then the little things became much bigger things. Much darker things.

Slowly the silt was stirred from the bottom of the once clear and perfect pool of my life until I got very scared.

Stopped telling the story at all.

And now it's too late. People are dead. There are police teams and white tents at our home. And in this surreal new version of my life, I am staring at the moon through a window with bars. Very soon my picture will be on news channels across the world and I'm realising much, much too late that 'the story' was never mine to tell.

That someone is out there right this moment.

Writing a different ending . . .

CHAPTER 1

BEFORE

Laura

The truth? It wasn't just the split-second pressure. That young woman heading out into the dark on her own.

Deciding whether to help her or not made me think of the *mess* I'd made with my own two girls.

Also – and this is key – the day this whole nightmare began was one of the most stressful I can remember.

It was that day when the UK's air traffic control system went down. Airport hell. Cancellation carnage.

It felt as if everyone in the world was trying to get back to the UK, and for a time no one had any clue which flights would get off the ground. And which would not.

I was in Barcelona on business, with a family party to get back home to finalise. It was Clara's eighteenth and I needed to make it special – partly because her sister might not be there (probably wouldn't be there) but mostly because Clara was still in such a muddle. Undecided whether to take a gap year or go straight to university. And I wasn't handling that very well. Just as I didn't seem able to handle anything in the mum department very well anymore.

At first, as my flight was called, I really thought I'd got away with it. As word spread around the terminal of the growing UK air traffic crisis, I was bussed to my plane and I remember clinging to the overhead strap in the packed bus as we were jostled at a higher speed than usual and then climbing the steps to the plane, thinking – *thank the gods.*

But the cabin crew seemed tense and our pilot soon confirmed why. *We have a slot . . . but we have to be ready. If we miss it, I don't know what will happen.*

I have never seen passengers load the overhead cabins so quickly, mothers having terse words with bickering children all round me, strapping them in with warp-speed efficiency. *No – you can't have your colouring book. It's in the other bag. Not yet. After take-off.*

I checked the drinks list, thinking a celebratory gin and tonic would very soon be very much in order. *I have got lucky. I am going home . . .* The engines roared.

And then? Absolutely nothing. Fifteen minutes. Twenty. At last, after half an hour of twitching and mutterings, the engines quietened and the pilot was back on the intercom to share that we had lost our slot and that the situation was 'evolving'.

How I *hate* that word. A sneaky little word that tries to hint at a range of outcomes, but is really camouflage for 'all hope is lost'.

Whatever. The pilot's decision was to stay on the tarmac ready for take-off, so that he could respond quickly to any slot he was offered and taxi straight to the runway. Technically our flight was cleared, not cancelled. We were at the front of the queue.

For a while we stayed in that tense little bubble of optimism, staring out of the windows as if we could somehow will the aircraft to move. A few people unbuckled themselves only to be pounced on by the air crew. It was like whack-a-mole. Staff in their navy uniforms and polka dot neckerchiefs darting from row to row. Firm tones. Stretched smiles.

We have to keep the seat belts buckled. You have to sit back down. We must stay ready for take-off.

But children will be children.

Can I have my colouring book, Mummy?

I need the toilet!

Tensions grew. The compliant phase passed. After nearly an hour on the tarmac, colouring books were fetched. Overhead locker doors slammed. *I'm sorry but we can't expect small children to just sit here!* Adults were showing their true colours too.

A large, pink-faced man in a navy polo shirt stood up to appoint himself spokesman.

We need information! I'm putting this all over social media, you know.

Next, the air conditioning was switched off. A malfunction or to conserve energy, I have no idea.

Polo-shirt man was close to spontaneous combustion. I imagined (or maybe secretly dreamed of?) him in a medical emergency.

The upshot – and I always shudder at the memory of this part of the story – is we were on the sweltering tarmac for four hours, most of the time without air conditioning.

And then they bussed us straight back to the terminal.

Where hundreds if not thousands of people were now ahead of us in the queues for information and alternative tickets.

This is when I blush. The champagne socialist. Me the middle child of a factory worker and a mechanic dad, now able – and apparently all too willing – to buy my way out of discomfort.

So – yes; I remember scanning the queues and the airline signs and thinking – *I will throw money at this.*

My original flight had been with a budget airline. Now I would flash my credit card at any big-name airline happy to take my euros.

I got in one of the shorter queues. And I watched, with that familiar frisson of guilt, the parents across the concourse on their phones, struggling with small children and multiple suitcases, and was just grateful that my two girls are grown. And that my business is doing well.

I was in the queue for more than an hour, scrolling social media and news channels on my phone. The information boards by now were showing most flights to the UK as *cancelled.* Passengers were accosting airline reps, who looked utterly defeated.

Some families were setting up little camps on the floor. Others were on phones trying to get hotel rooms.

News outlets were already starting to share that the traffic control blip would have knock-on delays for days. The cascade of cancellations leaving all the aircraft and crews 'in the wrong places'. It was 'leaves on the line' times a million.

There was advice on consumer rights. How to get your money back. What your airline should be offering you by way of food.

I decided to worry about all that later and just get out of Spain.

I'd overheard a couple mumbling in the queue ahead of me about trying to get a flight to France and then the Eurostar to London. This seemed to be my best bet too. Everyone was moaning that prices were rocketing. For flights and trains and hotels. I resolved to pay whatever it took to get myself home – first-class seats if that was all that was going – and worry about compensation afterwards. I had my younger daughter's eighteenth birthday to host. I also had an elder daughter who was living in the wilds of Scotland. And still wasn't speaking to me.

Would Ruby even come to her sister's party?

Bottom line was, I could not stay in Barcelona.

By the time I got to the front of the queue, the woman was on autopilot. 'We don't have any flights to the UK this evening or tomorrow. I'm sorry.'

'How about Paris?'

'Paris?' She started tapping on her keyboard. 'Do you mind which airport?'

'No.' I frowned. Didn't even realise Paris had more than one.

'Nothing for Charles de Gaulle but we have evening flights to both alternative airports – Orly and Beauvais. Are you interested?'

I was.

And while I waited for my new flight to an airport I'd never heard of but which, I assumed, had Ubers and buses that could get me to a Eurostar train the following morning, I was on my bookings site to clinch a hotel room near the unheard-of airport.

Bingo. Last one. Inflated price. Only three stars – everything else booked – but who cared? I put in my credit card details and waited for the confirmation email.

And that's where 'the story' begins proper.

The Paris airport, many kilometres from the city centre, had an industrial estate nearby with budget hotels, including mine, and some other unidentifiable buildings along with huge parking lots.

I queued for a taxi, gave the name of the hotel and expected to be taken to the entrance. But after ten minutes or so weaving through a concrete jungle, the cab driver stopped by a barrier, raised his arms in frustration and told me this was as close as he could get.

I was thrown. And anxious. It was pitch-black outside, and beyond the barrier there was a dark walkway leading to some kind of underpass with faint lights far in the distance. I didn't like the look of the setting at all. There seemed to be a sprawl of parking areas, possibly off-site airport parking, but no signs of life anywhere.

I asked him again to take me to the hotel entrance.

'*Pas possible.*'

He told me in poor English that the barrier system was broken so his pass wasn't working that evening and I would have to walk the final stint.

I complained that I couldn't even see the hotel. He simply shrugged and pointed through the dark walkway to the distant lights.

'*La bas.*'

I got out the maps app on my phone, and sure enough it didn't look *too* far. But I was shocked at how dark and remote it felt. A horrible industrial estate sprawl.

I asked if we could drive around a different route. Approach the hotel from the other side? I said that I didn't mind paying extra, but he was either not understanding me or pretending not to.

In the end he asked bluntly. Did I want to go back to the airport? My choice.

So I paid, got out and set off down the dark walkway with my keys between the fingers of my left hand, juggling my phone torch and my suitcase with my right.

It was a while before I heard the footsteps behind me, together with the sound of another case being rolled along. I picked up my pace. The footsteps picked up pace. I was too afraid to turn around to see who the person was for fear of inviting a chase.

By the time I made it through the walkway, the underpass and around the corner to the hotel I was almost in tears.

There were revolving doors and the relief of bright lights and a man on reception in a grey uniform. It was a modest chain long since past its best, but I had never been so relieved to check in.

My twin room was confirmed. And yes – I had got lucky with my reservation, he said. The hotel was now fully booked.

It was only as I stepped to the side to sort out my room key card and the mess inside my handbag that I noticed her properly.

Turned out the footsteps following me belonged to a young woman – early twenties, maybe – who had a similar small suitcase to mine, but in scuffed bright pink, and a large black rucksack. She looked about the same age as my eldest daughter and I remember clearly being relieved she was OK. Both of us safe now.

I was still putting my keys back into my handbag when I overheard her conversation at reception. The young woman didn't have a booking. Was hoping for a cancellation. This hotel had been recommended for its size when she couldn't find anywhere online.

The receptionist confirmed there was nothing. The woman practically begged. She said she would take *anything. A family room? A single room? A room that needs refurbishment?* But the pleas were pointless. There was absolutely nothing going.

She asked if she could camp out in the reception area. Company policy said 'no'. Next, she asked if he would call a taxi to take her back to the airport terminal, but the receptionist said he had tried for other guests and it was hopeless. There was an hour-to-two-hour delay given all the travel chaos, with so many passengers trying to transition through Paris. She would have to walk back to the airport. He offered to draw her a map.

I watched the young woman check her watch and glance at the dark beyond the doors and then look at the floor. Her face was so pale, I thought she was going to cry.

She stood very still for a time and then she let out this really long sigh and headed slowly back to the revolving doors. Towards the dark.

Which was when I realised I had to make my decision. My snap decision.

'Excuse me,' I said. 'I know this may sound odd. From a stranger. But I have a twin room. You could share with me if you like? Rather than walk out in the dark, I mean?'

CHAPTER 2

BEFORE

LAURA

The young woman looked shocked at first, and in the beat of that first reaction, I felt a little shocked too.

But I couldn't take the offer back, so I told her I had two daughters. That I would hate to think of either of them in the same situation. Walking alone in the dark. Everything shut.

'Obviously, it's entirely up to you. But I couldn't live with myself if I didn't at least offer.'

She looked at my luggage. She looked at me and then the colour in her face started to improve. 'You really wouldn't mind sharing?'

'Well – I'm not pretending it's ideal. But it's just one night. I'm trying to get back to the UK to organise my daughter's eighteenth birthday party. I'm going to try the Eurostar tomorrow. What about you?'

'I'm at university in York. There's no real hurry to get back. I'll probably find somewhere cheap tomorrow in the city. Do the galleries until all this craziness dies down.'

'Right.'

I could see that she still hadn't made a decision and realised she might see me as a threat. I remember looking at her luggage, her scuffed pink case, wondering suddenly if I was being a complete mug; if I was the one who should see *her* as a threat. What kind of crazy was it to go to sleep in a hotel room with a complete stranger? I was someone who always put the security bolt across. Sometimes even put a chair in front of the door.

So yes. I did have a momentary wobble. What if she stole from me in the night? My purse? My phone? My identity? What if there were no clothes in that suitcase at all. If this was all some scam with the taxi driver.

I would share this lightning flash of worry when I later told the whole story to other people. When the sceptics would list the very same fears – *What if it was a set-up, Laura? What if she was the taxi driver's daughter and there was nothing wrong with the barrier?*

Do you not watch Black Mirror*, Laura?*

But in the moment, in that hotel foyer on that dark and dreadful night, I watched relief flood across this young woman's face, and when she finally stretched out her hand – 'I'm Jade. I don't know how to thank you for this' – I felt completely and instantly reassured. And proud. Yes. Glad that she would later get on her phone and Jade's mother would be out there somewhere, so grateful for what I'd decided in that split second.

Of course, I didn't know a thing about StarBonders then.

Which meant I didn't recognise the pendant around her neck. Or any of the red flags.

It was a bit awkward – taking turns to get changed in the en-suite. Small talk. Me about my girls, skipping the truth that my elder daughter was still not talking to me. That I wasn't even sure if she would be coming to Clara's party.

Jade chatted mostly about her course. English lit. 'And no, I have absolutely no idea what I'm going to do afterwards.' She laughed. 'Please don't say *teach*. I have no patience.'

When I told her that I had read English too and now had a copywriting agency, her face lit up. 'That's crazy. So we're *both* writers. And I'm named after a rock. And so's your daughter.'

'Yes.' I was smiling. 'Though I prefer to say *precious stone*.'

'*Precious stone* then. And here we are at the same hotel on this same awful night.'

She had this excitement in her face which, looking back, was a bit odd. But I put it down to youth. Nothing more.

She changed into red checked pyjamas, and I asked what writing she did. She said, 'Just blogging. Nothing special yet.' Wouldn't be drawn.

We ordered sandwiches from room service, the only food going at the late hour. We chatted a bit more. She had this slightly weird thing of pointing out connections between us – *Oh look, we both have red phone cases too*, that sort of thing. She was very into horoscopes and positively squealed when she found we were both Librans. And then, just like my own daughters, she stopped talking as if her batteries had suddenly run out. She disappeared into her phone, glued to the screen, until I turned out the bedside light alongside my single bed.

'Night Jade.'

'Night Laura.'

When I woke up at just seven thirty, she was gone. There was a thank-you note on the bedside locker with euros for her share of the room. And that was that.

As I said, I hadn't recognised her pendant.

And I thought it was just my muddled mind that was confused to see my phone on the bedside locker when I thought I'd popped it under my pillow.

After breakfast, I walked back in the light to the airport to get my steps in, paid a king's ransom for a taxi to the Eurostar, and just thought I had a bit of a story to tell.

I had no idea where it would all lead.

How could I?

CHAPTER 3

BEFORE

LAURA

The first strange thing happened a few weeks later.

I was still playing catch-up after the chaos of only just making it home to host Clara's party and having my parents to stay for a week. I was also feeling down because Ruby hadn't attended either the family 'do' or Clara's more raucous nightclub trip for friends (which involved two limousines and a lot of sleeping bags and sick buckets).

It had been a busy time at work, rewriting a series of websites for a major client, and I had let things at home slide.

I find it easy enough to keep on top of food and laundry with online deliveries and a well-kitted utility. But I hadn't made it to the dry-cleaner's in a long while.

Every night I passed the door of Ruby's room with that familiar leaden feeling deep inside me. Every night I texted her to say *I love you and I miss you, Ruby,* waiting and longing for the three pulsing dots which never came. And every night I walked past the bulging dry-cleaning zipped hamper on the landing, thinking – *I really must take that this week.*

And then one Friday I raced up the stairs to get changed for a drinks party and the dry-cleaning hamper thingy was gone.

Joe, my husband, was meeting me at the party straight from work, and I had one of those moments when I realised I really should stop taking him for granted. I assumed it had to be him. He had a lot of stuff in that hamper too.

I'd been so busy for weeks and I'm not at my best when I'm stretched, so I ran my fingers along the dresses on the rail in our dressing room until I reached his favourite. An aubergine fitted number – shorter than I felt was wise for my age but which Joe loved. *You still have the legs, Laura.*

'Thank you,' I said, kissing him on the cheek as he turned up to the party about half an hour after me.

'For what?' he said, eyes evidently taking in the dress.

'For taking the dry-cleaning in.'

'I'm sorry but you must be mistaking me for one of your other husbands.' He just looked a little puzzled then smiled again. 'By the way, you look nice.'

'Seriously? You didn't take the dry-cleaning in for me?' I'd been mentioning it every night for a while. 'The hamper's gone.'

'Wendy?'

I frowned. I'd never asked our cleaner to handle our dry-cleaning before. It seemed unlikely.

'So – enough of airing our dirty laundry in public. Who's here?' He started to scan the room for familiar friends and I laughed at his small joke, then moved off to see who hadn't yet heard my airport story.

It was a nice party. One of those evenings when you know most of the people and drink just enough. But not too much. We'd planned for one of us to drive the other home but each went one glass of wine over the deal so booked an Uber instead.

Later, in our en-suite, I asked Joe again if he didn't think it was a bit odd. The dry-cleaning disappearing. By this time, I'd kicked off my heels and marched around the whole house, searching cupboards and the utility, in case Wendy had just tidied away the soft canvas hamper.

'Clara?' He was cleaning his teeth, spitting between words.

'The same Clara who still hasn't passed her driving test. And has an allergy to anything *household*.'

Joe smiled at me through the mirror and then I paused before asking the question that was always a risk. Especially after a nice evening together. An evening in which he had put his hand on the small of my back, a secret little signal between us. *Laters.*

'Have you heard from Ruby?'

It was like a slow drip of lemon juice on my open wound. The fact that Ruby and her father were still in touch. A part of me was glad, of course. Relieved. I needed to know that she had support; that she was not out there totally alone. That there was a line of communication at least. But a bigger part of me felt this unnatural tear in the universe. That the daughter I loved as much as him was in touch with Joe. But not with me.

I imagined this was what it must feel like to be divorced. To know there was a separate line of communication with children. A whole different relationship going on. One that was not supposed to be your business.

'She's fine.' He said it in that tone I had so come to hate. The tone that warned me – *Please don't ask me more questions. Please don't push it. Not tonight.*

'I just wondered if she'd sent anything for Clara's birthday. Clara won't say.'

'You know the deal here.' He put his toothbrush back into the glass tumbler and turned to put his arms around my shoulders. 'I check in every week with her and I always pass on your love. And I tell Ruby that I won't gossip. I won't take sides in this. But I am always here for her. As are you.' He let out a long sigh. 'She knows that you love her. She'll come round.'

'Will she? It's been nearly a year, Joe.' Saying the words out loud always made it all the more inconceivable. Horrific. My Ruby. No proper contact. *Nearly a year.*

'If I push it with Ruby, I'm worried she'll cut off contact with me too. You know that.'

'Sure. I know. Sorry.'

I reached for my own toothbrush and resisted the urge to ask for the millionth time if he blamed me too. For what had gone so horribly wrong between me and Ruby.

CHAPTER 4

BEFORE

Laura

The next morning the first girl died.

And the worst thing? The most *terrible* thing was that her death was only reported because of the delays it caused.

I had no idea at first of any connection. It was only much later at the inquest that the media used her picture. Wearing the same pendant worn by Jade at the airport hotel. Different girl. Same pendant.

No. The worst thing I will always remember is the first girl's death was only reported for the traffic hold-ups it caused on the M5. Imagine that? A beautiful girl dead much too young and on the radio news she was a traffic report.

I only heard about it because the morning after the party Joe messaged me on his way to Bristol to say the motorway was shut and he was being re-routed. I'd talked about meeting a client in Taunton and he wanted to warn me.

So I checked in with the local radio news and it came up that a section of motorway was closed because of a death being investigated by police. They said it was not a road accident. And that a bridge over the motorway was also closed. The presenter thanked drivers for phoning in with updates.

'It's on socials. Sounds like a suicide,' Clara said, biting into her toast as she checked her phone, her face pale.

'Well I hope they're not gossiping on social media. Because that sounds truly awful.'

'Yeah. Melody has to deal with that sometimes.'

Melody is my niece. Clara's cousin. A paramedic.

I scanned the website for the local newspaper on my phone and there were more details. No name but the reports confirmed the death was a twenty-year-old girl. The road was expected to be closed for some time.

'How terrible,' I repeated. And yes – I was thinking of Ruby. And I was thinking of the dead girl's family. And how the hell a girl with her whole life ahead of her could decide to end it so very brutally. From a bridge.

I remembered reading an interview with a mother who had lost a daughter to suicide. She said she kept her room exactly as it was, changing the sheets every week *because I like them to be fresh. Can't explain why . . .*

I looked again at Clara and she tilted her head, still very pale. I thought of that mother changing her child's bed and tried very hard to compose myself in front of my own daughter.

'So, what are you up to today, darling?'

I knew that for Clara's sake I needed to try to stop talking about the girl's death; to keep my tone lighter. My family are always telling me I take other people's troubles and tragedies too much to heart. That I'm prone to assume both responsibility and empathy for things that are not my problem. Sometimes I worry they may be right. Tragedies and reports of any kind of violence always cut me deeply. I took a quiz once which said I might be some kind of HSP – highly sensitive person.

I think Joe fears my worrying and this particular hypersensitivity is at the root of what went so wrong between me and Ruby.

So I masked it that morning. Pushed the feelings down. And as Clara finished her toast, I deliberately didn't say anything more about the girl on the motorway because I wanted Clara to know I was concentrating on *her*. Focused on *her*. I had messed up my relationship with one daughter and was determined not to make the same mistake twice.

'I might go into town. Just to potter,' she said finally, and so I offered her a lift, explaining I'd need to grab an Uber first as I'd left my car near last night's party. And that was when I remembered the dry-cleaning and made the phone call as I loaded the dishwasher.

'Hi. Mrs Harry here. I have an account.' I gave the number from my loyalty card and then explained there was a bit of a puzzle as we had a missing canvas bag of dry-cleaning. One of the company's branded little square zipper hampers. I hadn't been able to get hold of Wendy and was starting to think maybe she had done me a favour and dropped it off.

'Ah yes. The bag with your ID came in yesterday. It will be ready after four o'clock.'

I felt a sweep of relief. There were some favourite silk shirts in that hamper. And a very good suit of Joe's.

'Such a relief. I'll pick it up later. By the way – do you have a note of who brought it in? Was it Mrs Hawkins?' I was making a mental note to text a thank-you to Wendy with the rider to please keep me up to speed the next time. To spare more confusion.

'No. Note here says your daughter brought it in.'

'My *daughter?*'

I was stunned. I turned my face, phone pressed to my chest. 'Clara – you didn't take the dry-cleaning in, did you?'

'Sorry. Dry-cleaning? No. Was I supposed to?'

'No. And Ruby. She hasn't visited has she?'

'No, Mum.' Her expression looked appalled. I was breaking the agreement not to press her about Ruby. 'You know she hasn't. Why are you even asking? You know it always causes a row.'

I turned back to the dishwasher and put the phone back to my ear. 'Sorry. Just a bit of confusion this end. I'll see you after four.'

CHAPTER 5

LETTERS FROM A LIGHTHOUSE

THE STARBONDERS BLOG

Hello StarBonders!

How are you all this week? Apologies that this blog is a day late but I've been dealing with 'some stuff'. And I just know you are the people, maybe the only people, who will understand.

None of us have ever pretended this was going to be easy, have we? And this week, I guess it was my turn for a dip. I have always promised to be honest with you guys, and so the truth is things really haven't been easy for me at all these past few days.

I've had a few dark moments. Wondered if I was good enough for this calling. But that's all a part of this, isn't it? Doubting ourselves. Being forced to dig deep. After all, no one stared into the night sky without wonder and awe . . . and just a little bit of trepidation. That awareness that all the answers are out there. Our destinies set already . . .

So what I want to share this week is the need for courage. Because, hard as this is, I feel sure that I'm going to come through this wave stronger than ever – sure that very soon the stars will burn even brighter for me.

Because every level, every chapter on this journey, has its own lessons for sure. Which is why we're all here, isn't it? For the courage to . . . do . . . the . . . work.

So I wanted to remind you that I am always here for you. To learn with you. And to help you. I'm going through the ups and downs of this just as you are. So if your StarBonders journey is hitting some bumps in the road – or worse, entering some dark shadows – please know that you're not alone.

This path can be very tough. And not everyone around us is going to understand. Not everyone believes as we do.

But the important thing for you to remember is that the team here at the StarBonders Lighthouse always has someone at the end of our messaging service with the expertise and energy to help you.

Marie was the one on our team who really helped me this week – with one of her incredible readings. So I want to remind you that if you want a personal StarBonders reading to work through a particular problem you can click HERE and we'll get back to you as quickly as we possibly can. We can take all payment methods completely safely.

And if you want to purchase one of our new pendants – all now available in different finishes and with different-coloured leather cords – then you can click HERE to see all the updates on our shop.

I need to sign off now, but send you my love and my blessing for a good week ahead. Remember too that you have been chosen as one of the lucky ones.

Some outsiders – maybe even people we care about – may not understand or even believe in the things we know to be true. Try to be patient with them. Try to feel sadness and not anger towards them.

It is not easy to know that you have the perfect StarBonders partner out there already, waiting for you. Maybe someone you have yet to meet. Maybe someone you have already met. That cosmic certainty and that sure destiny can be both comforting and paradoxically scary. We all know that. But how much harder and sadder and more terrible to never know this journey at all. So you must try to be kind in the face of the jealousy of the doubters; of those outside our truths. Just don't let them steer you astray.

Next week I will be sharing the story of Alicia, who has made it to the next level. YES! A whole year apart from her StarBonders match and now at last they are reunited. She has done the work and has made it to that very special place we all long for. True union. True happiness. Until then, much love to you all.

Phoebe xx

CHAPTER 6

BEFORE

LAURA

After picking up the dry-cleaning, still utterly confused over what was going on, I ran into Ned's mother. And it was like a bomb going off.

It was not the first time I'd seen her since everything that happened. We live in the same area, after all. We share the same market town as our nearest shopping destination so I had always known – and to be frank, dreaded – that it would happen.

That last time I'd spotted Ned's mother in the street – maybe six months back – it was a shock how physical it felt. Like a slap to the face, pulling me up and bringing it all back so vividly. What happened to her son. And also what happened between me and Ruby as a consequence. But that first time his mother hadn't seen me. I had managed to cross the street and avoid her. I rushed back to the car park and remember sitting in my car with my pulse pounding in my ears. I felt so sad and so sorry for her. All that she had been through. But the truth is the extremity of my discomfort was really upset over all that Ned's death had meant for me.

Me and Ruby.

This time, in the coffee shop after I'd picked up the dry-cleaning, I wasn't prepared. I'd laid the dry-cleaning on its familiar grey hangers on the back seat of my car and decided on the treat of a cappuccino and carrot cake at my favourite place. I was still puzzling over how the mistake had happened. Who had taken the dry-cleaning in? And why did the shop think it was 'my daughter'? I'd pushed them for a description but the member of staff who'd taken in the hamper wasn't on duty. I was fobbed off. Told that maybe it was just a misunderstanding and they were confusing me with another customer.

And so I felt uneasy as I stirred the heart-shaped dusting of cocoa into the frothy milk, dipping my finger into the foamy top and licking my finger. I'm someone who always finds drinks served in coffee chains too hot, unlike Joe who has an asbestos tongue. And so I was waiting for the coffee to cool a little, scooping a small piece of carrot cake on to my fork, when I saw her walk through the door and join the queue.

It knocked me sideways again, and I'm not going to lie. It occurred to me to hide. To abandon the cake and coffee and dart into the toilets at the rear. My first thought was I could venture back out once Ned's mother was seated and hurry past, hopefully without her noticing.

I wanted to spare both of us the awkwardness, but it was too late. She looked across the room and clearly saw me. Locked eyes for a moment. A sweep of something deeply uncomfortable passed across her face. I had expected anger, not because I had ever felt genuinely responsible for what happened to Ned but because I knew she thought differently.

But it wasn't anger. It was just this deep sadness. True sorrow. It was that picture of grief which is the most haunting of all. When it catches someone out in a moment they're not expecting it.

I realised that she was thinking very suddenly and very intensely of her son. Her only boy gone. It had thrown her off balance. She looked down at the floor and reached her right hand to the counter to steady herself. It made me feel terribly sad for her and I looked down at my carrot cake, ashamed to be there. To have made her feel that way.

I thought about how often I'd been caught out myself when my father died. He was only in his late forties. A sudden massive stroke. And for years it would surprise me how some small thing would suddenly remind me of him. Catching the back of someone's head with the same kind of haircut. Hearing a favourite song of his. Remembering him getting home from work. *Hello, darling girl.* It still does catch me out sometimes, and I could feel my eyes tearing up as I stared at the cream frosting of my cake, wishing I was not causing that same discomfort in Ned's mother.

I kept staring at my cake, but out of the corner of my eye, I could see her fuchsia jacket moving forward. Soon she was at the head of the queue, ordering a coffee and toasted sandwich to go. I wondered if that had always been her plan. A takeout. Or if she had changed that plan because of me. She paid and, as she waited for the order, she walked across to my table.

'I just need to say,' she began, but her voice broke. She coughed. Her head twitched. She looked away and then straight at me again. 'I just need to say that Ned was not a bad person.'

'I do know that. I'm so sorry for your loss. Truly I am.'

'I think we both know that isn't true, Laura, is it?' She kept her eyes locked on mine for just a moment longer and then she held her chin up as if she had done something important. And it was honestly as if another little bit of me died inside.

Later I would think of many things I should have said. Added. But we are so bad at death and grief, aren't we? And in the moment, given the chasm between us, I couldn't think of anything to say at all.

And so I just watched her fetch her toasted sandwich and her coffee and then turn and leave.

I waited five, maybe ten minutes, to be sure she had moved well away from the shop, and then I got up and left, without touching my drink or my now ridiculous piece of cake.

CHAPTER 7

NOW

LAURA

Thursday. Some two months since I met Jade at the airport and my first full day in police custody.

It still feels shocking and frightening and, above all, surreal.

Until this nightmare, my only real contact with the police was over what happened to Ned. I thought it was the worst thing we would ever go through as a family.

How wrong I was.

Right through the night I have felt this rising panic, wanting to bang on the cell door to scream and scream – *I have done nothing wrong! Nothing . . . wrong!*

But I'm not going to be believed, am I? *Well, she would say that, wouldn't she?*

I keep thinking of those poor postmasters and postmistresses sent to jail for crimes they had never committed. Wrongly accused of stealing money when it was a computer glitch all along.

I became obsessed with that scandal because I did some copywriting for charities before I set up on my own – campaigns against scams and injustices. So when the entirely innocent postmasters told their stories of being sent to jail, I shouted at the television. *How can this happen in our country?*

And now, unbelievably, it's me.

Someone dead. Me a suspect.

They have used the word *murder*. At the front desk they actually typed the word *murder* into the computer alongside my name . . . *Laura Harry, arrested in connection with . . .*

Me, the woman who pays her taxes early and her parking fines the day they arrive. The woman who's never even had a speeding ticket.

I've turned down the duty lawyer and so we're waiting for my own solicitor. I haven't mentioned that he's only ever done our house purchases and wills . . .

What I'm trying to do is buy time. To go over it all in my head. Scene by scene. Week by week. Trying desperately to figure out what the bloody hell is really going on here.

And how I'm going to get myself out of this nightmare.

CHAPTER 8

BEFORE

RUBY

Ruby took in the view of the lake and tried not to think of home. The sea. The coastal paths. Scotland really was as beautiful and magical as she'd imagined. But it was very different from all that had once been her anchor.

She was seated outside a favourite café. It was chilly with a strong breeze but she'd layered up rather than sit inside. This vista too good to miss.

And then another text pinged into her phone.

We cannot fight this Ruby. RING me . . .

The sixth message from Scott today.

A familiar unease growled in her stomach. The view and the calm shattered. Ruby closed her eyes and slid her phone into her pocket. How she wished now that she had never met Scott. Never made the terrible mistake of imagining they could just be friends.

The problem was she'd been so very lonely when she first arrived in the Highlands, and Scott was the first person to be kind.

Sometimes she agonised over whether she had unintentionally sent any mixed messages; but she can't see that she did. From the off she had made it clear she was not ready for any kind of relationship. Not with anyone. Not after Ned.

It was actually how they'd bonded, her and Scott. He'd had a traumatic break-up too and implied he was *over all of that nonsense*. So she mistakenly saw him as safe company.

They hung out a bit. Then a lot. Cinema. Cocktails. Takeaways and Netflix. He confessed more details of his romantic tragedy. The cliché of his girlfriend sleeping with his best mate. Ruby could not bear to share what exactly had happened with Ned. All she said was she too was scarred.

And then, over time, Scott started to talk about something called StarBonders. He dropped it into conversation lightly at first and Ruby was surprised. She'd seen some stuff and nonsense blowing up on socials, endless misquoting of Plato, and didn't think Scott would fall for that kind of thing. But he was lonely and hurt, she realised. And so she bit her tongue.

She imagined Scott would drop it. See through StarBonders over time once he regained his confidence. But it went the other way entirely. He started to talk more and more about StarBonders readings and blogging. More ominously, he then started to claim he and Ruby were some kind of 'cosmic match'. Became borderline obsessive.

And now?

Ruby took the phone from her pocket to look again at the message.

We cannot fight this, Ruby.

A chill passed through her, and not from the weather. Last night there had been a scene at her house and she'd really thought Scott would get the message. Leave her alone.

Ruby took in the sprinkling of cocoa on her coffee. Pretty. The shape of a flower. She was surprised to find this really did take her home. Made her think of Clara. This strong image suddenly of the cream-and-chrome coffee machine in the kitchen. Her sister had worked as a barista one summer and was for a time almost obsessively into coffee art. She'd made everyone proper coffee every morning during that fad, creating hearts and animal shapes and all manner of fancy finishes to the frothy milk.

Clara. It was so hard to think of her. Ruby missed her every day, and though they FaceTimed occasionally, it wasn't enough. She was surprised to feel this pang of longing. Not for home as it was now but for home as it was long ago. *Before.* For that other version of her life which was so full of fun. And hope. And all good things. The problem was thinking of home and Clara meant thinking about Ned and the awful memories of everything that had happened. Reality versus nostalgia.

Reality was why she had moved to Scotland.

She'd had this idea that putting miles between them plus the beauty of the Highlands would allow her to be an entirely different version of herself. Erase the hurt. But it hadn't worked.

'Was that Scott again?' Natalie was back at the table now after a visit to the ladies. 'I saw you looking at your phone. Looking worried. Was it another message from Scott?'

'It's fine.'

'It isn't fine for someone to bombard you with messages when you've asked them not to.'

Ruby shrugged as Natalie sat down and pulled her cake closer.

'How do you manage to eat cake and never put on weight?' Ruby raised her eyebrows at her friend.

Natalie was one of those natural beauties. Dark features. Strong eyes and eyebrows. The infuriating kind who didn't need make-up. Slim too.

'Nice try but don't change the subject. We need to talk about Scott. I thought you said the guys warned him off last night.'

Ruby shrugged. She wasn't going to be sucked into talking about Scott again. Not today. She was exhausted by it. 'I mean it. The cake thing. How do you manage it?'

'It's called the gym.'

'I hate the gym.'

'So do I but I like cake.' Her friend sipped her iced water. 'So, enough of your distraction tactics. If Scott isn't taking the warnings, you should go to the police.'

'He'll get bored. I'm not worried about it.'

This was a complete lie. Scott was not only leaving texts and voice messages but had started to turn up at the hotel when he was off shift and she was working, looking for her. Just hanging around. And last night, even worse, he'd called at her house share while she was still on a bar shift. Scott had been carrying a large box. He said he had brought some vinyl she had asked to borrow – not true – and he was let in by one of her housemates. He'd then been waiting for her in the kitchen when she got off shift.

It took an argument and the intervention of two of her male housemates to get him to leave. It had been unpleasant and at one point Ruby had feared Scott was going to hit someone. All five housemates had a meeting about it later and everyone had now agreed he was never to be let in again. They were a good crowd, Ruby's housemates, but the problem was they all worked very different shifts in restaurants and hotels across the lakeside resort. Ruby would sometimes be at the house on her own, so the whole episode had freaked her out.

One of her housemates, Shelley, had also suggested involving the police. *It's getting a bit like stalking, Ruby.* But Ruby didn't want that. No way was she having the police involved in her personal relationships. Not that. *Not again.* And no way could she explain to everyone why.

'Are you listening, Ruby? I think it might be time to talk to the police. Get some advice.'

The shock of this same advice from a different friend was too much. She was remembering the message from Ned's mother when the police had turned up at the house that awful day.

'No. I'm not going to the police,' she repeated. 'He'll get bored. Back off. I'm sure of it. I'm going to wait it out.'

And then Natalie's own phone pinged with a message. She checked it and her face darkened.

'Your mum?'

'Yeah.'

'Does she need you?'

Natalie nodded. Natalie's mother had multiple sclerosis and Natalie often had to fly south to support her through hospital appointments in London. She'd had to take a lot of time off lately and the hotel wasn't keen.

'I'm getting worried Letitia will sack me.' Letitia was the hotel manager. Something of a nightmare.

'You're on a zero-hours contract. They can't sack you. And in any case, they're always short of staff. Always thrilled to have you back. You'll be fine.'

Natalie shared a small smile and typed a reply to the text.

Ruby stared again at the mountains across the lake and thought of the irony. Natalie who couldn't do enough for her mother.

And Ruby who tried not to think of her own at all.

CHAPTER 9

BEFORE

LAURA

The pendants arrived the week after the dry-cleaning mystery.

At first I thought it was a legitimate order. I often use Etsy, and so when I saw the company logo on the packing receipt, I assumed it was an item that had been delayed; an order I'd forgotten about. But as I ripped open the bubble wrap there were two pendants inside, both in chrome on thick chains.

I order many things from Etsy but never jewellery, so this was obviously some kind of mistake. I turned over the package to check the label but weirdly that was completely correct. My name in full and my address, complete with the right postcode.

I laid the two pendants on the kitchen table in front of me and frowned. The more I stared the more puzzled I became, because although I knew I hadn't ordered them, there was something weirdly *familiar* about the design.

The pendants had a circle with a star inside and some kind of central logo that looked like a fancy letter S. I was just sitting there, narrowing my eyes and trying to figure out the familiarity, when Clara appeared.

'Any coffee going?' She was still in her pyjamas, her hair in a top knot with a thick pink band at the hairline, as she slumped into the chair opposite.

'I take it you don't want the machine switched on?' I glanced across at the expensive espresso machine. Now sorely neglected. 'Put it on if you like.'

'Nah. Can't be bothered.'

'OK. Well, I've just made a pot of filter. That OK? It's on the counter.'

'Sure.'

She didn't move. I was tempted to tell her to help herself, but I took in her exhaustion and I thought of Ruby. So I moved to the kitchen counter and poured her a large mug, adding just a dash of skimmed milk. As I moved back to the kitchen table, Clara was holding one of the pendants, running her finger across the design.

'Why have you ordered StarBonders pendants?'

'I didn't order them. It's some kind of mistake. And what is StarBonders?'

'You're kidding me. You seriously don't know what StarBonders is?'

I shook my head, sipping my own coffee, noticing that Clara was now blushing.

'Jeez. I know you're old but that's ridiculous. It's getting huge. All over Insta and TikTok.'

'Well I don't do TikTok as you know. So enlighten me. What is StarBonders?'

'Cosmic love. Destined partners finding each other through star mapping. Based on Plato. Everyone knows about it.'

'Well, apparently not.' I picked up the second pendant and turned it over to look for a maker's mark. There was nothing. 'So

I was going to ask if you ordered them using my account? Is that what's happened?'

'Er, no.' Clara pulled her chin in. She tried her coffee, then went over to the counter to add more milk and a spoonful of sugar, keeping her back to me.

'I thought your body was a temple and sugar was the devil.'

'That was last week, Mother. Keep up.'

'So you didn't order these?'

'I said no.' Clara's tone was now irritated, her face oddly flushed as she turned around. 'Are you accusing me—?'

'I'm not accusing you of anything. I'm just puzzled.'

'Maybe they mixed up an order. Or you clicked on the wrong thing by mistake.' A pause. 'After *wine*.'

Her face was colouring even more and it made me uneasy. And that was when the puzzle clicked into place and I suddenly remembered where I'd seen the pendant before.

'Hang on. You remember that student I shared my room with? When air traffic went down?'

'How could any of us forget. You tell that story on a loop, Mother.'

'Well *she* was wearing one of these.'

Clara put the pendant back on the table and drank more of her coffee.

'So she's got a StarBonder. The girl you met. Lucky her.'

'But don't you think that's a bit weird?' I could feel a shift in my stomach. I certainly thought it was weird.

Clara just shrugged. 'It's not that weird. Like I said. StarBonders culture is getting huge.'

'Is it? And why did you say she was lucky? To have this StarBonder match thingy. Is that some kind of big deal?' It all sounded a bit woo woo to me.

Clara suddenly checked her phone. 'Sorry. Gotta dash. Get dressed. I've got a Zoom booked.'

'Is that about your gap year?'

Clara had been driving me and Joe frantic the last few weeks, wavering between confirming her uni place and researching gap year options. She'd made the grades for her first choice but time was running out for her to decide. She'd swung from being dead set on a degree in computer science with web development to toying with the idea of a one-year internship, which sounded odd to us. Shouldn't that come *after* her degree?

'It's a Zoom interview for a paid internship,' she said, slurping the last of her coffee.

'I still don't understand. Why would you do that first?'

'Duh. Because they might sponsor me through my degree. Loads of people do it that way.'

I looked at Clara but she refused to meet my gaze, fiddling with her hairband. I took in her hair and felt that familiar unpleasant shift in my stomach again. It reminded me of the time Ruby had started lying to us. That awful gut instinct when you know something isn't quite right and you can't figure out if it's just teenagers being teenagers or something more serious.

'Well, you'll keep us in the loop? Yes?' I widened my eyes, but too late. She was already heading for the door. 'We just want to support you. And we do have life experience, your dad and me. And if you want to talk this—'

'Sorry Mum, but I really do need to get a shower.'

Her voice trailed away. Footsteps on the stairs. And all at once I was in the kitchen alone again, just staring at the two mystery pendants.

CHAPTER 10

BEFORE

LAURA

I was totally unprepared for the row those pendants would cause with Joe. Or that two cheap bits of tin and leather could create yet another schism I wouldn't be able to fix.

What I really wanted to share with Joe was my worry over Clara. Her strange reaction to the Etsy mistake and her increasingly secretive behaviour over her personal plans. All those Zooms in her room with a 'Do Not Disturb' sign on the door.

We were having pasta with pesto for dinner together. I was back on top of my work and had finished early so I'd pushed the boat out – made the pasta and the pesto sauce myself. I wanted it to be nice. Dinner just for the two of us. Clara was out, heaven knows where, and I wanted to talk properly so I showed Joe the pendants and asked what he thought.

'Maybe you ordered them and forgot? Clicked on the wrong thing?'

He looked tired. Also distracted.

'I didn't click on the wrong thing. I know I didn't.'

And then he rolled his eyes.

I tried not to bristle. Failed. 'Look, I'm sorry if you find my conversation dull but this matters to me.'

'And where's that come from?'

'What?'

'That tone.'

'Well, you've hardly looked at me since you came in. I've made us a nice dinner. And now I try to talk to you about something which is important to me and you look as if you can't wait to get up from the table.'

'You're being dramatic.'

'*Dramatic?*' I was not expecting that. Again I tried not to overreact. Again I failed. 'I suppose there's a game on Sky Sports you want to get to. Or one of your endless gardening programmes.' Even as I heard the words leave my mouth, I realised I should have tried harder to press pause. Too late.

Ridiculous how quickly rows can blow up. Over nothing. But on we plunged . . .

'So I enjoy sport. And gardening shows. What does that make me? A criminal?' His face was flushed. Voice raised. 'I work hard. I get tired.'

'Sorry. I'm sorry. I shouldn't have said that. I'm just feeling a bit, I don't know. Disorientated. You know. The dry-cleaning. These pendants.' I was about to add that the girl at the hotel in France had been wearing one when he interrupted.

'Look, I don't want to fight either, but I'm glad you said that because I've noticed you've not been yourself and I've been a bit worried about you.' His tone was quieter.

'Worried? What do you mean – worried?'

'Well, I just wondered – and please don't bite my head off – if it might be a good idea to have a chat with the doctor again?'

'The *doctor?*'

'Yeah. I mean you remember how bad it got when you started with the whole . . .' A pause. '*You know.*'

I couldn't believe what I was hearing. *You know.* He meant the menopause. Couldn't even bring himself to say the word. I could feel the anger bubbling back up inside me.

'I was wondering if you maybe took the dry-cleaning in yourself. And then forgot. Maybe ordered these pendants. And it slipped your mind. I mean – it happens. Forgetting things. I do it too. Maybe the HRT needs tweaking?'

I just stared at him, the anger turning to something much, much worse deep inside me. I looked at the home-made pasta and the stupid bloody pesto sauce and I felt this complete disconnect. This aloneness. 'So that's your verdict. All this weird stuff going on and you think it's mad old menopausal me *forgetting*. That's what you think?'

'No darling. I didn't say that and I don't think that.' He had calmed his tone but his eyes looked somewhere else entirely. And then came the salt. 'I mean, it's just not like you. Not like old you. When the dry-cleaning thing happened, I thought that maybe your HRT wasn't working so well?' He paused again. 'And now this.' He picked up one of the pendants which I'd put on the table between us. 'Getting worked up over a couple of cheap pendants when the NHS is going down the tubes, the planet is imploding with global warming. And our family is still broken.'

It was too much. *And our family is still broken.*

I was so afraid of losing all control and saying something I would seriously regret, I just pushed away the smart blue-and-white striped bowl of pasta and stormed out of the room.

Upstairs I sat on the bed, listening to my heart pounding. And waiting for him to follow. I was still angry but regretting the flounce. I was sure Joe would come upstairs. We'd say sorry. Sort it out. But he didn't. I waited and waited.

And that was when I noticed this weird beam of light through the curtains. It was incredibly bright. Like a torch beam but with some kind of serious strength. I marched to the window, still angry, and wondering what the hell the light was. I drew back one curtain to see the shape of someone in the alleyway at the end of the garden, someone in a hoody, and this really fierce beam of light directed at the window again.

I turned my face away, worried about the impact of the beam. For a moment I thought it might be a burglar trying to get into the garden. But that was bonkers. Our lights were on in the house. What kind of burglar would snoop about with a high-beam torch when people were home? I stepped to the side and waited. Any other day, I would have called out immediately to Joe to come and look. I felt torn. If there was someone genuinely targeting our house, I would have no choice soon but to call him upstairs, row or no row.

I waited for another minute, maybe two. And then I moved the curtain slightly again. But this time all was darkness outside. All I could see was a figure running away along the alleyway.

I sat down on the bed, realising that I would have to be alone with this; that I could not tell Joe about the odd light across the garden in case he put this too down to my age. And my bloody hormones.

And it just made me feel terribly sad. Sort of hollowed out and, yes, terribly alone because it felt in that moment in the bedroom, with the faint smell of pesto sauce still wafting from the kitchen, that I had no one to talk to about anything that worried me anymore.

Not Ruby. *Gone.* Not Clara – *always in her cave.*

And not my husband either.

CHAPTER 11

BEFORE

LAURA

The next morning a second girl nearly died and StarBonders suddenly hit the headlines.

I was watching the local TV news from the breakfast bar when the story came up. The most shocking thing was a big picture of the pendant behind the newsreader. The same pendant that had so weirdly turned up at my home.

I quickly stretched for the TV remote to press pause and record. There was this huge shift in my stomach. I stared and stared at the pendant on the screen as the wave of unease spread right through me. It felt surreal to see the now-familiar symbol of the bizarre-sounding organisation – so oddly in my own orbit – now on my TV.

I read and re-read the ticker-tape headline frozen on its first line at the bottom of the screen.

Mother demands investigation into StarBonders as a second young woman tries to take her own life . . .

I frowned first at the seriousness of the story, and second, wondering how on earth the channel could run this story without the risk of being sued. It was such a grave accusation, and years of working in copywriting had taught me how careful you had to be pointing fingers at companies and brands. Especially any brand with funds. And hot-shot lawyers. So the channel must have more than just the mother's word, I thought.

My mind was racing now, and what I wanted, I realised, was to call Joe. *Come and see this.* That's why I'd instinctively paused the bulletin. And that was when I felt this horrible sinking feeling inside again. Just like last night with the torch outside.

I glanced at the counter where a plate of crumbs sat by the sink and closed my eyes.

Joe had slept in the spare room last night, and I was shocked when I got up to find he'd left early for work without even saying goodbye. This was unheard of. The only trace of him was that plate of crumbs suggesting he'd had toast for his breakfast.

For just a moment I kept my eyes closed. Overwhelmed. Once upon a time we had this strict rule, never to go to bed on a row. I felt so strongly about 'the rule' that sometimes I'd eat humble pie and say sorry, even if it wasn't my fault. Anything to close down conflict before lights out.

So how had we come to a place where I had shared no olive branch? And Joe was gone with no word. No kiss to make up?

I took a deep breath, opened my eyes and pressed play.

The newsreader summarised the accusation against StarBonders. That local police had been asked to investigate messages from StarBonders to two young women – one who had taken her own life and a second woman who had attempted to end her life.

The drive for an investigation was being spearheaded by the mother of the second young woman, who was now seriously ill.

The report cut to a clip of the mother speaking outside our regional hospital.

'Something needs to be done about this. An investigation,' she said. 'I have reported this to the police and to my local MP and I am making complaints to all the social media platforms. They should freeze the accounts of these people peddling this rubbish. I want everyone, parents especially, to be aware of the dangers.'

'It is of course terrible, the tragedy you are dealing with in your family,' the reporter said. 'But some people are saying that StarBonders is an entirely positive movement. The belief in destiny and true love. That for some people it can be uplifting. A lifeline. What do you say to them?'

'I say that they should see my daughter linked up to machines in her hospital bed and tell me how positive and uplifting they find that.' She paused, her voice cracking with emotion. 'Here,' she added, fumbling in her pocket before she lifted out her phone, scrolled its content and suddenly held up a picture of her daughter in her hospital bed. 'Here. This is my Zoe. This is what StarBonders and its popcorn Plato and twisted ideology is about. Misleading young and vulnerable minds until they can't cope. You think this is positive?'

The camera zoomed in on the photograph of a white-faced teenager wired up to a host of machines and intubated too – fat tubes and ugly apparatus clearly breathing for her.

I could feel my own breathing faltering, my heart thumping in my chest.

'The police have the bullying messages StarBonders was sending my daughter. Charging money for ridiculous readings and then getting nasty when she ran out of money. And I am not alone. I am in touch with other parents whose vulnerable children have been targeted,' the mother said.

'Can you tell us more about that?' the reporter asked.

'Not right now. But soon.' The mother paused. 'I will share everything, all of it, very soon.'

The report finished with a statement onscreen from a StarBonders representative, expounding the spirituality, the compassion and the positive energy of the movement. The statement expressed huge sympathy for the young woman's 'personal crisis' and wished her a speedy recovery, but said her 'tragic situation' had absolutely nothing to do with StarBonders.

I rewound the TV and watched the whole thing again. And then I stared once more at the plate of crumbs, feeling confused and hollowed out.

And yes. Above all, very alone.

CHAPTER 12

BEFORE

Clara

Clara could hear messages pinging into her phone. At first two or three, then a cascade.

She did not know the time, only that it felt *too early*. She must have forgotten to switch the Do Not Disturb mode back on. She opened her eyes to the glare of sunlight through the white slatted blinds. A sigh left her body as she shut her eyes again, thinking of her mother. Clara had wanted a blackout roller blind. Practical and essential, as the window was directly behind her computer desk. But her mother had said a black blind would look depressing. *This room is already like a cave, Clara. You need brightness in here.*

There had been a tussle of two, maybe three days. Clara had tried to rope her father into the row but he had raised his hands in surrender, having learned long ago to stay out of anything he perceived as 'drama'.

Her mother had argued that she had found a nice white blind with wide slats that would 'practically' shut out all the light when

Clara was gaming or designing *or whatever it is you do on that computer at all hours.*

The stand-off had continued. Clara wanted black. Her mother wanted white. *How about we just try the white slatted blind and see how it goes? Then you can have a nice bright room some of the time. Yes?* In the end Clara had caved. Which was every bit the mistake she had known it to be, and now she was stuck with sunlight streaming into her room and waking her too early every single day.

She reached for her phone, planning to silence it until she saw the WhatsApp group. Clara felt a strange unease sweep right through her body as she read the messages visible on the lock screen.

Have you heard about the girl?

Isn't it awful?

What do you think we should do?

My parents are going nuts. Should I say anything?

No. Don't say anything.

Should I stop wearing my pendant?

I don't know. I'm scared now . . .

Clara shuffled to a sitting position, her eyes still struggling against the sunlight. She opened the phone. Just 8.30 a.m.

She accessed the WhatsApp group to find the discussion verging on hysteria. Clara had no idea what they were even talking about. Some girl in hospital. *What girl?* She followed one of the links to a news website and started reading.

The strange feeling in her stomach spread until she could hear her pulse in her ears.

She swept the chat away to access another contact. Started typing.

We need to talk. The Retreat Group is going crazy. Can we do a video call?

Clara waited. The message registered as delivered but there was no reply. She went back into the retreat group chat to see the panic continuing. But there was no message from Phoebe. Nothing to calm things down.

Clara tried a few news websites. There was nothing on the national news sites yet but local papers and broadcast media all had fuller explanations of the story that had kicked all this off. Some mother blaming StarBonders for her daughter's attempt on her own life. There were clips of the mother holding up a picture of her daughter Zoe, wired to machines. She said she had discovered her daughter had become obsessed with StarBonders and had been paying a lot of money for 'personal readings', which her mother felt had made her mental health worse. Zoe had an eating disorder and was already fragile. 'No one should have been taking her money and pouring petrol on her troubles.' The mother claimed that when her daughter's money ran out, StarBonders got nasty. Pushy. Telling her daughter that she was destined to be lonely and unhappy forever.

Clara felt that horrible feeling deep in the pit of her stomach again. She thought about her cousin who had told her how awful it was to deal with that kind of self-harm call on her paramedic shifts. *I dread it. I absolutely dread it.*

And then she thought of Ned. That day they got the call and Ruby had to be sedated. All the shouting and the crying and the disbelief that someone you knew could be there one day. And not the next.

What happened with Ned was her only close experience of death, and Clara still could not process it. Still woke sometimes in the night, remembering it all. The doctor. The police. Ruby shouting. Ruby sedated. Ruby packing her bag.

Her mother pleading. Sitting on the stairs right outside Ruby's door. *Pleading.*

Clara tried to breathe in and out slowly as she had been taught. Two cycles. Three. She opened her eyes and looked back at the phone.

It was awful what had happened to this girl Zoe, and the previous girl on the bridge who was mentioned in another story. Also *allegedly* linked to StarBonders. But how could this truly have anything to do with the group? It just couldn't.

Clara skimmed through the rest of the story to see a statement. So Phoebe *had* responded? Good. That was good. Well, maybe not exactly good but it was something at least.

Clara checked her message to Phoebe again but there was no reply so she typed a new one.

I REALLY need to talk. WhatsApp video? Please?

This time three dots appeared. She waited, her palm up to her chest. At last the message loaded.

Sorry. Talking to police about this very sad story. It is AWFUL. So tragic. But absolutely nothing to do with us. Talk later. I'll message when free.

CHAPTER 13

BEFORE

Ruby

When Ruby first took the job in Scotland, she had no idea how long she'd stay. All she knew was she couldn't be at home.

It wasn't hard to get the job. Throughout her A levels and the disaster of her two terms at university, she'd worked in cafés and pubs so had a decent hospitality CV. The hotel in Scotland, still struggling with recruitment and staffing levels after Covid, bit her arm off. One quick online interview and she was offered a month's trial.

Her father had begged her to stay and let things settle down. Her mother had sat on the stairs outside her room, crying and pleading with her to reconsider. But Ruby was in this haze of shock and grief and anger. She'd never known anything like it. Ned's mother had sent a message to say she didn't want Ruby at the funeral and so she took the job, booked a train and a flight, and packed her suitcase.

She had wanted to take a taxi to the railway station but her father insisted on driving. *Please, Ruby. Let me drive you. Please let me do that.*

And so she had stood in her childhood bedroom one last time with her large roller case and her backpack ready. She looked at the corkboard where she had once pinned the revision timetable for her A levels. She stared at the books on her shelves, wishing she had more space to take her favourites. *Wuthering Heights. The Goldfinch. The Life of Pi.*

She took in the duvet cover with its primrose design, a pattern chosen by her mother who knew how much Ruby had always loved primroses in the hedgerows. And then her eyes blurred at the confusion. The memory of that day her mother had brought the duvet cover home as a surprise and Ruby was so happy. The contrast with this rage at her mother that was so huge and frightening that it felt as if her insides would explode like a bomb, splattering every part of her across the yellow flowers she had once loved. Now hated.

Ruby moved across to turn out the lamp at her desk in the corner, then pulled herself up and left the room, leaving the suitcase upright and the rucksack alongside it on the landing for a moment. Alongside the bathroom, Clara's room had the 'Do Not Disturb' sign on its white hook. Normally it was a signal she was on her computer – always on her computer – but that day it was a sign she was fed up with all the shouting and the drama.

Ruby knocked. No reply.

'It's me, Clara. I'm going now.'

There was a pause, the sound of shuffling inside the room and then the door clicked open. Clara was standing in her pyjamas, white background with pink hearts, her hair in a top knot with a wide yellow hairband and her face red from crying. She looked more like a child than a teenager.

'You're really going?'

'I have to. I'll keep in touch.'

'Please don't go, Ruby. I can't be here on my own. Not after all this. I can't do it.'

'You can and you must. You need to get those grades and get to university. You hear me?'

Clara just started to cry again and so Ruby put her arms around her sister and they held each other.

'It will all calm down, Ruby. It always calms down. You could just stay. Wait for everything—'

Ruby pulled back and held her sister's head between her hands and kissed her on the forehead. 'Not this time. I'm sorry, bunny. I've got to go.' She had called her bunny when they were younger. When Clara had a favourite story book with a family of rabbits. A lifetime ago.

She heard footsteps on the stairs and turned to see her father, reaching for her suitcase and backpack. He watched the two sisters for a moment, his skin grey, and then silently carried the bags down to the hall.

Her mother was standing in the kitchen doorway. *Please, Ruby. Please stay. You know how much I love you. I'm so very sorry. I had no idea—*

Ruby had looked at her mother, who held out her arms with her head tilted, her eyes still beseeching for some kind of reconciliation, but Ruby had stood very still and in the end had chosen not to go to her. Not to accept that hug goodbye; not even to say goodbye out loud. And some nights since, she had lain awake wondering if she had been wrong to do that. Wishing she could travel back in time.

But the problem was Ruby had no idea how to find a real path back to her mother and so she was mostly just terribly sad. Deeply and horribly sad, right down to her bones.

◆ ◆ ◆

The hotel was a good deal shabbier than the photographs on the website. Its position right by a loch was every bit as magnificent as Ruby had hoped, but it clearly lacked the investment to keep it in good condition. And, oh, my goodness – there were major staffing issues.

Ruby was completely exhausted from the long journey. A train then a flight and then another local train in Scotland. She'd been told she could have a room in the 'staff accommodation' for her trial month and would shadow a couple of shifts before she was assigned a full rota. The job would be full-time but on a zero-hours contract and would see her sharing her time between bar work, front of house and occasional cover on reception. She had expected to be given training on each section as promised in her interview.

The reality? She was met at reception early evening by a very harassed-looking manager called Letitia who said she would need to show her straight to her accommodation.

'You have black and white to wear – yes? White blouse and black skirt or trousers.' Letitia was walking very fast through the rear hallway, past the doors to the kitchen and through a covered passageway to a courtyard containing a myriad of large waste bins. Across the courtyard was a rather shabby square block. The staff accommodation, Ruby assumed.

Her room was on the first floor. Sparse with a single bed, small chest of drawers and single wardrobe. 'Showers and toilets along the hall,' Letitia said, looking at her watch. 'Shall we meet back in reception – say half an hour?'

Ruby tried to find a smile. 'Is that for paperwork?'

'Well, actually we have a bit of a situation today. I wouldn't normally ask but I'm going to need you on the bar this evening. Is that OK? Your CV said you have extensive bar work?'

'This *evening?* But I thought the email said I would start tomorrow. Shadowing first. And it's just I've had a really long journey—'

'And I appreciate this *so much*, Ruby. In at the deep end. Not ideal but I promise you we'll get a rota sorted very soon so you know where you are. Half an hour then?'

Ruby nodded and watched Letitia retreat with a very bad feeling in her gut. She would come to learn very quickly that the hotel was understaffed every single day. Unreasonable requests the norm. Serving breakfast after a late finish in the bar. 'Covering reception' when she was supposed to be on a break. The list went on. And on.

That first evening Ruby worked from 7 p.m. to midnight on her own in the bar, fulfilling orders on trays for the restaurant as well as the bar customers. She was used to pressure and could serve quickly, but she was unfamiliar with the layout and the till and some of the cocktails on the bar menu, so she had to keep summoning a waiter or waitress to help her. It was a complete nightmare. Customers complained about delays. Ruby came close to tears several times, disappearing for a 'comfort break' while a waiter held the fort.

The truth is she was still in shock after Ned's death and hadn't given herself time to get over that shock, let alone grieve.

The only thing that made her smile was Scott, one of the chefs who was leaning against the outside wall of the kitchen as she was crossing the courtyard back to her room.

'Hi. I'm Scott. We saw you arrive earlier. Did it go OK? Grapevine said they put you straight on the bar.'

'Yes. I'm Ruby. It was manic, to be honest. A nightmare. I'm done in.'

'Did Letitia have *a bit of a situation*?' He mimicked Letitia's voice exactly, and for all her exhaustion, Ruby couldn't help but laugh.

'Top tip now is to turn your phone off. Otherwise, they'll text you for the breakfast shift.'

Ruby pulled in her chin. 'I hope you're kidding.'

'Wish I was. Just stand up for yourself, don't answer your phone unless you're happy to take an extra shift and you'll be fine. Oh – and demand a rota. They can be . . .' He paused. 'Elusive.'

'I will. Thank you for the tips.'

'You're welcome. Good luck. I'll see you around.'

Then Scott raised his hand in farewell and was gone. And Ruby made the terrible mistake of feeling she had made a new friend.

CHAPTER 14

BEFORE

LAURA

When Joe didn't come home on time on Wednesday – the day after our row – I assumed he was still sulking.

I didn't even text him. I was still cross that he had slept in the spare room then got up early to leave for work without even talking to me.

Why should I text him, I thought, *when he never makes the effort to resolve conflict. When he hasn't had the courtesy to text me that he's going to be late.* Once upon a time he would always message. I thought about all the effort I had made over the pasta and pesto dinner and look how that turned out. *Pizza tonight. See if I care.*

Seven o'clock came and went. Seven thirty.

At seven forty-five, I caved and sent a very short text. No kiss. No reply.

I went upstairs to see if Clara wanted pizza yet but the 'Do Not Disturb' sign was in place. I knocked. Nothing. She probably had her headphones on. I turned off the landing light and looked down at the carpet. Sure enough there was the bright yellowy glow under her door which signalled her ring light was on inside, which meant she was on yet another Zoom call. I stood for a little longer outside her door and texted the pizza offer, wondering how many parents were reduced to the same sad and ridiculous style of communication.

And then the doorbell rang. I remember frowning – still irritated with Joe. It was the wrong time for anyone to call on spec. Too late for a delivery. I imagined someone from a charity, pushing for a monthly sign-up. *Do you like animals?* I sighed and checked my watch again. Nearly eight o' clock.

It was only when I was near the bottom of the stairs that I could make out the shapes through the rectangle of frosted glass in the front door. They were distorted but still recognisable. Something shifted inside. Police uniforms. Two people. One short. One taller.

I think I sat on the stairs for a moment then. I heard a question pop into my head – *Ruby or Joe?* – and remember feeling giddy. And sick. I also decided quite firmly not to answer the door. To get the supper on instead.

The doorbell rang again. They could see me through the frosted glass and one of the two figures knocked on the glass with their knuckles over and over.

I don't remember the next bit too clearly.

'Is it Mrs Harry? It's about your husband. Would it be OK if we come inside?'

I said no. That I was busy and needed to get some supper for my daughter, but one of the officers held the door and so I let them into the cramped hallway. I didn't want them to come any further into the house so we stood, all three of us, too close. Sort of huddled. I remember that I didn't want them that near to me. Right from the beginning I wanted to say no to them. *Go away. Take your uniforms and your bad news away from me . . .*

It was a blur. Something about an accident. Joe in the hospital. They wanted to know if there was anyone who could drive me to the hospital. I said there wasn't. *I'll drive myself.*

And then I remembered Clara and I think I must have tried to move back up the stairs to see her. To tell her. But I felt dizzy again and the next thing I was sitting on the stairs and the female officer had a glass of water in her hand.

I didn't understand where it had come from – the glass of water. And I was thinking she must have been in my kitchen and that upset me. I didn't want them in the house, let alone in my kitchen. I still had this really strange notion that if I could get them to leave, I could put the pizza on. *Clara's favourite margherita. And an American hot for Joe.*

'You need to go now. I need to get the supper.'

The two officers exchanged a strange look.

'It's a shock. Just sip the water and sit there a moment. If there's no one who can drive you, how about we give you a lift to the hospital. You and your daughter. You can talk to the doctors. See what's happening. Like we said, we don't know the details of your husband's condition but he'll be getting the best care.'

'I have to tell my daughter.'

'Yes. In a moment. Take your time.'

It suddenly dawned on me that I needed to find the right words for Clara. But I didn't have any words. Any details.

'So what happened? You said an accident. What kind of accident?'

They said his car had left the road about a mile from home. On Anstey Way. No other car was involved. It was a mystery but it was being investigated.

'He's a very good driver.'

'Yes. I'm sure.'

'So could they have made a mistake? Got the wrong person?'

'He has his photo driving licence with him, Mrs Harry.'

I sat thinking some more and very soon I was remembering how cross I had been with him for not texting, realising that at the very time I was angry, sending him a text without a kiss, he was in his car, all twisted up somewhere on the side of the road. Me angry. Him all twisted up. Someone checking a pocket for a wallet. Blood on his pocket. Blood on his photo driving licence?

'So is he badly hurt. Is he—?'

'We don't know details. We just need to get you to the hospital.'

'I thought you only made house calls if people were dead. Is he dead? Because if he's dead, you really do have to tell me right now. My daughter is upstairs and I have another daughter—'

'Your husband is in the hospital. Our patrol car happened to be nearby so we said we'd call on you. Our understanding is your husband is going into theatre for an operation. We don't know any more than that.'

I don't remember how I told Clara. Much later she said that in the back of the patrol car, I was rambling. Muttering about pizza. I feel terrible about that. Failing to hold it together.

But I do know why I lost it. I remember that, in the car, I kept thinking that my mother had been right. She was the one who'd told me – *never go to bed on a row*. I had rolled the wrong dice. Tempted fate.

I had failed to say sorry. To patch up my row with Joe.

And I was terrified that I was going to be punished. That I would never get to look my lovely husband in the eyes to say how sorry I was.

CHAPTER 15

BEFORE

CLARA

In the back of the police car, Clara could hardly bear to look at her mother. The change in her mother, the state of her mother, was every bit as frightening as the news of her father's accident. She was like a different person. Her eyes and her mind somewhere else entirely.

It was the moment Clara realised that she was supposed to step up; be an adult too. And she didn't feel up to the job. Not at all. Her mother kept rambling about supper – *I don't know what to do about the pizzas*. Clara reached out to hold her hand but it was shaking. For the whole twenty minutes of the journey, she realised her mother was in shock and Clara had no idea when she would come out of it.

The police officers were very kind. At reception, they checked which ward they should go to and made sure they took the correct lift. The female officer whispered to Clara that they should try to phone another relative. *Is there a grandparent you can call? Someone else who can be here with you?*

Clara shook her head. She wasn't thinking of her grandparents, who were frail and lived in France; she was worrying about Ruby in Scotland, worrying if it was now her job to tell her sister this terrible thing? In the car she had very nearly texted her. Needing her support in the panic. Her mother this stranger suddenly. But she realised she didn't know what to say to Ruby and so decided to wait until she knew what was happening with their father.

It was the mention of her sister that seemed to suddenly bring her mother back to herself.

'Should I ring Ruby, Mum?' They were in the lift and Clara had her phone in her hand, no idea what to do for the best.

Her mother was breathing in and out very strangely, and then, at the mention of Ruby's name, she narrowed her eyes. There was this confusion, this question mark in her expression. A deep frown and then a sweep of change suddenly. She closed her eyes and kept very still for a few moments, and then she opened her eyes to give Clara this big hug.

'Oh, my poor girl. I'm so sorry, darling. I've been a bit . . .' She looked away and then back again. 'I'm so sorry. It's going to be alright, Clara.'

It was like a switch. The relief so intense that Clara burst into tears.

Her mother squeezed her very tightly and then, as they walked along the corridor, following overhead signs to the ward, she said that they should find out what was happening first.

'I'll see where we are with your dad and then I'll text Ruby and tell her to call you urgently. Would that be OK? Do you feel up to talking to her?'

Clara just nodded and her mother's face looked really sad then. 'I mean – I hope she'll want to speak to me. But just in case she doesn't, we need to make a plan. We have each other. But we need to think of Ruby. It will be very hard for her. Up in Scotland. I can send her the money for the train fare or a flight. She needs to get here as soon as she can. Is that OK?'

Clara nodded again, relieved that there was some kind of plan now. How to tell Ruby. She was so used to having her father as the other go-between with Ruby that it had honestly never occurred to her to worry about this scenario. Ruby and her mother still not talking.

She closed her eyes, thinking of that awful scene when Ruby left. Her father carrying Ruby's suitcase down the stairs. Her mother in the kitchen, crying.

At the reception desk for the ward, there seemed to be confusion. At first they couldn't find the name. *Harry. It's Joe Harry.* And then a different nurse appeared to say that her father had already been taken to theatre for an operation. She was really kind, the nurse. Said that he had suffered a collapsed lung in the crash along with serious crush injuries to his chest. Also head injuries. They needed to do an urgent operation to stabilise him.

'Is he going to be OK?' Clara was crying as she spoke.

'He's in great hands. We have brilliant doctors here. They'll do their absolute best for him.'

'So can we wait outside the operating theatre? What should we do?' Her mother's voice was cracking as she spoke. 'Where should we go?'

'You won't be able to see him up on the operating floor. There's a relatives' room. G3. Just along the corridor.' The nurse pointed. 'I'll take you there and fetch some drinks. And then I'll update you when we know which ward he'll be on.'

'So he won't be coming back to this ward?' Her mother looked confused.

'Possibly but not definitely. It depends. He will probably go straight to ICU.'

'What's that?' Clara was struggling to follow all this. She'd expected to find her father in a bed on the ward.

'It's intensive care. But that's normal after an operation.' Her mother put her arm around her shoulders and Clara could tell that she was back to herself completely. Back in reassurance mode. 'Come on, darling. We can get in touch with Ruby from this relatives' room.' She turned to the nurse to explain further. 'That's my elder daughter. She's in Scotland. We need to get her here.'

'Of course. I'll stay in touch with the team upstairs. I'll let them know where you are so we can update you as soon as we know any more.'

The relatives' room was painted green and Clara remembered reading somewhere that it was meant to be a calming colour. Only it wasn't working. Her heart was beating so fast as she dialled Ruby's number.

'Hi Clara.' Ruby's voice. 'Look – I can't talk now. I got Mum's text to say to ring you but I'm right in the middle of a shift. Nuts here. Can I call you when I'm done?'

'Ruby. I'm really sorry.' She started crying. 'But Dad's been in an accident. A car accident. We're at the hospital. He's having some kind of operation. We're waiting for that to happen.'

There was a terrible beat of silence. Clara didn't know how to fill it.

'Would you be OK to speak to Mum? She said to ask.'

Suddenly there was a loud crashing sound at Ruby's end.

'What on earth—'

'It's OK. Something fell.' Ruby paused for a moment. 'It's being sorted. So is he going to be OK? How badly is Dad hurt?'

'I don't know. We don't know. So are you OK to speak to Mum?' Another pause. 'Yeah. OK. Put her on.'

Clara passed the phone to her mother, who shut her eyes tight as soon as she had the phone up to her ear.

'Hello, darling. I'm so sorry we're having to do this on the phone, especially after we haven't spoken for so long.' A pause. 'Such an awful shock for you. For all of us. I'm hoping you'll be able to head home straight away and I'll transfer some money to cover the rail fare. Or flight. Whichever is quicker.'

Clara could hear her sister's voice but not loud enough to make out what she was saying.

'Well let me do that anyway. Is there somewhere you can sit down? Catch your breath? Is there someone there who can help you? Support you? Book the train and everything, maybe take you to the railway station? Or the airport.'

Clara watched, aware that there was another long silence at the end of the phone.

'OK.' Her mother had tears running down her face now. 'I'm here if you want to talk. But if it's easier to talk to Clara, I will completely understand. I love you, Ruby. And I'm so sorry that you're so far away and alone facing this. They have great doctors here and they're going to look after your father. I'll make sure of that.'

And then Clara heard her sister break down at the end of the line before the call was ended.

'She's gone. She's hung up. Will you give her a moment, then ring her back, Clara?' Her mother's face was completely white. 'Can you do that for me? Is it too much?

'I can do that.'

'Good. Thank you, Clara. Tell your sister to get a lift or book a taxi. I'll start checking which will be faster. Train or plane so she can make travel plans. And reassure her that we're here for her if she wants to ring again. And we'll send updates as soon as we know anything.'

Clara looked into her mother's pale face and her worried eyes and realised something properly for the first time.

When she had thought about phoning Ruby privately when her mother was still in shock, all she had wanted was an ally. Someone to cry with. *Lean* on. She wasn't thinking of the shock to Ruby. All alone, dealing with this news in Scotland.

But her mother was now worrying about Ruby in an entirely different way. With this different lens. And Clara felt momentarily ashamed for all the times she had misjudged her mother. Lied to her mother about all the Zooms and her new plans. Moaned with Ruby about their mother. Failed, in short, to even notice this difficult and essentially selfless aspect of their mother stepping up always to be the true grown-up in the room.

'I love you, Mum,' she said suddenly, pulling her mother into another hug.

'I know, darling. You too.'

CHAPTER 16

BEFORE

JOE

It happened so fast. No warning.

Joe knew as he checked the dashboard clock in the car that he should have texted Laura to say he was going to be home late.

It was on his mind as he turned into Anstey Way. That growl of guilt in his stomach. And it was still on his mind when he first saw the sudden beam of light.

The problem was the picture from the awful woman in the nightclub was also on his mind; *uppermost* in his mind. Would she really send the photograph to Laura? And would their family survive another bomb going off in their lives?

It had been a long day with a lot of driving. His shoulders and his back were aching. His eyes were tired too and he was fed up, not just with that particular day but with a job he'd grown this past year to despise. Some days Joe wished he could just drive in the wrong direction. Take a random turning and disappear for a bit.

He had this ridiculous fantasy of living in a shepherd's hut on his allotment. Just him and nature. Growing things. Experimenting with new seeds and different varieties of plants. Nurturing the plot properly. Putting in the time until he could live off the land.

It wasn't that he didn't love his family. He loved them more than ever. He just needed a break. A change. The problem, this past year, was that everything had become so very complicated since the schism between Laura and Ruby.

Once upon a time he could talk to Laura about anything. His work. The girls. His worries. But since Laura's business had taken off and she was so busy and sad over Ruby, he felt too guilty to moan about anything.

He was proud of all Laura had achieved with her business, but the reality was it had been tougher than expected trying to juggle two demanding careers. When the girls were small, Laura had worked part-time from home and was happy to manage her freelance work around the school run. The sports days. The Christmas panto. She was just establishing herself as a copywriter and it seemed back then to suit them both.

At first she did the copywriting and social media accounts for two or three small charities. But as the girls got bigger, her contracts got bigger. Soon her work brought a whole stable of hobby horses. Campaigns against scammers. Campaigns against housing proposed for green field sites. There seemed always to be something for Laura to be wound up about and to write about for her clients.

She was very good at all that. She blogged for the charities, updated their websites, shared their work on social media and sent out press releases too. But as Joe watched her reputation grow, he could see that she was overstretching and also underselling herself. She was struggling to keep the plates spinning without fair reward. Her day rates were much too low.

You work all hours around the kids, you should be charging more.
They're charities, Joe.
It's business, Laura.

Joe was relieved and proud when Laura finally set up officially on her own. Bigger contracts. Better pay. She stopped working for small charities. The better income meant they could afford a cleaner and a part-time assistant to help with the family. The balance. But he knew that deep down Laura now felt guilty about the money her business was bringing in. Feared she had 'sold out'.

He thought of her text. No kiss. Their constant bickering of late.

The problem was not so much their jobs but the fracture with Ruby. This permanent elephant in the room. Joe tried so hard to mediate but he hated being stuck in the middle. He had never imagined it would go on for this long and it had dragged him down.

And so somehow over the past year Joe had gone from being fed up with his job to hating it. He couldn't talk to Laura and so he had become passive-aggressive at home. Irritable. He could see that now, after the stupid row over the stupid pendants.

Joe thought about why he had not replied to Laura's text, asking where he was. And he realised with a sweep of shame that he had become sort of permanently angry with her. Not on the surface but deep down. He thought about how very lovely she had looked at the party they went to recently; how much better they'd been together that evening. Another sweep of guilt.

He realised as he drove that the anger at Laura was his fault and not hers, and could see that they needed to talk about his need for a change. *Really* talk.

In the past he'd always relied on Laura to patch things up between them. But she'd stopped reaching out. Rightly or wrongly, he'd assumed she had simply stopped caring so much.

Checking the dashboard clock again, Joe thought again of the *real* problem. The woman in the nightclub. He felt his cheeks colour. Fear. Would she send the picture?

He decided he needed to tell Laura first. And share his mad idea. The idea of a sabbatical. Not just for him but for her too.

They could afford it, so why not? Six months off, even a year, to try to reset everything. Not just their work lives but the family. Their relationship.

Very soon Clara would be leaving home too. They really needed to make some plans. To make a change. He felt a sigh leave his body as he imagined it. Sorting things properly with Laura. And time away from his job.

Joe was now the regional sales manager for a major breakfast bar brand and he hadn't always hated it this much. Once upon a time it had provided the security and the income the family badly needed. But it was a career he had fallen into by accident, starting as a stopgap graduate position soon after university. The truth was he had never wanted to work in sales. His real passion had always been the outdoors. Joe was happiest in the garden. At the allotment. In his shed, pottering about with landscape plans. Muddy hands and big dreams of all the things he might do once he had more time.

Joe was still thinking about his fantasy of working outdoors when the beam of light first appeared.

He narrowed his eyes at the intensity of it, imagining a motorbike in the distance. He put his hand up and the visor down. But the light became brighter still.

He checked his side mirror and then, as he glanced forward again, the glare suddenly filled his whole windscreen. He was completely blinded, his eyes burning. He felt the car swerve. Slammed on the brakes.

There was a scream from the tyres.

And then . . . just blackness.

CHAPTER 17

BEFORE

Ruby

Ruby was serving main courses to a table of six in the restaurant when the call from Clara came through.

Technically there was a rule that two members of staff had to work on a table that large so the food would not go cold. But there was 'a bit of a situation' on the restaurant rota, and Ruby was racing from table to kitchen and back to table to get everything out as fast she could. She was not supposed to take personal calls on shift and the stress was heightened because Scott was in the kitchen, stealing glances her way when he thought she wasn't looking.

She had a large platter of cauliflower cheese in her hand when Clara told her their dad was in the hospital. *Will you speak to Mum, Ruby?*

There was a crash as she dropped the platter. Cauliflower cheese all over the floor. And her shoes.

Two chefs stepped forward – one cross, one kind.

What the hell.

Calm down. It was an accident. She didn't mean it. I'll get another.

Ruby just stepped away to the pantry area, phone pressed to her ear. It was like being sucked into a parallel world suddenly. A slap to her face to remind her she had a family. A father. A whole different life once. Not that long ago, and yet forever ago.

It was surreal to hear her mother's voice. Also terrifying because she and Clara didn't seem to know much. Ruby's heart was racing because she wanted them to say her dad was going to be OK. But they didn't say that; didn't know that yet. He was still in theatre.

'What's going on?' Letitia's voice. She had been called through from the reception area.

'I'm sorry but my father is in hospital. I'm going to have to go home.'

Letitia looked sorry and Ruby mistook this.

'Is there any way you could drive me to the railway station?' She didn't know who else to ask. Her closest friend in Scotland, Natalie, was away. Two weeks off to visit her poorly mum.

'You mean tomorrow? I'll have to look at the—'

'No. I need to go now. See if I can get a late flight or a sleeper or something.'

'*Now.* You want to go now? Right in the middle of a shift? I'm sorry but you can't possibly go now.'

Ruby stared into Letitia's face, anger bubbling up inside. She saw that Letitia was indeed sorry. Upset. But not for her father. Letitia was upset at the inconvenience to the hotel. And Ruby thought suddenly of her father driving her to the railway station after she had stormed out. Left home. How in the car he had told her that it would all come good. That she just needed to give it a bit of time. *It will be OK, my darling girl.*

'My father has had a car accident and I'm going right now, Letitia. I'll let you know when I can come back. If I can come back.'

With that she pushed past Letitia into the main kitchen as her waitress friend and housemate Shelley came over to offer comfort. Asked for details. Quickly offered to call a taxi.

To her horror Scott then stepped forward to offer to drive her to the nearest railway station, but Letitia shut this down. *I can't have you leaving as well, Scott. We'll sort a taxi for Ruby.*

Ruby liaised again with Clara and her mother. It was still so strange to hear her mother's voice. She was too confused and worried about her father to even know how she felt about them speaking again.

In the taxi, she just stared ahead unblinking until her eyes were at first hurting and then watering. She tried to make a conscious effort to blink, but it was as if her brain had forgotten what to do. How to breathe. How to blink. How to sit.

She was on her phone in a panic, also trying to figure out the best way to get home – sleeper train or flight? – when a text came from her mother with links to the various timetables and options. Also confirmation that she had sent money to cover the fare.

Six months back Ruby would have been furious. Seen this as controlling. Infuriating. But in the back of that taxi, there were suddenly tears dripping down Ruby's cheeks. Not just for her father but for her mother – so quick and capable and organised – whom she had not allowed herself until that very moment to miss.

Her mother's message said flying would probably be no quicker because of the awkward timetables. She wouldn't make the late flight from Edinburgh but she would make the sleeper to Euston. So she clicked through to the first train on her mother's list. She checked the time on her phone; she should just about make it. Which meant she would make the connection to the sleeper which would get her on her way properly tonight.

The sleeper on which she was pretty sure she would *not* sleep.

CHAPTER 18

NOW

LAURA

'How the hell do they think I could kill someone when I've been at the hospital, looking after my husband?'

'They claim to have *strong* evidence.' My solicitor is sitting across a Formica table.

'What evidence?'

'I don't know exactly. We'll find out in the interview.'

'But don't they have to tell you now? Disclosure rules?' I feel dizzy. Cannot understand any of this. Why the finger is pointing at me.

'Disclosure is only a thing when a case goes to trial,' he says, leaning forward. 'There's no obligation for them to share evidence before a police interview.'

I run my hand through my hair, my heart pounding.

'But it's all ridiculous. I've never even *heard* of this person who's died.'

'Like I say, I'm as in the dark as you are. So what do you want to do? Do you want me to oversee this first interview and then refer to a more experienced colleague if they charge you?'

'You seriously think I'm going to be *charged?*'

His face is grave. 'Like I told you. This is not my area these days, Mrs Harry. You might do better with the on-call lawyer.'

'No, no. I'd like you there with me. So how long can they hold me like this? Without charge, I mean.'

'Up to thirty-six hours on a murder case, if a senior officer approves. Longer if they refer to a magistrate.'

'So what are my options? What do we do? I have my daughter to think of.'

'We look at confirming an alibi for you. How about you talk me through your movements the past few days. Everything you've done. Everywhere you've been. Yes? All the places that might provide CCTV confirmation.'

I nod. And he opens his notebook and takes out a smart fountain pen from his top pocket.

'You seriously think they might charge me?' I feel light-headed as I whisper this again.

A murder charge?

Me?

CHAPTER 19

BEFORE

LAURA

I remember the trip to the hospital after Joe's accident very differently from Clara. She says I was 'out of it' and I feel bad about that. What I recall the most is the shock at all the media outside the main doors. The police gave us a lift as a favour, and that was the only reason we were able to get close to the entrance.

Lots of other cars and taxis weren't able to get through at all. There was this big throng blocking the road in front of the entrance – a crowd of TV crews, photographers and journalists.

Clara was already very pale and obviously fragile sitting in the back with me, and I felt irrationally angry as the police car was forced to reverse. I was in shock. Confused. Also worried about my younger daughter being filmed when she was so upset.

'Sorry. But we're going to have to drop you here,' the policeman driving said. 'We'll find out what this is all about, call this in and meet you at reception.'

I was slowly emerging from the shock and pulled Clara close as we got out of the car and manoeuvred past the media, me turning my head away and holding up a hand to shield my face.

The police were true to their word. After five minutes or so, they met us at reception. A member of staff shared that Joe was not well enough to give any kind of statement to the police, so the officers said they would return to conduct an interview once his condition was more stable.

They wished us luck, and again asked if there was anyone else they could call for us.

I shook my head, then turned to look again through the main doors at the throng still outside.

'So what's all that about out there?' I assumed it was a continuation of the story I'd watched from home at breakfast.

The two police officers exchanged a wary glance. 'It's a watch-and-wait situation for us. Try not to worry about it.'

Another woman alongside reception then chipped in. 'Some mother campaigning about her daughter.' She shook her head in apparent disapproval. 'Hospital security's on the way.' She then turned to the two police officers dealing with Joe's accident. 'So why don't you step in now? Get them to move away. It's trespassing, isn't it?'

The police officers said nothing so I linked Clara's arm with mine and we headed for the lifts.

As we waited in the narrow alcove by the lifts, a hospital posse appeared – a procession of security staff and officials with matching lanyards marching in the opposite direction along the main corridor, presumably to deal with the press.

Finally, up on the third floor, we were told there was no news from the operating theatre yet and directed to a relatives' waiting room. A young nurse said it was not clear which ward Joe would be transferred to after his surgery.

'Right. I guess we'll just have to wait here then.' Again I squeezed Clara's arm. 'Do you want a drink? Coffee? Water?' I noticed machines out in the corridor but she shook her head. I paced the room, a small space painted the inevitable calming green, and then moved to stand by the window to watch the pantomime continuing far below us outside.

The security team had moved the media from the road to a car park opposite, but there was still a large huddle with lights glaring alongside TV cameras, and I could see the mother in a deep-green coat being interviewed, several microphones thrust close to her face. The same woman on the breakfast bulletin.

'I think there's another TV interview going on right now,' I said.

'Yes. I've got it up on my phone. The story's on the nationals now. I've got Sky News playing.' It was one of the other relatives, sitting in the corner of the room. A tall woman in a red shirt holding her phone in front of her with one earbud in her left ear, the other hanging loose so she could also hear what was happening in the room.

'So what's she saying now?' I asked. 'Why's she still talking to the media?' It felt every kind of wrong to allow myself to be distracted by this when I should be concentrating on Joe, but the commotion was upsetting.

'Ignore it,' Clara said suddenly, standing to join me at the window. 'It's being blown up. How are they being allowed to do this at a hospital? Why didn't the police step in?'

'I suspect the police don't want to escalate things,' I offered. 'With all the cameras. They won't want a scuffle all over social media.'

I put my arm around Clara's shoulders. I could understand why she was both upset and cross, just like me. But I didn't understand her phrasing. *Being blown up?* Why had she said that?

'I'm surprised the hospital is allowing it as well.' The woman in the red shirt was now speaking more loudly, forgetting she had the earbud in. 'She's warning about some organisation I've not heard of. Star-something. Some sort of dating or relationship thing. She claims it's a cult. That it was manipulating her daughter. Taking money. She says she has emails to her daughter to prove it all.'

'It's not a cult,' Clara said.

'So you know about it? This group? This Star-thing?' The woman in the red shirt's tone was curious as she turned to Clara. 'It's just I have a daughter about the same age and I've never heard of it. All sounds a bit alarming. What do you know about it, then?'

'Well, I don't know about it *personally.*' Clara was blushing. 'But it's all over TikTok and Insta. It's just like all the other relationship stuff. You know. Reality dating programmes. Dating apps. It's not really that different.'

'Wait a minute. The mother's saying something else.' The woman in red held up her hand to quieten us. I moved across the room so I could see her phone screen and she pulled out the earplug lead and turned up the volume so we could all listen.

'*I only found the emails today. My daughter was paying for some kind of star readings and therapy. Readings. Stuff and nonsense. It was supposed to help her find her one true love through star mapping. That's what they told her. But it was pricey. She signed up to monthly payments and when she couldn't afford to keep going, they got pushy. And then nasty. Said maybe she was destined to be alone. That if she didn't read the stars properly and follow her correct path, then her destiny was to be lonely. And miserable. That she would never find her star mate. Imagine being told that. At nineteen?*'

'Star mate? What's that exactly? Like a soul mate?' I said, frowning, but the woman with the phone waved her hand to shush me again. A hospital spokesman then stepped into view on the live Sky coverage. She said she could not comment on individual patients due to confidentiality.

'*Our concern here today is the safety and well-being of all our patients and staff, and we're asking the media to respect that. We are always open to legitimate discussions but we need the media to keep away from the entrance and not to interfere with patient traffic and parking. Any questions should go to our press office through the normal channels.*'

The woman in red shook her head. 'Well, I don't blame the mother for being so angry. I would be. Sounds like a scam to me.'

'I sympathise with this mother too but I think they should get the media off site,' I said, moving back to the window. 'We all have sick relatives here and we need this hospital and all the staff to be concentrating on them, not dealing with cameras and journalists wandering about and getting in the way.'

Clara moved to my side and I kissed her on the forehead, thinking again of Joe in surgery. How long would it take? *How long?*

'I think you're right. The hospital is frightened of a public clash being filmed.' The woman in red now had both earphones back in place and was again forgetting herself, speaking much too loudly.

I decided to say nothing more. When I'd worked for charities, I was all for free speech. Campaigning against scams. But today I was annoyed by the circus. The distraction. The upset.

I was also confused, and deep down I was unsettled, thinking about the pendants that had turned up at home. And Clara's comment. *It's not a cult.* How did she know?

'She's saying something about a pendant now.' The woman in red was frowning, her voice still too loud. 'Apparently her daughter bought one but took it off before she tried to hurt herself. An overdose, they're saying. The mother found the pendant on the floor of the bathroom.'

I felt a shiver go through me.

'Are they showing a picture of the pendant?' I asked, remembering it from the breakfast bulletin.

'Leave it, Mum. They're just stirring up rubbish,' Clara said, her face flushing again.

'Yeah. The mother's got the pendant. I'll do a screen shot.' The woman in red clicked her phone to capture the image and then turned the screen to show me. 'Never seen anything like it. Looks and sounds all a bit woo woo to me,' she continued.

I leaned in closer to take in the image. The freeze frame was a close-up of the mother's hand, holding the pendant in her palm to show the media.

Sure enough, it was just as I remembered from the breakfast bulletin at home. Identical to the pendants that were sitting on the kitchen worktop of my house.

And that had been around Jade's neck. The girl who'd shared my Paris hotel room.

CHAPTER 20

BEFORE

JOE

It was the weirdest sensation. Joe was lying down but the bed felt all wrong. Too hard. He tried to open his eyes but the lids just wouldn't budge.

Next he tried to lift his right arm but again it wouldn't move. He felt panic rising within. He could sense light bleeding into his eyes so wasn't in complete darkness. But *where was he?*

Joe thought again about the unfamiliar mattress. Harder. The sheet crisper. Not soft. There was also the sound of unfamiliar bleeping nearby. And then voices – at first whispering. Not close by – as if across the room. But which room?

Joe paused. He tried once more to open his eyes and move a limb, any limb, but nothing worked. He tried desperately to remember what had happened. How he'd got here. What was this? But his brain felt blank. As if someone had pressed 'delete'. Wiped everything . . .

This paralysis, this inability to even open his eyes, was unbearable. Joe decided he must be in some strange dream. Still asleep. Yes. That would be it. He remembered having an awful nightmare once where he felt pinned to the bed. Paralysed just like this. That time he had sensed something bad in the room, like something was coming for him, meaning harm. But in the end, he had just woken up. Realised it was a nightmare. So maybe this was like that again. He just needed to wait until he woke up. Safe on his soft mattress and his soft sheets at home.

'Heart rate's up a bit.' A female voice. Nearby.

Joe tried to speak. *Who's that? Where am I?* But the words echoed inside his head, not out loud. Mute as well as frozen. And yet he could now hear and sense his own breathing and also his heart rate increasing. He made a conscious effort to try to calm himself but it didn't seem to work.

'Heart rate's not steadying. Think I may need to call for help.' The same voice.

'Sats seem OK. Let's give it a minute. If it doesn't settle, I'll page someone.' A second voice. Also a woman but with an accent. Irish. A soft and pleasant accent. One that Joe liked.

Sats? A medical term. So was he somewhere medical? A hospital possibly? Was that what this was?

Joe tried to think why he would be in a hospital. A heart attack? A stroke? An accident? He tried very hard to scan inside his brain to find a picture, some flash of something, anything that might explain this.

If he was in a hospital, where was Laura? And Clara and Ruby. Why weren't they here? Why couldn't he hear their voices too? And then Joe felt a sweep of relief, pleased to think of them. His family. Face by face. Name by name. So he hadn't forgotten everything. His brain wasn't blank after all. It was just the most recent bits that were for some reason missing.

Next, a terrible new thought landed and Joe wondered if he was actually dead. That perhaps this was what death was like? Maybe he was not in a hospital at all . . .

And then suddenly there was this flash behind his eyelids. This glaring light. And Joe remembered.

He was driving. Yes. In the car. It was late. He was driving home to Laura. She had sent a text with no kiss – pissed with him for not warning he would be late, and he was feeling guilty about that. He wanted to apologise. Make up after a stupid row. But he didn't know how because he was worried about the message from the woman in the nightclub. And then there was this sudden flash of light. He was blinded. And then the screeching of brakes . . .

And then *this*.

'His heart rate's still increasing. I don't like this.' That Irish accent again. 'I'm paging the on-call.'

CHAPTER 21

BEFORE

THE POLICE

Special Constable Amelie Hill turned the tap on to wash her hands, only to underestimate the flow. Cold water sprayed so furiously into the sink that it splashed upwards all over her front.

'Oh good grief!' She spun the tap to reduce the spray and quickly washed her hands before shutting off the water completely and marching to the air dryer on the wall. She dried her hands first then tilted the blower upwards to dry her front. Her stab vest was waterproof and took only moments to return to its usual colour, but her right sleeve, which had taken the worst of the soaking, was uncomfortable. She sighed. Activated the dryer again.

Finally sorted, she turned then to check her reflection, and was struck with the familiar shock of it. Special Constable Amelie Hill. It was surreal every time she caught sight of this new version of herself in a mirror. Hair in a neat but unflattering bun at the base of her neck. The bulk of the uniform and all its equipment.

It had taken most of her first year at uni to get through the training. Her fellow students still considered her completely bonkers, giving up her free time and most of her holidays. But Amelie had a point to prove. This was a deliberate step on a determined path, and now she was officially a 'special' – committed to a few hours every single week of term time and more in the holidays.

She had just finished the second year of her degree in criminology and her special constable status meant she could work some of the summer break in Cornwall with her mentor DCI Melanie Sanders. Mel was something of a legend. A family friend – a close pal of her father, Matthew, who had left the police force many years ago and still thoroughly disapproved of Amelie's career plans.

But she remained resolute. Or perhaps the word was *stubborn*. She was doing this stint as a special to get in flying hours and to hopefully earn some brownie points before she applied for a graduate detective position after her degree. Hand on heart, it had all been much tougher juggling everything than she'd expected. But no regrets. Not really. She had seen at first hand the dark side of crime and wanted to be on the *right* side. Just one more year before she could start her career proper.

Amelie tilted her head. She was trying to picture her father in uniform. He had worked as a private investigator after leaving the police, but was now semi-retired in Devon. She didn't fancy life in uniform herself long-term – detective work was what interested her. Amelie let out a long sigh, feeling her slightly damp cuff again.

She checked her watch – 9.45 p.m. – and hurried to join her colleague Ben outside.

'Why do women always take so long?' he moaned. It was his default setting, moaning. Ben was *never* happy. He'd confided long ago that he was only working as a special to please his family. There was money at stake. Ben's plan A was to finish university and live off his trust fund, but his father had other ideas. Ben had apparently been presented with a choice. A stint as a special or a short term in the military. No access to the trust fund unless he *gave something back* first.

It was not going well. Ben hated his shifts and so Amelie was bracing herself for more negative banter when she spotted a young boy clocking them from a bus shelter further along the road and then suddenly running in the opposite direction.

Amelie started to give chase, wondering what the boy had to hide. *Drugs? Something stolen? Worse?*

'Really?' her colleague complained, the tone all sarcasm, before hot-footing behind her. 'Why do you always have to go looking for trouble?'

'I think that's actually our job,' Amelie said, increasing her pace.

'But it's nearly the end of our shift,' Ben panted from a few paces behind her. 'Anyone else would be phoning ahead for a kebab. This is so *typical* of you.'

Amelie was not a bad sprinter. She kept her position several strides ahead of Ben and it wasn't long before she caught up with the boy. To her surprise he finally and suddenly stopped running and turned and put his hands up.

'I ain't done nothing.'

He was much younger than she'd expected. Tall and skinny but more like twelve than the thirteen or fourteen she had imagined. She felt a bit conflicted. He was just a child. And yet?

'So how about you turn out your pockets? If you haven't done anything, why did you run the second you spotted us?'

'Breaking news. Not everyone likes the police. Especially pretend police. You one of them specials? You look too young to be a real one—'

'Breaking news. I'm not pretending. Or joking, so you can cut the lip. I have full police powers so turn out your pockets.'

The boy let out a huff of annoyance and reached into his right pocket to take out sweet wrappers.

'And the left pocket.'

He finally drew out a strange, black, pen-like device which at first Amelie didn't recognise.

'I found it,' the boy said defensively as Ben finally caught them up.

'Is that a laser pen?' Ben asked, leaning in closer.

'Might be. I told you I found it. Anyway, they're not illegal.'

'But they are potentially very dangerous,' Ben said. 'So what would you be doing with a laser pen out on the street? Late. In the dark.'

'I told you. I found it.'

'Well, we're going to need your name and your address and to have a word with your parents about this,' Amelie added, her mind whirring. It was the first time she'd seen a laser pen and was grateful Ben had done the ID. She'd read about them, and they'd been mentioned in a training exercise after a teenager was caught with one near an airfield.

'So what's your name and how old are you?' she said, turning the laser pen in her hand.

'I'm Daniel and I'm fourteen.'

'No. You're not. Try again.'

'OK. Twelve. But I'm nearly thirteen.'

'Have you been using this near the traffic?' she asked, leaning in to look the young boy in the eye. Amelie was now remembering a story about a boy in Greece who had accidentally blinded himself in one eye with a laser pointer. This lad could hurt himself or someone else very easily. It was bad news for him to be out late on his own with this in his pocket. She definitely needed to have a word with his parents, both to give him a scare and to keep him safe.

He didn't reply.

'I asked if you've been using this thing near the traffic?' Amelie glanced at the main road.

'No. Course I haven't. I told you. I found it.'

'And where exactly did you find it?' Amelie was trying to read the boy's face. Was he lying? Been up to no good? Ben was now checking his watch as if tiring of the exchange, but they needed to get to the bottom of this.

'Down the road, near the bridge.' The boy was pointing. 'Near the dual carriageway.'

CHAPTER 22

BEFORE

Ruby

Phone in hand, Ruby sat on the bed of her sleeper cabin and felt completely overwhelmed.

Checking in at Inverness had been stressful. She'd only just made the train. Now she was worrying if she had even made the right call. Should she have waited for the early flight tomorrow? With streaks of lights punctuating the darkness through the window, it was too late to change her mind . . .

She could hear voices in the corridor. Staff checking on passengers and offering more information. *Luggage goes under the bed. Not in the en-suite, please.*

In the end, she'd decided on the train over flying because she'd missed all the evening flights and the only early flight went into Gatwick, which was a nightmare logistically. The sleeper at least meant she was heading south already with the option of phone contact the whole journey. The last text from Clara had said there was no fresh news, and Ruby couldn't bear the thought of being out of contact on a plane in case something happened. And what if the morning flight was cancelled? Bad weather?

The sleeper got into London before the flight would get into Gatwick. But Ruby still felt disorientated. She'd never been on a sleeper. In the past it had been parked in her brain as something potentially romantic. Sleeping on a train. But the reality, as she used the card for her cabin in this stressed state, was the whole thing felt all wrong. As if she were taking some kind of 'treat' when her father was in an operating theatre, enduring goodness knows what.

From the chatter on the platform earlier, Ruby had picked up that not all passengers had private rooms. There was a cheaper option of seats only. But once she had plumped for rail, her mother sent cash for a 'double cabin', insisting it would be more comfortable. Ruby was now thinking how typical it was of her mother to throw money at this. As if money could ever patch up anything.

As for the reality? The room was nice enough – a small, neat and well-designed space with a double bed, compact en-suite and just a little floor space – but because it was all so unexpected, it felt alien. Also – in these stressful circumstances – claustrophobic. Ruby checked her phone again. Still no new messages.

She texted Clara to say she was onboard and her phone rang instantly.

'So you made the train?' Clara's voice.

'Yeah. Just. I'm on the way now. Is there any news?'

'No. He's being moved to ICU after surgery. It's awful here. The waiting. I hate it. All of it.'

Ruby pressed the phone tighter to her ear.

'Listen. Mum's getting coffee so I need to tell you something quickly.' A pause. 'There's this big kerfuffle. At the hospital.'

'What sort of kerfuffle? To do with Dad?'

'No, no. It's some mother sounding off against *StarBonders*. Have you not seen the news?'

'No. I've been busy getting the journey sorted. So what's going on?'

'This woman's daughter hurt herself. She's blaming StarBonders. The mother's getting a bit hysterical. I thought I should tell you. Warn you. Because didn't you say your friend Scott got into it – StarBonders?' Clara was speaking more quickly. 'The thing is, Mum's getting herself into a state about it. She may mention it. There's media outside. I'm surprised you didn't see it online?'

'No. I was working earlier and then frantic sorting the journey.' Ruby felt a new tightness in her chest. 'So does she know we discussed it? You and me. Did you tell her my friend was into it?'

'No, of course not. I didn't tell her *anything*. I tried to calm her down but you know what she's like. This mother is saying StarBonders is a cult.'

'A cult?' Ruby wasn't wholly surprised to hear this. The organisation had always sounded dodgy to her.

'Oh. I don't know. It's getting ridiculous.'

'Right.' Ruby felt her stomach lurch. Because of Scott, she sorely wished she'd never heard of StarBonders. But she didn't want to discuss Scott's obsessional behaviour with her mother. 'Don't say anything to Mum about us discussing Scott and StarBonders.'

'I won't, but there's something else.'

'What?'

'You know the pendants they sell?'

Ruby frowned. She remembered that Scott had tried to give her a StarBonders pendant once but she had said 'no thank you'. It was when he first started getting seriously weird. Pushy. Claiming they were a match.

'Someone sent two to Mum.'

'*What?*' Ruby couldn't quite take this in.

'Two pendants in the post. I know. It's really weird, isn't it? They came from Etsy and she swears she didn't order them. And I just wondered . . .'

'You think I sent them to her?'

'Well, no. Not really. But I thought I should at least mention them.'

'*Of course* I didn't send them.'

'Right. No. Of course. I just thought you should know because it's all so very weird. I'm trying to distract Mum. But it's difficult.'

Ruby let this bizarre update sit between them a moment. For the most part, she and Clara had avoided discussing their mother since Ned. Since the rows. And the drama. And the funeral. And the decision to move to Scotland. It had become this unspoken pact. The same with their father. They spoke on the phone and sometimes FaceTimed, but they never discussed the elephant in every room.

'OK,' Ruby said finally. 'Thanks for the heads-up. Maybe the pendants were just a mistake?'

'Maybe. Mum will be back in a minute. I just wanted to tell you when she's not here. In case she mentions it to you.'

'Thanks.'

'So what's it been like? Talking to Mum again? You OK?'

'No. Not really. It's weird. Hearing her voice. Stressful. I don't know.' A pause. Ruby closed her eyes, suddenly picturing her mother in the kitchen, reaching out her arms for a hug goodbye that day she left. The hug that Ruby had rejected. 'How about you? Are you holding up without me? Worrying about Dad.'

'Not really. It's awful.' Clara started to cry. And sniff. Ruby could feel her own tears coming.

'Ring me any time,' Ruby said. 'Through the night. I doubt I'll sleep at all. I'll keep my phone charged.'

'OK.' Clara sniffed again. 'I miss you, Ruby. I'm really scared.'

'I know. Me too.'

CHAPTER 23

LETTERS FROM A LIGHTHOUSE

THE STARBONDERS BLOG

Dear StarBonders,

This week's blog comes early, as I know many of you will have seen on social media and in the press alarming reports which totally misrepresent all that StarBonders stands for.

We at the Lighthouse will, of course, never betray our followers' privacy. We keep all the exchanges between us confidential. For this reason, we cannot comment on the details of the distressing and inaccurate stories that are circulating this week.

But we can say this.

We have nothing but compassion for any young person suffering a mental health challenge, for whatever reason. The health and happiness of our followers is of the utmost priority here at StarBonders. Given it's a sad fact that a percentage of society will at some time in their life face mental health challenges, it is inevitable that a percentage of our members will at some point be similarly challenged.

Resilience is something we aim to teach, and we support all our members in their relationships and with their mental health in general.

Honesty is something we value highly. We do not pretend that any journey through life, and in particular our very special journeys to union with a true StarBonder match, will be easy. But our teaching and our readings are all very carefully structured to nurture this critical resilience so that our StarBonders will have the strength to navigate the downs as well as the ups.

Again, we will not be drawn into detailed comments on an individual case. But we can reassure that if any StarBonder presents with anxieties that worry us, we always refer them for support.

Sadly, it is our belief that some in the media, who simply do not believe in the cosmic powers all around us, seek to attack that which they do not understand. And that's what is happening right now.

We are a caring organisation but we do also have to protect our reputation, and so we are consulting lawyers about the inaccurate stories that have been circulating in print and on social media – and, make no mistake, we will not hesitate to take action against anyone who misrepresents what we stand for.

You all know that we are here for the journey towards TRUE love. And TRUE (and lasting) happiness. We are here for insight and positive support for every single one of you. So if you have any worries about the stories circulating, do reach out to your StarBonders coach or arrange a reading to discuss this further.

We, none of us, expected this to be easy. Challenges are a part of this. But just as Plato said, we are all connected to our companion star at all times. And that connection and that strength will keep us going. Through this. And through everything ahead of us.

If you need calm in these turbulent times, remember always to find the best stretch of night sky with the least light pollution and spend some time gazing at the stars.

One of the reasons I chose a retired lighthouse for StarBonders HQ was the isolation and the limited light pollution.

So I will be calming myself also, examining the wonder of all your companion stars tonight, and will be thinking of each and every one of you.

With love from the whole team at the StarBonders Lighthouse.

Phoebe xx

CHAPTER 24

BEFORE

LAURA

'Hey darling, we're here now.' I smoothed Joe's hair back from his forehead, trying to keep the shock from my voice at the large bandage around the left side of his head. At the cuts and the bruises. And the grim, stitched wound down his left cheek.

Instead I leaned forward to kiss his forehead ever so gently, careful of the bandage and the bruising but hoping that he would at least feel my touch.

'Can he hear us?' I turned to the nurse who was checking the alarming bank of machines alongside the bed.

'We can't know for sure, but we hope so. It's good for you to talk to him. If he can hear you, that will really help him.'

'Clara's here,' I said. 'Come on, love. Step forward. You heard the nurse. Daddy may be listening.'

Clara was still standing near the door. She was trembling and I could see that the shock of her father's reality was even worse for her than for me. It was as if she were frozen to the spot, too afraid to edge closer.

I stretched out my hand. 'It's OK, love. I know it looks a bit scary – all the machines – but they're doing an important job. And you heard the doctor earlier. The operation went really well. They're just keeping him asleep for a bit to let him rest. To let everything calm down and heal after the operation.'

'So, is it a coma?' Her voice was almost a whisper.

'It's a medically induced coma. So it's deliberate and it's temporary, love. Like a special sleep to let Daddy heal. Come on.' I tilted my head. 'Would you like to come and stand a bit closer?'

At last she moved, but she remained deathly pale. There was just one chair alongside Joe's bed and so I stood. 'Do you want to sit down?'

'No. No. You stay there.'

'OK. No worries, honey.' I turned back to Joe and again stroked the little bit of hair poking from his bandage, wondering if the rest of his hair was shaved.

'Like I said, Clara's here and Ruby's on the way by train. It's still the early hours but she'll be here tomorrow to see you. Isn't that great? All of us here so we can see you when you get strong and wake up.'

'That's lovely,' the nurse said suddenly. 'You can take turns to keep each other company.'

I frowned, not understanding.

'It's two visitors at a time at the bedside in ICU,' she added, lowering her voice to a whisper. 'Just to keep things nice and calm in here for all the patients.'

'Oh right. That's no problem,' I said. 'Once Ruby arrives, we can take turns to fetch coffee and snacks.' I squeezed Clara's arm but she was still pale as snow, her eyes staring.

'So the important thing, Joe, is not to worry. Just to rest. It must be confusing if you can hear us. But don't be afraid. You had an accident in the car but the surgeons have done a terrific job, sorting you out. They say you're going to be just fine. So your only job now is to rest and let us take care of you while you heal.' I took his hand and gently squeezed it for reassurance. I was tempted to ask him to squeeze my hand back but didn't want him to feel under pressure, just in case he really could hear us.

I took in his closed eyes. All those bruises. And I wondered how scary and difficult it must be in there, trying to figure out what was going on. Out here.

And then I felt this sweep of panic, worrying what was going on in his head. What on earth must it feel like in there? And instantly I swung from hoping he could hear me to realising it might actually be better if he couldn't. For him. Because it occurred to me that it must be terrifying . . . to be able to hear but not to move. And so I told myself that I must keep talking to him, just in case, but deep down I rather hoped he was completely out of it and that to him it would just be like a long sleep until he woke.

CHAPTER 25

BEFORE

RUBY

It didn't take long for the sleeper compartment to feel even more claustrophobic to Ruby. She looked around again. Took in the neatness. The clever design. It wasn't that it was too small or disappointing. In other circumstances she might indeed see it as cosy. A big treat in a little space.

The problem was she felt so alone in the space. And the circumstances were just too awful for her to see it all as anything but confining.

Ruby was again wondering if she should have plumped for the early morning flight just as her phone rang. Clara.

'What's the news?' Ruby felt her heart quicken as she put the phone to her left ear.

'OK. So he's out of theatre. In ICU now. The surgeons say it went well.' Clara paused and Ruby picked up on the 'but' in her tone.

'But *what?*'

'He's in a coma, Ruby.'

'A *coma*?' Ruby couldn't keep the panic from her voice. Back in their old life, when they were a proper family, she was the one who had always tried to protect and reassure Clara. Her sister was always the more nervous of the two. A worrier. Not good at stress. Deeply sensitive to rows and conflict. 'Sorry. Take your time, Clara. I didn't mean to make it harder for you.'

'It's medically induced, apparently. Deliberate. They're keeping him unconscious so his brain can rest. There's swelling or something so it's best for him to rest before they bring him round. But it's so hard to see.'

'Right. OK. So talk to me. You know you can be honest with me. How are you holding up?'

'Not good. I had this idea that when we saw him, he would be coming round from the anaesthetic. I thought he would be groggy but OK. It was such a shock to see him just lying there, eyes shut, with all the machines. I expected to feel relief, but I didn't. I hated it. It really frightened me. Mum wanted me to talk to him and stuff but I just wanted to get out of the room.' Clara started to cry. 'What kind of person does that make me?'

'It makes you human,' Ruby said quickly. 'Don't be so hard on yourself. No one can know how they'll react when something bad happens. Look at me with Ned. I was useless. I couldn't even go to the funeral. His mum said she didn't want me there but I should have pushed back. Phoned her. Asked to go. I should have been there.'

'This isn't like Ned. Dad isn't going to die, is he?' Clara was struggling to speak through the sobbing.

'No, no. I'm not saying this is like Ned. I'm just saying it's very tough when something emotionally big happens. With Dad, we just have to listen to the surgeons, and if they say it went well, we have to believe them. Yes?'

'Yes.'

'So where are you now, Clara. Is Mum nearby?'

'No. I'm in the toilets. I said I needed the loo so that I could ring you without Mum hearing.'

'How's she doing?' Ruby felt her throat clamp as she thought of her mother. Her strong and capable mother who was every bit as infuriating as she was capable. Always stepping up in a crisis, making decisions and sorting logistics like the conductor of an orchestra. Never missing a beat . . .

'She went into shock for a bit. In the taxi. It was frightening actually. I've never seen her like that. Out of the loop, I mean. But she's OK now. Running the show. Staying positive. You know what she's like. How about you?'

'Oh. I don't know. Still not sure it was the right decision to take the train. The sleeper's comfortable but my head's in the wrong place. I'm finding it claustrophobic on my own.'

'But better to be moving, you said. Heading towards us.'

'Yeah.' Ruby looked out at the darkness, with the shadows of buildings and trees streaking past the window. 'I may go to the seating area. The club car or whatever they call it, just to be in a bigger space. Get a drink. Feel like something strong, actually. A brandy or something.'

'OK. But keep your phone with you. Yes?'

'Of course. And text or ring if there's any news at all or any change?'

'Sure. I promise. Bye for now.'

'Love you, sis.'

'You too.'

Ruby put her phone back in her pocket and for a time just glanced around the room, again taking in all the details. The bag on the floor containing the towels. The little vanity gift pack of sleeping mask and earplugs. The shelf above the bed with a charging point for her phone. She let out a long sigh, reached for her bag, checking that she had her card key for the room, and headed out into the corridor.

The steward earlier had said the club car was to the left. She needed the space. A wider view. Change of scene. And yes – a drink. She made her way along the narrow corridor, passing room after room. It was further than she expected, but on arrival she was relieved to find a bright and quiet space with just three or four people sitting with meals and drinks.

She picked an empty banquette for privacy and smiled as a server immediately caught her eye and raised his hand to signal he wouldn't be long. Ruby returned the smile and put her thumb up. Her time in hospitality had made her a patient customer. It was as the server turned away from her that she suddenly caught sight of a flash of distinctive maroon coat at the far end of the club car. The wearer was facing the other way, getting up from his seat.

The server now turned again, moving down the aisle presumably to take her order, momentarily blocking her view. But the jacket was unmistakable. Maroon with black edging. And as the wearer stood and exited the far end of the carriage, Ruby caught sight of the back of his head properly. Mid-brown hair. Long on top and much shorter at the nape of the neck.

She couldn't quite take it in.

It's Scott.

Or rather it looked very much like Scott. His hair. His jacket. And then a voice in Ruby's head replied that it couldn't possibly be Scott. That the stress must be making her see things. Imagine things?

Because these tickets cost a small fortune and Scott was always broke. And in any case, what the hell would Scott be doing on this train?

CHAPTER 26

BEFORE

CLARA

In the toilets still, Clara put her phone back in her pocket and moved into the middle of three cubicles. She didn't actually need the loo but didn't want to risk anyone seeing while she made her 'adjustment'.

Her head was itching. It happened whenever she got stressed and overheated. She tore off a piece of toilet paper to protect her hand, then put down the toilet seat lid. Next she lay several pieces of toilet paper across the top of the lid before sitting down gingerly. Then she pulled off her wig and closed her eyes, feeling the sweep of relief at the coolness to her head.

Clara let out a long sigh. She tried to make her heartbeat settle but it was racing. She thought of her father lying in the hospital bed looking nothing like himself. And then she thought of her conversations with her sister.

Ruby didn't know about her hair loss. Clara always wore her best real-hair wig and an expensive, vibrant band from Etsy over the hairline when they FaceTimed. Clara knew that Ruby would blame herself if she found out and it would become another fault line in their family. *No one is to tell Ruby about my hair . . .*

Clara's hair had begun falling out not long after the huge storm over Ned's death. And Ruby disappearing to Scotland. At first it was just extra hair in her hairbrush every day. Then there was quite an obvious bald patch on the back of her head which she managed by always wearing a ponytail to cover the area. Next quite a significant bald patch appeared on the right-hand side of her head too.

For a time she took to wearing brightly coloured berets and scarves to try to keep her secret from her mother, who was already in an emotional state over Ruby leaving. But finally the hair loss became so bad that she couldn't cover it up anymore, and her mother caught her weeping in her bedroom.

'Oh my darling. Why on earth didn't you come to me sooner?' Her mother pulled her close. 'We are going to get proper advice and help for this.' She leaned back to cup Clara's face between her palms, kissing her forehead. 'Lots more help, darling. This is an illness. Something biological. It's not your fault and no way should you be trying to handle this on your own.'

Clara was already seeing a counsellor for her anxiety. She wasn't like Ruby – all confident and sassy and beautiful and cool. Clara was a geek. Happiest on her computer in her bedroom with the blinds shut. Out in the real world and most especially at school, she always felt as if she were playing a part. She had read all the self-help stuff online. *Fake it until you make it.* In class, she tried to make out that she was comfortable when she was anything but. She had a few friends, but that was mostly because she went out of her way to be good to people. A good listener. A good helper with homework. A support system for anyone who needed it.

A people pleaser, her therapist said. Trying to buy the company and approval of others because her own self-esteem was low.

But why was her self-esteem low? Clara didn't know. And her counsellor didn't seem to have figured it out either. Clara was loved and had a happy and stable home. And apart from wishing she was more like her confident and beautiful big sister, she was content. Until the whole Ned debacle, that is.

Clara had always thought there was something not right about Ned, but she was too afraid to say anything to Ruby, who was so instantly and completely besotted with him. They had always been close, Clara and Ruby, despite their very different personalities. Ruby looked out for Clara. Helped her with her shyness and her anxiety. *You can talk to me. You know that you can always talk to me . . .*

At school, Ruby warned off any bullies and gave Clara advice on how to fit in. She styled her hair. Taught her how to wear the uniform so that she would not be pulled in by prefects but would also not look quite so 'geeky'.

But everything had changed when Ruby started seeing Ned during the upper sixth form – the final year of Ruby's A levels – and Clara had no idea how to navigate that change.

Ned went to the local private school. He was older, redoing his sixth form for some reason, and Ruby met him at a party. The lunchtime afterwards, a Sunday, Ruby called Clara into her room and said that she had met the 'coolest and hottest snack you can imagine'. She showed a picture from his social media.

Ned was indeed a looker. Dark brown hair and huge, dark eyes with lashes that looked as if he were wearing mascara.

'Does he do something to his lashes?' Clara asked.

'No. Of course not.' Ruby enlarged the picture onscreen. 'I mean, I know it looks as if he does. I asked a few people but apparently he just looks like that naturally. It's infuriating, isn't it. My lashes don't look that good even with extensions.'

The following week, Ruby met Ned for drinks at a popular cocktail bar. Next it was the cinema. Then a meal. And then, very quickly, she confided in Clara that she was officially his girlfriend.

'What? Exclusive already?' Clara didn't know why she wasn't that keen on this turn of events. But Ruby was already like a different person. All she talked about was Ned. How clever he was. How incredibly good-looking he was. Knowledgeable about the world. A rebel, too, who was anti-establishment, in fact anti pretty much everything, by the sounds of things.

Clara bit her tongue. And it was not until she met Ned that she realised what was troubling her. It wasn't the lashes – as impressive as they were; it was Ned's eyes. Or rather his pupils.

Ruby introduced them in a coffee shop in town, paying for carrot cake all round. It was around 11 a.m. but Ned was weirdly hyper, as if he'd mainlined sugar. Or alcohol. Or both. He was all opinions. Politics. The patriarchy. And constructs. Everything was a construct, according to Ned. Clara wasn't entirely sure what he meant but wasn't convinced that Ned was either. Words seemed to just spew from his mouth. He spouted his opinions with huge gestures of his hands and arms and hardly drew breath for anyone else to speak.

Clara didn't like how showy he was. How he demanded centre stage. But Ruby just sat there, her face glowing with admiration while Clara narrowed her own eyes and looked at Ned more closely. Yes. There was definitely something up with Ned's pupils.

Later, when they were plaiting each other's hair in Ruby's room, she tested the water.

'So – don't take this the wrong way, sis. But why is Ned redoing his sixth form? Does he use at all?'

Ruby stopped stock still, holding Clara's hair tighter. 'What do you mean, honey?'

'Drugs? Does Ned use? I only ask because he looked a bit – I don't know. Sort of high today. His pupils. And I wondered about him redoing his A levels.'

'*Excuse me?*' Ruby's tone was all indignation, her expression appalled, pulling her chin into her neck.

'I'm asking you straight if Ned does drugs?' Clara kept her gaze fixed on her sister and her tone determined. It was rare for her to find the courage to speak this frankly, but the situation felt serious. Not OK. And she wanted an answer.

'Only a bit of weed.' Ruby shrugged. 'But not all the time. And it's no big deal. And I would have thought you of all people would sympathise with someone needing a break from school. A reset.'

'So do you do weed with him?' Clara felt a sudden sweep of alarm. She knew that a lot of people at school did weed but she'd never seen her sister's pupils enlarged like Ned's and they were both quite anti-drugs. A mug's game, both their parents had warned. And up until now, she and Ruby had agreed.

'No. Not my thing. But I don't judge. It's not a big deal. You really do need to lighten up, sis. I keep telling you. If you want to fit in at school, you really need to chill about this kind of stuff.'

Clara had not answered. But she had felt that her sister was lying to her. And with that came a creeping sense of dread.

CHAPTER 27

BEFORE

THE POLICE

It was early on Thursday, not quite 7 a.m., when Amelie pottered into the kitchen, still in her dressing gown, to find Melanie already up and dressed, serving breakfast to both her husband, Tom, and son George.

'You lot get up so early every morning,' Amelie said, groaning. Her clock struggled between the vampire hours of university life and her stints as a special. But even when she was in the rhythm of her volunteer work, she hated both late finishes and early starts, and secretly wondered how she would manage as a detective.

'We're larks,' Melanie said. 'While you clearly are not. Want coffee?'

'Oh yes please.' Amelie watched Melanie pour it into a generous-sized mug. An attractive artisan affair. Bulbous turquoise with a dark blue handle. Everything so tasteful in Mel's house, much of it sourced from the many galleries around Truro and also the Lizard peninsula. A favourite place for both Mel's family and her own.

'So how was your shift yesterday? I thought you'd be having a lie-in.' Mel had been out with Tom at the cinema when Amelie got in. Date night, they called it, which she found rather cute.

'Interesting shift actually. I woke up early thinking about it and couldn't get back to sleep. I caught a kid with a laser-pointer-type thing. Expensive and powerful one. We looked it up. Took him home to his parents and his story is that he found it and was hoping to sell it. It's a good one. Parents agreed we could confiscate it, so it's at the station.'

'Did you believe the kid? How old? Those lasers can be very dangerous.'

'Yeah, I know. Actually I do believe him. I watched him really closely with his parents. Not been in trouble before. Good school record, blah blah. His parents said he wouldn't have the money to buy it. I think he was telling the truth. So I'm left wondering who dropped it. And what they were doing with it. Probably up to no good. It was by a dual carriageway. But also near a road that leads into residential areas.'

'We can try for prints, but I'll be honest it's not likely to lead anywhere.'

'Actually, I had a slightly off-piste idea I wanted to bounce past you before you head out.'

'I like off-piste. Bounce away.' Mel bit into her toast, and at the sound of the crunch, Amelie suddenly felt hungry. It was like that advert for cheese on toast. You saw it. You wanted it. She moved across the kitchen to the bread bin, to take out two slices. It was so good of Mel to put her up in the holidays so she could do her special shifts more easily. Her parents back in Devon missed her, but Mel's place in Truro really felt like home now.

'I had this idea about checking local traffic accidents throughout yesterday to see if anyone reported anything odd. Bright light that might be a laser pen. But my teammate Ben says I'm being ridiculous. He says I go looking for trouble when we have enough trouble already.' Amelie popped the bread into the toaster and set the timer. 'He calls me Roger, as in Roger Rabbit. *Too much energy and always down rabbit holes*,' she mimicked Ben's grumbling. 'What do you think, Melanie? Am I ridiculous?'

Melanie started to laugh. 'What I think is that you are your father's daughter.'

Amelie smiled too. Her father Matthew, both as a private investigator and previously in the force, was renowned for his strong instinct. And also his stubborn determination.

'The thing is, I'm not supposed to be on shift today,' Amelie added. 'But I'd genuinely like to check this out. Follow it through. Ben says if I pester Traffic to check local accidents for me, they'll think I'm bonkers. Laugh at me.'

'Well. I can see this is a long shot. Odds against it. But you never know. If you fancy following it through on your own time, I'll back you up and clock it up as work experience, with me overseeing. How about that?'

'I thought you were going shopping today?' Mel often worked weekends and took Thursday off when the shops were quieter.

'Well, apparently not. Apparently, I'm popping into the office to catch up on admin while you check yesterday's traffic reports to see if any witnesses reported a blinding light.' Melanie winked at Tom, who also smiled. 'I'm teasing. I mean it when I say I like the way you think, Amelie. And even if it comes to nothing – which I have to say is quite likely – you'll feel better for scratching the itch. A lot of detective work involves accepting time spent on dead ends. So are we on? Day in the office together?'

'Yes. Definitely. But I need more coffee first.' Amelie yawned as the toast popped up, nice and golden. 'And fuel.'

'Help yourself. Oh wait. I see you already did.'

Melanie's tone was clearly teasing again. This time they all laughed, and Amelie beamed and blushed and felt this really nice feeling deep in her gut as she fetched butter and strawberry jam from the fridge.

CHAPTER 28

BEFORE

JOE

Joe felt himself coming to again, and with this strange sense of 'surfacing' came the accompanying and now all-too-familiar wave of panic. He listened but could hear nothing bar the beeping of the machines. No voices. No Laura reassuring him that everything was going to be OK.

Where is she?

He paused and wondered if she was nearby but just silent. Reading maybe? Or had she left the room? Joe tried to calm himself. If he failed to, his heart rate would go up and the machines would kick off. And if Laura was there, she would get so worried.

Laura, Laura, Laura . . .

Joe listened. Longed for her voice but there was nothing. Just the machines. He concentrated on his breathing. In and out. In and out. No alarms pinging. *Good.* And then he tried to regroup; to go over what he knew. So it seemed that he was regularly falling in and out of what he assumed was some kind of deeper sleep. But he had to find a way to stop the panic and the worrying as he resurfaced.

Listening to the machines and the occasional voices in the room and not being able to respond was pure purgatory. But he reminded himself that he was at least beginning to piece together from the whisperings a little of what was going on.

According to the chats he'd overheard between Laura and the medical staff, he was in some kind of induced coma after surgery. He'd found it difficult to pick up the exact details. It depended where Laura and the staff were standing. If they were talking at what he assumed was the nurses' station, he couldn't make out the words at all. Just mumbling. It was only when they were right alongside the bed that he could hear properly.

In between the medical updates, Laura often sat right beside the bed and talked to him directly. He found this really comforting. But she kept it generic. Upbeat. All reassurance and pleas not to worry. But how could Joe not worry?

He was afraid that the deeper 'sleep' he experienced wasn't sleep at all. Some different phase of the coma? It was like living underwater. Sometimes you were right near the surface and aware of life above and beyond the water. And sometimes you sank uncontrollably deeper where everything was much darker.

It frightened him. The spells of greater unconsciousness made him fear he would eventually sink way too deep – so far away from Laura and Clara and Ruby that he wouldn't be able to get back to them.

So every time things became more silent and more distant, he didn't know whether to fight to keep nearer the surface. Or not.

Laura kept saying that his brain needed to rest to recover, but was she right? Should he be letting go? Allowing himself to sink deeper so that his brain could rest? Or was he right to fight it?

He tried for the millionth time to open his eyes. Nothing. He tried to move his hand – first his left and then his right. Again – nothing.

And then, at last, he heard some distant click. The door? And Clara's voice. *Dear, sweet Clara.* She had a very distinctive and very lovely voice, his younger daughter. Higher pitched than Ruby's. Sing-song. Gentle and melodic. He loved both his daughters very much but was constantly surprised at how different they were. Equally lovely but in entirely different ways.

At nursery school, they were chalk and cheese. Ruby had loved it from the off, skipping off to play with hardly a backward glance. But Clara? She had been clingy and tearful at every single drop-off. Joe was ashamed to admit he had been glad that it mostly fell to Laura as it was so traumatic. *Don't leave me here. Please don't leave me . . .*

◆　◆　◆

More voices now. Joe tried hard to listen. Laura was trying to encourage Clara to come closer but the conversation quickly became tense. Furious whispering. Not quite an argument but not relaxed. *Please don't argue*, he was thinking. There had been so much conflict these past few months. He was so tired of it all.

'I need to go home, Mum,' Clara said suddenly.

'How about I ask if there's a family room? Where you can get your head down for a few hours. Some proper sleep?'

'It's not just sleep. I find it really hard here. My stomach's kicking off. My IBS.'

There was a long pause and Laura sighed, changing her tone and reassuring Clara that she should do whatever was right for her.

Joe didn't want Clara to leave but he also didn't want her to be stressed. It had become such a worry to them, Clara's health. She was seeing a counsellor. Laura had encouraged that and was very good at making sure Clara got all the help she needed. But Clara still kept too much to herself. Always holed up in her bedroom.

They didn't like to push but didn't really know what to do for the best. It was like this tricky decision over whether she took a gap year or went straight to university. They were leaving it to her but it was a worry. With the hair loss. And the anxiety. Would she be OK, living away from them?

Joe wondered if it was like this for all parents. The constant worrying.

'I'm sorry but the truth is I need to sort my hair out at home,' Clara said finally, and there was this rustling sound. Fabric on fabric. He imagined it was Laura giving their daughter a hug.

She was a very good mother, Laura, but she could be a bit full-on and it had not been easy since the mistake she'd made over Ned. The thing she wished she could undo. She hadn't voiced her regret out loud because that would be too painful for her, but Joe knew she wished she could go back in time. Undo it.

The consequence for all of them had been so terrible. Ruby and Clara especially.

'Here. Take a taxi. Have a rest at home if that's what you need, but keep in touch with me and with Ruby, will you, darling. Yes?'

'Of course.'

Next there was another door click and he could only assume that Clara had left.

For a time there was just the noise of the machines. And then there was a new sound – something soft and stifled. And Joe felt wretched and utterly helpless because he was pretty sure it was the sound of his wife trying very hard to cover up the fact that she was crying.

CHAPTER 29

BEFORE

Ruby

Ruby could not know it at the time but replying to the text from Scott would become the worst mistake of her life.

The text pinged into her phone on Thursday morning as she was eating breakfast in her little compartment. A bacon roll. Quite nice, though she lost her appetite the moment her phone vibrated.

How's the sleeper? You OK?

Ruby's heart instantly began to race. The text seemed to confirm what she'd lain awake worrying about all night. Scott knew she was on this train. Hell. There was a possibility that Scott might be on this train himself.

After catching what she thought was a glimpse of his coat in the club car last night, she'd phoned a friend, Anna, back at the hotel to check that Scott was still there. She'd expected reassurance. Confirmation that he was still in Scotland and she was simply being paranoid. That it was a horrible coincidence; someone with the same coat on the train.

But the reply from her friend chilled her to the bone. Anna said Scott had left the hotel very suddenly, not long after Ruby. No one knew where he was. The gossip was that he was facing a 'final warning' or even the sack over it.

Ruby had kept her call to Scotland short. She'd pretended it was nothing to worry about because she didn't want more gossip back at the hotel.

But now *this* text. How could he know for sure that she was on the sleeper? She'd not told anyone her final travel plans as she was still torn between the train and the plane when she left the hotel.

So had he followed her? Was it really him in the restaurant car last night?

How's the sleeper?

Ruby, her heart palpitations increasing, started to type her reply, panic and anger coursing through her.

Are you on my train? I thought I saw you last night in the bar. What the hell, Scott?

Three dots came and went for what felt like minutes. Finally the reply landed.

Just looking out for you. Here if you need me.

Ruby closed her eyes, feeling dizzy suddenly. So this was not paranoia. Scott was definitely on . . . this . . . bloody . . . train. Her heart was still racing as a million thoughts started to fire around her brain. She remembered him turning up at her house share, lying that she had asked him to bring his records round. He was crossing all the lines now. Out-and-out harassment. Borderline stalking. Her housemate and friend Natalie had been right. She should have reported him.

So what to do now? Should she contact staff on the train? The transport police? Clara? No. Clara was already stressed enough.

Ruby's breath was feeling strained, her chest tight. It was not long after eight and the train was coming into Euston. Very soon, she'd have to get off. She opened her eyes as the phone vibrated with another message.

Shall we grab a coffee together? Here for you.

Fight or flight mode now. With her adrenaline pumping, she started typing as fast as she could.

You should not be following me. I have told you to stay away from me.

Just being a good friend.

This is stalking, not friendship! STAY AWAY.

We could travel to Cornwall together. I can help you.

Ruby was horrified. Scott must have found out back at the hotel that she was going to the hospital in Cornwall.

NO! You come near me, Scott, and I swear to God, I will make you VERY sorry.

Even as she pressed send, she could see that her message looked a bit like a threat. But Ruby didn't care. She meant it. She was sick to the back teeth of Scott and his StarBonders nonsense. His bonkers narrative that they were somehow 'destined' to be star mates, whatever that was supposed to be.

She was alarmed but not entirely surprised to hear from Clara that StarBonders was in the news. The fact a mother was talking to the media about the organisation had shaken her; made her realise that she should have taken action much earlier over Scott. And yes. Involved the police.

Staring at the message exchange in her hand, Ruby realised that grief and loneliness had skewed her judgement in Scotland. She should never have struck up the friendship with Scott and she should have run a mile once he became so clingy. So strange.

She remembered now that awful evening when he had declared his feelings for her.

I've had a reading. You need to look at the star chart with me. Seriously, Ruby. We are meant to be. We can't fight it . . .

And now he was seriously harassing her. At her house. At the hotel. And now on this bloody train while she needed to concentrate on her family. Her poor father in hospital . . .

Ruby threw the remains of the bacon roll in the bin and gathered her things, checking the small en-suite bathroom before zipping up her case and putting on her coat.

She stared again at her phone, dreading another reply. But there was nothing.

If her calculations were correct, Scott was at least two carriages away from her. She would get off the train as quickly as she could and take a taxi to Paddington for a train to Truro. Sod the Underground.

If Scott was waiting for her on the platform and approached her in any way at all, she would call transport security. Or the police. She would remind Scott there was CCTV everywhere and he must leave her alone.

Ruby kept staring at her phone screen, her palms sweaty. No further reply from Scott. Good.

She quickly messaged Clara, wondering why there had been no more updates.

What's happening? Any change with Dad? I'm just about to get off the sleeper.

A few minutes passed before a slightly baffling reply came back. Clara said there was no change in their father's condition but she was now going to take a taxi home. Not feeling well. She would be returning to the hospital when she felt better and would see Ruby there.

Ruby was both confused and worried. She dialled Clara's mobile and her sister picked up immediately.

'You OK? What's going on? What's wrong, lovely? Why are you going home on your own?'

There was a long pause. 'Some kind of stomach thing,' Clara said. 'My IBS is kicking off. It'll pass. Probably just the stress. I'll go back to the hospital as soon as it settles.'

'OK. Well, I'm so sorry you're not good.'

'It's fine. Look. I need to go. Sort the taxi. You know what it's like when I get this. I'll speak soon.'

'OK.' For a beat, Ruby considered telling Clara about Scott being on the train. But it was clear that her sister was far from OK herself. She didn't want to add to her worries. Her stress. And so Ruby took a deep breath. 'Lots of love to you. And to Dad if you get back there before me. I'll update when I'm closer.'

'OK. I love you too.'

And then she was gone and Ruby was left feeling oddly empty. And afraid. And very alone.

She had so wanted to confide in someone about Scott.

But something in her sister's tone had really worried her.

Or rather added to her list of worries. About her father. About what it would feel like to come face to face with her mother after all this time.

And how the hell she was going to deal with Scott.

CHAPTER 30

BEFORE

LAURA

I'd been warned to expect more contact from the police about Joe's accident. But so soon?

I was sitting beside Joe's bed drinking coffee from the machine in the corridor when I saw them arrive. Two women. One very young in uniform and one much older in a navy skirt and polka dot blouse. It was Thursday morning, barely breakfast time. Why so early?

Late last night a constable in uniform, an older guy, had called in with an update on the accident investigation. He'd pretended it was all about family care, but I saw him talking with staff and suspected he was really tasked with finding out when Joe would be well enough to give a statement. He told me that no other vehicle seemed to be involved, and it would take time to appraise the various photographs from the scene. The car would be evaluated for faults. They were still looking for witnesses and checking local CCTV, also waiting for various test results.

He didn't spell it out but I picked up they were also waiting for blood test results to see if Joe had been drinking. I knew he'd be in the clear. Joe would never drink and drive.

Knowing how stretched the police were these days, I hadn't expected to hear any more from them for a while, especially with Joe unable to give a statement himself, so I watched these two new officers talking to the nurse, wondering what the hell was going on. Had something changed? New information?

Finally the nurse glanced my way. There was more whispering and nodding which made me feel seriously uneasy, until at last the nurse moved across the unit to approach me.

'It's the police again about the accident. They'd like to have a word with you if possible.'

'I don't like to leave my husband. My daughter's had to go home for a bit, and I don't want to talk alongside the bed in case he can hear. In case it upsets him.'

'How about I sit with him while you talk to the officers? They said it wouldn't take long.'

I agreed to this, picking up my handbag before walking across the unit, taking a long, slow breath as I reached the two officers.

'I'm Laura Harry. I understand you may have some more information. About my husband's accident?' I kept my voice low, aware of other relatives at bedsides. There were six cubicles in the unit, all the patients clearly very unwell.

'I'm sorry to intrude at such a worrying time. I'm DCI Melanie Sanders.' The older woman stretched out her hand and shook mine. Warm face. A small smile. But what the hell was such a senior officer doing investigating a road traffic accident? 'And this is Special Constable Amelie Hill, who's working with me this week.'

'A DCI on a road traffic accident?' I said. 'Should I be worried? Is there something I should know?'

'Do you mind if we step into the corridor?' Melanie Sanders' voice was gentle. Confident.

I nodded and followed them to seating just outside the unit entrance.

'You're right. It would normally be uniform. And not normally a senior officer.' She smiled again. 'But I'm supporting Special Constable Hill on her inquiries into an unusual find near to your husband's accident, and so we're just trying to see if there might be any connection.'

'What sort of unusual find?'

'A laser pointer. Or laser pen. Have you heard of them?'

'Yes.' I frowned and noticed that DCI Melanie Sanders was watching me especially closely. It put me on edge and I wondered what on earth was going on.

'A laser pointer was found not far from where your husband's accident happened. We've been looking into that. My colleague has been cross-checking witness statements and it turns out there was a woman on the street where the accident happened who saw a strange bright light in the road. Just before the crash. She was closing her curtains at the time.'

'Are you saying this laser pointer may have caused my husband's accident?' I felt stunned. 'That this may have been *deliberate?* I had imagined Joe being tired. On his phone. Changing the radio station and getting distracted for a moment. It had never occurred to me that someone may have caused his accident on purpose.

'I realise this must be upsetting. At this stage, we don't have clear evidence what exactly happened. It may have been random. Someone being reckless with a laser pointer. But we'll be making more inquiries and we need to ask if you're aware of anyone hassling your husband. Threatening your husband. Anything unusual going on within the family or at work for him?'

'No. No. Absolutely not. My husband is a really gentle man. He wouldn't have any enemies. So this could just be random? Some nutter with a laser pen in the street?'

'As I say. That could possibly be it.'

'Do they have the results yet from the car? Could it not have been brakes or something like that?' I was reeling. Not wanting this to be deliberate.

'We're fast-tracking the checks on the car now,' DCI Sanders said. 'I'll let you know as soon as we know anything.'

I wondered if they knew yet whether he had been on his phone. I wanted to say that his phone connected to the media unit by Bluetooth but decided to keep shtum. Just in case.

'We've checked his phone records this morning after the laser pointer came into play as a possible line of investigation.'

So she was sharp, this DCI Sanders. It was as if she were reading my mind. 'Your husband wasn't on his phone.'

'Right. Good.' I paused. 'In any case we both use the Bluetooth connection in the car. For Spotify and for calls. It's perfectly safe.'

I could feel myself flushing as I said this.

'And you don't remember anything unusual happening lately? Or your husband mentioning anything worrying him?'

I thought for a moment and suddenly remembered the figure in the alleyway behind our garden. The weird bright torch. Hang on. Maybe it *wasn't* a torch? Maybe . . .

I looked at the two women, my frown deepening.

'What is it? What is it you're remembering?' It was still the senior officer speaking.

'There was someone checking out my garden this week. With a very bright torch. Or at least I thought it was a torch. I thought it might be a burglar or just kids mucking about. I was going to call my husband, but whoever it was ran off.'

'You saw them?'

'Well, not clearly. Just someone in a hoody at the back of our rear garden. There's an alleyway.'

'And when exactly was this?'

I frowned again, remembering our argument. Joe sleeping in the spare room. 'Tuesday night. Yes. The night before his accident.'

'Do you have any security cameras at your home that might have picked this up?'

'No. Sorry. Nothing like that.'

'And could you give a description?'

'Not really. Like I say, it was late. Just a figure in a hoody, with what I thought was a strong torch. But it could have been a laser. It was certainly exceptionally bright. So piercing that I had to move aside from the window.'

'Right. OK. Well – we'll need to take a statement about this. Do you mind if Special Constable Hill does that? I need to make a call, get uniform to speak to your neighbours to see if anyone else saw this. Or if there are any security cameras nearby that may have picked it up.'

'Right.' Still I felt winded. And then for the first time in a while, my mind suddenly travelled to the young woman at the hotel in Paris. And I wondered if I would sound like a complete lunatic if I told them that I was getting more and more alarmed that so many odd – and now dangerous – things seemed to be happening in my life. All of them since I met her . . .

Should I tell them? Mention her? The dry-cleaning mystery and the pendants turning up. StarBonders all over the news suddenly. Or would that just sound stupid? Undermine my credibility because how could it be connected?

I considered everything for a beat. Felt overwhelmed.

I took a deep breath and decided – *no*. I needed them to see me as steady, not hysterical. I needed them checking what had really happened here to my husband. I didn't want them thinking I was paranoid. Unhinged.

I wanted them putting all of their energy into finding out what had happened to Joe.

CHAPTER 31

BEFORE

CLARA

Clara sat at her dressing table and checked the latest from the WhatsApp group to find that the messages about the retreat were finally starting to calm down.

Everyone had read the latest StarBonders blog. Most seemed to be reassured that this was just the media targeting StarBonders unfairly.

For herself, Clara wanted to trust the blog and all the reassurances, but she was still very stressed. She felt guilty. And conflicted. What if there *was* something to this story? She thought of her mother, back at the hospital on her own now, and was petrified she would find out about everything.

She couldn't bear to think how she would react. Clara loved her mother very much but the problem was her mother saw everything in black and white. It was literally like that row over the stupid blind in her bedroom. Her mother always thought she was right. She saw everything as her business. And she was a classic catastrophiser.

Clara felt overwhelmed. What if her whole family rumbled the truth about her and StarBonders?

What if she'd made a terrible miscalculation?

She moved across the room and lay down on her bed. She so wished Ruby was there. Before all the trauma over Ned, she and Ruby had shared this really important bond over their mother. They would joke about her. Roll their eyes at her panics and her drama. But they knew deep down that for all their moaning and their eye-rolling, they both loved their mother very much. And to have lost that bond – to be in this awful place where Clara did not even know for sure what Ruby truly felt about their mother anymore – was beyond terrible.

Because if you didn't have family, if you weren't a proper family, what the hell did you have?

Clara turned on to her right side so that she could see the window. Thinking of Ruby and lying on the bed, staring at the window with the curtains open, made her think of Christmas when they were little. She and Ruby had always shared this room on Christmas Eve and would lie together, curled up in this very bed with the curtains wide, staring at the night sky.

Do you think we will see him? Do you think we can stay awake?

Ruby always fell asleep first and Clara loved it. The quiet and the calm with her sister fast asleep and close by. The excitement of Christmas ahead of them. The hope that she might, just might, manage to stay awake to see Santa and his sleigh cross the night sky this one time. This one year . . .

She clenched her right fist and felt a churning in her stomach at the contrast to all these years later. So *alone*. It would be hours yet before Ruby made it to Cornwall. Clara felt so conflicted and also a little ashamed. She should be with her poor father. With her mother. But the truth was she didn't feel strong enough to face all that. The hospital. The machines and the smell and the fear deep in the pit of her stomach. It had so shocked her to see her father, eyes closed, head bandaged and his mind who knew where?

Clara let out a long, slow sigh and realised there was no choice. She would have to stay put here at home and try to calm her own thoughts before returning to the ward.

She turned over again to lie flat on her back. Once more it was good to feel the cool of the cotton pillow against her scalp. She wished some days that she had the courage to forget the wig altogether.

But Clara didn't want people to think she was having chemo for cancer. Couldn't face all the explaining that would involve.

The wig her mother had bought was one of the best on the market. It was convincing – made of real hair – and most of the time she didn't think anyone rumbled she had a problem at all.

Problem?

Her counsellor said it was quite possible her hair loss had nothing to do with her anxiety. It was an unpredictable and unfair disease which could be completely unrelated. Could happen to anyone at any time. Sometimes it could simply resolve as quickly and surprisingly as it arrived. But Clara also knew that hair loss could be linked to trauma and anxiety, so it was all, of course, a vicious circle. Worrying on a loop.

She worried that the hair loss was somehow her fault. And she couldn't know if it continued precisely because she was anxious about it.

When Clara was managing her anxiety and looking after her diet and her health, she had spells of hair regrowth which suggested it *was* linked to how she was doing and feeling. A part of her just longed for the day this was all behind her. When she might look back on all of this as a temporary nightmare.

For now it was her father she was worried about. And also her sister's reaction.

Ruby would notice the wig for sure. Ruby would then ask questions and blame herself. For leaving. Which was bonkers, because it wasn't Ruby who'd started this. And secretly Clara did not believe it was their mother's fault either.

It was Ned who had started this.

Ned with his loud opinions and his obsession with 'constructs' and long lists about everything wrong in society. Ned with his weird pupils. And his drugs.

Ned.

Clara closed her eyes as the familiar picture flashed into her brain. In the kitchen downstairs. Everyone else out. The first time she had started to seriously worry about him.

It was autumn, the lawn covered in leaves from the three trees nearest the house. Her father had been saying for days that he would sweep them up but Clara had begged him to leave them for a little longer. She loved to put on her short wellingtons and march through them. Crunch, crunch. Clara had stared out at the garden, the myriad colours – brown and orange and yellow – and decided on a cup of tea to break up her studying. She'd been revising for exams; she couldn't remember which ones.

She'd thought that Ruby and Ned were downstairs watching a film together in the sitting room, but when she reached the kitchen Ned was fumbling through her mother's large red money pot on the windowsill.

'What are you doing?' Clara was shocked.

'Nothing. Just looking for change for parking.'

'That's my mum's. You know that's my mum's.'

'Yeah. Sorry. I was going to leave a note and get change.'

'Why do you need money for parking? And where's Ruby?'

Even as she asked these questions, Clara knew that something bad was going on. The huge ceramic pot was a sort of holiday savings fund. A family joke. A bit of fun. Her mother put all her loose change in there – pound and two-pound coins – over the whole year. Then just before each holiday, they would have a ceremonial counting. It was surprising how it added up. Hundreds of pounds. Her mother would transfer the money into euros and split it between Clara and Ruby as extra spending money. Some years it was nearly two hundred pounds each.

'Ruby's gone into town. I said I'd pick her up. I don't have any change for parking.'

'There are loads of places you can just pull in to park. And there are apps to pay. No one uses cash anymore. And anyway – why didn't you just go with her?'

Clara didn't like that Ned was in the house without Ruby. It felt every kind of wrong. Why would he feel it was OK to hang around their house without Ruby? Fool around with her mother's savings pot?

'Look. I'll get going now. If I can't find anywhere to park, I'll message her to meet in a lay-by. You're right. I should have thought of that.'

'You shouldn't be taking money from my mum's pot. That's not OK.' Clara could feel herself flushing, surprised at how angry the whole scene made her.

'There's no need to make such a big deal about it. It's only loose change for parking.'

'I'm not making a big deal. I'm telling you not to touch my mother's things. My mother's money.'

He locked eyes with her and then rolled his own. 'Ruby's right. You really can be so dramatic, Clara.' A pause. 'You need to chill.'

'Ruby said that?'

Clara felt a punch to her gut. To think of her sister bad-mouthing her to him. To horrible Ned. She could feel her face flushing again and the anxiety building in her stomach as he reached for his car keys from the kitchen table and marched through the hall to the front door.

'Bye, then,' he called out. 'Try not to miss me.'

Clara heard him pull the door shut and went to check the ceramic pot. It was, of course, impossible to know how much he'd taken – the large pot around three-quarters full. Clara remembered frowning and wondering why the hell he would need to sneak money – small change from a savings pot – when his family were so well off?

It was no secret that Ned's mother came from money. *Proper* money. A trust fund born of property development by her father and grandfather. Ned's mother wore expensive clothes and drove a very expensive car. Enormous house. So why the hell would Ned be angling for small change?

He didn't have a job but he had a car, and so Clara assumed he had some kind of allowance. Bankrolled by his mother?

She would like to have asked Ruby about it, but realised she couldn't. She was still very much in the honeymoon phase with Ned. Besotted. Bewitched. Ruby was choosing to believe that his use of drugs was no big deal.

Clara heard the echo of Ned's taunt. *Ruby's right. You really can be so dramatic . . .*

She felt so torn over what to do for the best. She couldn't bear to think of Ned rifling through the family's things. But she also couldn't bear to imagine Ruby's disapproval. Ruby and Ned laughing at her behind her back.

Later Clara would come to bitterly regret not speaking up that day; would wish she'd had a quiet word, at least with her mother. Maybe all the terrible drama that followed could have been cut off at the pass?

But the fact was, she didn't say anything.

The family was on a path to disaster already. The juggernaut was gathering speed. No brakes.

And Clara had absolutely no idea how to stop it.

CHAPTER 32

BEFORE

Ruby

It was nearly 8.30 a.m. and the final passengers were leaving the train. Ruby had her handbag across her body, holding her small suitcase in her left hand with her phone in her right-hand jacket pocket. Heart pounding. Eyes darting left to right.

She waited until a staff member appeared to her left, moving along the corridor.

'Excuse me.' She raised her voice. 'I'm sorry, but would you mind helping me off the train?' She signalled to her small case, and only then realised the request for assistance probably sounded strange. Healthy young woman. Small suitcase. 'It's just I have a shoulder injury. Finding any kind of lifting tricky.' She tried to find a smile.

'Oh right. Sure.' The male attendant smiled back and strode forward to pick up her case before opening the door and stepping down ahead of her.

'Actually. I'm sorry to be a complete pain.' She was still glancing left to right. 'I hate to ask, but actually would it be a nightmare to help me along the platform?'

'Does the case not have wheels? I can set it up for you to pull.' The attendant's tone was now curious. Wary. He perhaps thought she was a weirdo. Or worse – was hitting on him. There was clearly a lot of activity on the train behind them. The changeover for new passengers. He probably had work to do.

'OK. I am going to be straight.' Ruby lowered her voice then took a breath. 'There was a guy bothering me in the bar last night and I'm a bit worried he's going to be a nuisance. On the platform. I'm nervous he might look out for me.'

'Oh right. Goodness.' The attendant now frowned. Face flushed. 'Do you want to file a complaint? Do we need to get anyone involved officially? Transport police?'

'Oh no, no, no. Nothing like that. Just a bit of a tryer. I'd rather avoid him, that's all. If he's on the platform at the same time.'

'No problem. I'll help you to the barrier but then I'll have to come back. Press on. It's a bit busy after debarkation.'

'Of course. I appreciate this.' Ruby again glanced both ways. No sign of Scott. Good. The attendant wheeled her case at a lick ahead of her, but as she marched behind, past the length of one carriage, Scott suddenly stepped down from the train, clearly looking out for her.

'Ruby. Ruby? It's so great I caught you. I can help you with the luggage—'

'You stay away from me, Scott! You hear me.' Ruby was shaken. Raised her voice.

'Is this the gentleman you mentioned?' The attendant turned as he spoke, his expression more concerned.

'It is. Scott. You need to leave me alone.' Ruby began moving again, increasing her pace as the attendant took her cue and walked close beside her, wheeling her case.

'Look. I'm just trying to help. To be a good friend.' Scott reached out his hand as if to take the handle of the case from the attendant.

'The lady doesn't want your help, thank you, sir.' The attendant stepped further away from Scott and kept up his pace. 'She's made that very clear, so how about you get on with your day. And you leave her to get on with hers. Yes? Hope you had a good journey with us.'

'And how the feck is this any business of yours?'

'Sir?'

Scott then suddenly lunged to grab hold of Ruby's arm. 'We need to talk. You have a lot on your plate, Ruby—'

'Get off me!' Ruby jolted her arm to shake him off. 'I swear to God, you touch me again and I will not be responsible for my actions. You hear me? I'm warning you to stay the hell away from me!'

At this Scott finally stepped back and raised both hands in mock surrender. 'I was just trying to help.'

The attendant narrowed his eyes as if assessing this update, and then marched faster to the barrier, waiting until Ruby had used her digital ticket to move through to the main concourse. 'I think this really is a matter for the transport police, miss. I don't feel happy—'

'No, no. There's no need for that. I'll be fine from here. Thank you. If you could just ask the gentlemen to hold back a moment. Leave me be.' She hurried forward then, almost running with the case click-clicking across the uneven tiles and different surfaces. Ruby felt her heart pounding in her ears as she scanned for taxi signs. She turned her head very briefly to see the attendant still talking to Scott, who stepped back from the barrier and seemed to be remonstrating with him.

And then finally she got lucky. Only two people ahead of her in the queue for a taxi. Plenty of vehicles lined up. Within just a couple of minutes she was sitting in the back of one, her hand shaking as she took out her phone, relieved she had put the number of the transport police on speed dial if she needed it.

'Paddington, please.' Ruby clicked her seat belt into place and turned her head again, surprised that for now at least there was no further sign of Scott.

But there could be no relief.

Because Scott had crossed even more lines now. He had followed her. Hassled her. And worst of all, she'd told friends at the hotel which hospital her father was in. So it was almost certain that Scott knew precisely where she was going.

CHAPTER 33

BEFORE

THE POLICE

'So what did you make of the wife, Laura Harry?' Melanie turned towards Amelie to check her expression as she spoke. They were at traffic lights, not long after leaving the hospital site.

'Don't know. A lot on her plate. But . . .' Amelie paused.

'But what?'

'I can't explain it. To me, she seemed to be holding something back.'

'*Exactly* what I thought,' Mel replied, pulling away.

'So what now?' Amelie asked.

'Well, I think we should check out the neighbours on the Harrys' street. See if anyone else saw that possible laser pen beam around the rear gardens on Tuesday evening. Or the person in the hoody. But before that' – Melanie indicated to overtake a parked car – 'first I think it's worth you rechecking Anstey Way. Try to find anyone *else* that saw that laser pen in use at the time of the accident. Wednesday.'

'Definitely up for that.' Amelie knew there had been door-to-door inquiries already. But they were notoriously random. Some people wouldn't have been in. And the initial checks had been made before they knew what evidence they were really looking for.

'OK. Should also mention that I've just had a message from your dad.'

'And what did he want?' Amelie felt suddenly conflicted. And guilty. She had become so embroiled in the investigation she'd forgotten to make her usual call to her parents the previous evening.

'Don't shoot the messenger but he asked me to remind you to FaceTime.'

'Oh crikey. I'm sorry about that.' Amelie flushed. It was an odd dynamic, this. Melanie both a family friend and professional mentor.

She'd known Melanie since she was a little girl. Since something *terrible* had happened to their whole family when she was a little girl. Something she preferred not to talk about these days . . .

Melanie and Amelie's father had always been close friends, inside and out of work. And Mel had always been kind to Amelie as she'd grown up. Even when Amelie and her parents moved to France, Melanie would bring her family to visit once or twice a year. And Mel was the one who'd helped talk her father round when Amelie announced her grand plan to follow in his footsteps. Become a detective.

'I'm sorry,' Amelie repeated. 'He's right. I forgot. Got a bit wrapped up in this laser pen stuff.'

'Yes. I've been telling him how well you're doing. Good instincts and all that. Hand on heart, I hadn't expected your inquiries to come to anything, but I'm having a big rethink now. That new witness. And also the way the wife was in hospital.' A pause. 'We need to get to the bottom of this.'

'Agreed.'

'So I drop you at Anstey Way and will pick you up after I've done my admin. And the deal is you—'

'Will FaceTime Mum and Dad tonight. *Promise.*'

'Thank you.'

They both smiled, still facing forward, watching the road. And then they switched gear, Melanie worrying about supper. She'd put a chicken dish in the hotpot before they left, dashing around the kitchen to chop vegetables and find stock. She was now regretting not adding dumplings.

'Do you like dumplings?'

'I do. But it will be fine without.'

Truth was, Amelie was in awe of the way Melanie juggled everything, just as her mother did. The job. The family. All the chores. Tom stepped up too, but it always seemed to be Melanie striding around the kitchen doing a million things at warp speed the same time every morning. She'd even somehow managed to put a wash on before they left. All while Amelie wolfed down her toast and jam.

Half an hour later, Amelie was on the street where Joe Harry's accident had happened. Anstey Way – a wide, tree-lined road with Victorian terraced and semi-detached properties, most in red brick with bay-fronted windows. She first tried number twenty-four, home of the witness on record as having seen an odd beam of light in the street the previous night when the accident happened. A woman answered the door in a grey sweatpant ensemble with huge pink furry slippers. She seemed stretched. And distracted. 'I'm sorry but I gave a statement on this already. I saw it as I was about to close the curtains. Why do you need to go over this again?'

'Sorry.' Amelie shared her best smile. 'It's just I wondered if anything else had occurred to you since you spoke to the police. Gave your statement.'

'Only that the lady at number eleven saw exactly the same thing.'

'*Another* witness?' Amelie felt a little lift inside.

'I don't know her name but I bumped into her in the duty chemist's first thing and we got chatting. Anyway. She said she saw exactly the same thing, a sort of piercing beam of light across the street. She was out when the police did their door-to-door last time. I told her I'd already reported it so she didn't think it was worth phoning in.'

'Thank you. That's actually really helpful. I'll see if she's in now.'

Amelie marched down the street, taking in the numbering system. Even numbers this side of the street. So odd numbers opposite. She crossed the road carefully, noticing there were few parking spaces even during the day. The familiar problem of two-car families in a road with no off-street parking.

She took in a long, slow breath as she approached the bright green door to number eleven, where she couldn't quite believe her luck. Both a large warning sign and familiar apparatus confirming she might be on to something.

Number eleven had a doorbell camera.

CHAPTER 34

BEFORE

JOE

Joe felt himself near the surface again. He no longer thought of this as being 'awake'. He still couldn't move or speak. But he was getting more used to this sense of coming and going. Surfacing and sinking. It was a bit like sitting in a room and sometimes finding ear defenders had been put on your head without your knowledge. You were still there. Sort of. Just not one hundred per cent aware.

He was now putting all his effort into fighting the panic. Dreadful as this limbo was, he was learning that it did more harm than good to allow his fears and frustrations to bubble up inside. It simply sent his heart rate racing. Which set off alarms on the machines wired to him, causing all manner of panic among the nursing staff, while achieving precisely nothing.

So his priority now was trying to stay calm. Sometimes he tried to take his mind outdoors. A sunny day at the allotment. He imagined looking around the plot and drawing up a new design and wondering what new plants and vegetables he might try. And sometimes it worked. Soothed him for a while to picture the sun on his face, his hands in the dirt. No sales talk. No worrying over the row between Laura and Ruby. It seemed to calm his heart rate.

But the comfort never lasted. In the end, his mind was always sucked back to the ward. The frustration of his inertia. The need to piece together what had happened. And to listen out for any useful information.

Last night two nurses were discussing a book one of them was reading. A time travel thriller. Right now, he could hear different nurses gossiping about who was having to work the next bank holiday and who might be up for a swap. But still he could not speak. And still he could not move.

So what he tried to do instead now was to concentrate on what Laura had asked of him. To rest. *You need to let yourself heal, Joe. Just take it easy and rest.*

It was so comforting when he could hear her voice, and there was so much he needed to tell her. *Oh, Laura.* Things he should have said already. And so, while he waited to find his voice again, he tried with all his inner strength to fight the internal panic and cling on to the hope that this state, whatever it was, was temporary.

Part of this acceptance and new routine involved letting himself sink deeper, chanting inwardly, 'I will resurface. I will surface.'

And when he was back in the room? He replayed scenes in his head. All the things he needed to tell Laura.

Not just the beam of light before the crash. But the picture of the wretched woman in the nightclub. His brain seeming to ache in his skull as he tried to figure it all out. The guilt now burning inside his trapped body.

Joe was, of course, much too old for clubs. The problem was that some of his clients were not. He now headed a shrinking sales team for his company's cereal bars. Back in the pre-Covid days, Joe had a big team and could delegate wining and dining the younger business contacts to the club-loving members on his team. But the whole landscape was tipped on its head by the pandemic, and his sector had been hit hard. Once everyone was stuck at home, they'd started buying multi-sized boxed cereals. And if they fancied a cereal bar? Well, they were watching YouTube videos on how to make your own, simply for something to do.

Post-pandemic, Joe had lost half his team to redundancy. No one knew what the future held. At one point, Joe feared he might lose not just most of his team but his own job too, and though Laura's content company had ridden the pandemic brilliantly, he felt very uneasy about losing his income stream. It was the first time he'd started to think seriously about what else he might do.

When people finally returned to the workplace, there was a sudden reset of the market. His company's premium low-sugar and high-fibre bars were back in business. But everyone wanted to reinvent themselves. Gut-friendly was the new mantra. And so there was a new formula and new packaging with 'good for gut biodiversity' in gold writing.

I no longer feed people, Joe often reflected. *I feed gut bacteria . . .*

Joe was under new pressure to reclaim the big buyers. So he was back on the circuit of his early years, wining and dining some of his best supermarket clients while also courting new ones.

Hence the wretched nightclub. Last week, after a very nice dinner, three of his new contacts had wanted a nightcap. Joe suggested they head back to their very smart, all-expenses-paid hotel. He imagined a nice single malt on the rocks. But no. The younger gang fancied a club. And cocktails. Joe's heart sank.

He had never much liked clubs, even when he was younger. The lights. The noise. The mayhem. But one of the clients (two hundred high-end supermarkets) was on the verge of saying yes to a big new order. So Joe messaged Laura to say where he was going to try to clinch a deal. She sent back a laughing emoji.

He wasn't laughing. He was suffering. And then the night took a turn. At the club, he and his business companions were approached by three women who, quite frankly, did not look much older than Joe's daughters. Joe was mortified.

'Think I'm probably going to turn in,' he said, standing and brushing down his trousers. 'I'll get another round in then leave you to it. See you at breakfast.'

'Oh don't be so boring,' said Todd, the senior partner of the chain of supermarkets who had been negotiating the big new deal. Todd was newly single after a messy divorce. Evidently in an entirely different place. 'The girls tell us there's a much better place across town. I've ordered a taxi.'

'And I hope you will have a lovely time, Todd. But it really is time for me to turn in.'

'Mate. Mate. I am on the verge of making a decision about your proposal. And I think this place across town might be perfect for us to finalise numbers and then celebrate.'

Joe felt a sweep of anger at the emotional blackmail but did his very best to conceal it. It was in that moment, staring at pink-faced Todd alongside a woman young enough to be his daughter, that he realised he absolutely had to talk to Laura. About the idea of a sabbatical. About feeling too old for the sales circuit with all of its nonsense.

'One drink. To toast the deal. And then I'm back to my hotel,' Joe said, trying to find a smile.

'Good man.'

And so he found himself in the back of a taxi alongside a blonde woman who seemed intent on taking photographs. 'No. Please. I don't do selfies. Family man. You're wasting your time,' he whispered.

But still she stretched out her phone, held up high of course, and took the selfie, deliberately kissing him on the cheek – which made him feel deeply uncomfortable. And even more cross that he had allowed Todd to manipulate him.

At the club bar he paid for the champagne, lined up a second bottle for the gang and shook Todd's hand. 'I'm delighted we have a deal. Let's say we go with the last numbers we discussed. An excellent decision. There's a second bottle of Bolly lined up. Great night, guys. I will see you and your hangovers at breakfast.'

The small group laughed. Joe laughed. And at last he was able to leave.

It was just an hour later, back at his hotel, that the photograph pinged into his WhatsApp. A close-up of the girl kissing him with a short message: One for the wife? Plus a laughing emoji.

Joe went cold. How the hell had the young woman got his number? Drunken Todd must have shared it.

He did not reply. Was not entirely sure what that meant. If he failed to acknowledge the message and the new contact, would it disappear? Could he just delete it? Was WhatsApp like Snapchat? He had no idea.

A second picture then landed – in the taxi but a wider shot featuring more of the group. So where the hell was all this nonsense going? How he was wishing he had listened to his gut in the first place. A part of him felt he should message Laura, tell her about the stupid picture and ask her advice on what he should do.

But just a few minutes later – another ping to his phone. Another photograph. A more graphic photograph from the girl, her top and bra removed, with another short message.

Because you asked me so nicely . . .

CHAPTER 35

LETTERS FROM A LIGHTHOUSE

THE STARBONDERS BLOG

Dear StarBonders,

It has been an upsetting and difficult week here at the Lighthouse, but I've always promised to be open so I want to put everyone fully in the picture.

First – I know that many of you have been concerned whether our first retreat will be going ahead as planned, given all the distressing and wholly inaccurate speculation about StarBonders in the media. I'm very happy to tell you that the retreat WILL happen. But we've decided to put the date back by a month. All those who have paid their deposit or been added to the waiting list will be getting an email very soon, explaining everything in more detail. But I wanted to share this update with everyone.

As you may know, we have been receiving some very unpleasant messages on social media – mostly linked to the coverage of the poor girl who is still in hospital but whose sad circumstance is no one's business but her family's . . . and is absolutely nothing to do with StarBonders.

We had planned to just sit this out and show compassion and patience, as outlined in our first blog about the media coverage. But sadly that is no longer possible. The media frenzy is damaging not only our reputation but also the plans for our retreat and hence our financial situation.

Please don't worry. We have resilience . . . AND reserves. StarBonders is secure. We will always be here for you. But our lawyers have advised that we cannot allow these unfounded attacks to threaten how we operate.

For this reason, to protect StarBonders, our reputation, the retreat and our future, we are taking legal action against those who are libelling our company. This is not a decision we have taken lightly. Legal action is complex, expensive and a distraction we could well do without. But our critics have stepped over the line and there is a danger that failing to react will add fuel to the ridiculous accusations being made.

I promise that I will keep you in the loop going forward. If the revised retreat date is not suitable to you, we will organise a refund of your deposit, and your place will be reallocated to those at the top of our long wait list.

Many of you have asked for more information on the setting so you can plan your journeys. We had intended to give you the address of the Lighthouse and our retreat accommodation this very week but, given the media activity, we're exercising caution to keep everyone on our team safe. So I promise more details will be coming soon. But for now, look out for your email which will include pictures of the retreat's internal accommodation (spoiler alert – it's GORGEOUS!) and also, most important, of the night sky here at HQ with all YOUR stars and star matches shining brilliantly, in defiance of those who are choosing to misunderstand all we stand for.

As always, do reach out to your team mentor or arrange an additional reading if you have any worries.

In the next blog, I will be putting all this distraction aside to bring you up to date with Alicia's story. Second spoiler alert. We have a proposal to celebrate, people!!! He asked . . . and she said 'YES'. Alicia, like many of you, feared she would never know true happiness. But thanks to StarBonders, she's looking forward to the future she deserves. So do not lose faith. We are here for you all. And we will not let others pollute our pure and beautiful sky.

Phoebe xx

CHAPTER 36

BEFORE

THE POLICE

Amelie looked at the young man's distorted face – a plastic bag over his head tied in a small, grim knot at the back of his neck – and felt the first muscular roll of a retch.

'You OK. Need some air?' Melanie crouched alongside the body as she caught Amelie's eye.

'No, no. I'll be fine.'

Amelie dug her nails into her palm and felt a very long way from fine. She didn't want to say out loud what she was thinking – that seeing her first dead body was so much worse than she'd expected. The eyes were the thing – open and bulging. For some reason she had expected the eyes to be closed. And the body was twisted into a position that signalled the desperate fight for air.

It was like looking at a still photo but having the violence of the scene playing simultaneously in your head. She could imagine it so vividly. Viscerally. The recent struggle right here in the room. This young man arching his back and fighting for air. Fighting for his life.

When the call first came in, Melanie had warned her it would be grim. Said that Amelie did not have to attend. Amelie had stubbornly insisted she would be fine.

'Right. So what do we have?'

Melanie was now looking at the detective inspector in the room. Amelie imagined he wasn't thrilled to have 'the boss' checking out his crime scene. But Melanie was known for this. As the head of CID, she had oversight of several cases at once and was always juggling data and teams and budgets. But she was famous for turning up on the front line when she was least expected. Especially at a murder scene.

'ID from his wallet says this is Scott Crawford. Twenty-seven. Driving licence has current address listed in Scotland. Some money in the wallet too, which suggests theft was not the motive. There's also a leaflet and freebies from the sleeper train from Inverness in the room. We'll be able to check for train tickets when we get into the phone.'

'So we have the phone?'

'Yes, boss. Found right alongside the body.'

Melanie paced, glancing around the room and briefly into the en-suite, and then returned to look again at Amelie. She'd already introduced her to the team onsite as her 'mentee'.

'OK, so what do you make of the crime scene, Amelie?'

Amelie cleared her throat and forced herself to look again at the body. *Do not retch. Do not retch.*

She could hear the click of photographs being taken by the forensic team. And she was remembering again the conversation in the car when Melanie had made such a fuss, worrying about her response.

Have you seen a body before?

I've seen pictures, really nasty pictures at college—

So that's a no.

I'll be fine.

'So what are your first thoughts?' Melanie's voice was raised as if repeating herself.

Amelie snapped back into the moment. Glanced around the bedroom. Remembered what the DI had summarised from the hotel records when they arrived. That the victim had checked in for only one night. Had said his plans were 'fluid' and he might extend.

She again took in those horrible bulging eyes and the twisted position of the body so close to the door.

'Looks like he was shutting the door when he was attacked from behind,' she said. 'So he let the person in. Knew them. Or hotel staff. Someone not out of place. Something that did not at first frighten him.'

The DI turned his head and raised his eyebrows.

'Possibly a woman?' Amelie was turning over this option in her head as she spoke. She was wondering why a plastic bag. Was that because the attacker was slighter? Wanted something quick and silent. Something they could manage without too much noise? 'Maybe that's why he underestimated. Didn't feel threatened.' Amelie stepped back from the body and turned her head to look around the room. A small black rucksack on the floor and a scruffy holdall on a chair beneath the window. It was unzipped. Little inside.

'Looks like he didn't bring much stuff with him. So either a typical bloke or this was a last-minute trip.'

'Can I have her on my team?' The DI was smiling as he spoke.

'No you can't.' Melanie was still casting her eyes around the room. 'So let's get everything bagged up, yes, and update the coroner. I'm heading off but I want an update later this evening. I want to know why he was in Truro. Where he was working. Anything that CCTV throws up. Oh – and let's get into that phone asap. Yes?'

'Of course, boss.'

With that, Melanie led the way out. Amelie followed, so relieved that the internal retching had passed. Just outside they took off their protective shoe coverings and unzipped their white coveralls.

'You did well, Amelie.'

It was not until they were in the car that Melanie continued. 'Did you know your dad threw up when he saw his first body?'

'You're kidding me?'

'I wish. Vomited into his shoe.' Melanie was shaking her head as she pulled away, again checking the time.

'He threw up *into his shoe?*' Amelie couldn't help herself. She let out this sort of snort, halfway between astonishment and a laugh. 'His shoe? Why the hell would he puke into his shoe?'

'Heaven knows. Exactly what I said. He tripped. His shoe came off. He turned as he held up the shoe, took one look at the body and chucked. He told me later that he didn't want his vomit on the floor to confuse the evidence in the room. So he hopped about on one leg until he was given a plastic covering for his foot.'

Amelie bit into her bottom lip. This was not a story her father, the esteemed detective turned private investigator Matthew Hill – so often in the news – had ever told her.

Later, as Melanie saw to the chicken hotpot in the slow cooker, Amelie retreated to her room and sat on her bed. Part dazed. Part confused. Part exhilarated – which made her feel guilty. She let that settle for a moment. The buzz of being involved in a murder case. But what she realised she felt most of all was determination. She thought about what Mel had said in the car. She had talked a lot on the journey home about using the shock of the crime scene to *focus*. Amelie took out her phone from her pocket and pressed the button to FaceTime her father.

'Hello there, darling.' The tone was a mixture of delight and surprise as her father came up onscreen. The backdrop was shelving and pine slats. Ceramic pots stacked between plastic containers and two rusty watering cans.

'Are you in your shed?'

'Mancave, if you don't mind. And yes. I'm checking my cuttings. Trying to grow a range of chillies this year. Your mother says I'm nuts and that it would be cheaper to buy them at the supermarket, but she forgets how bored I get. It gives me something to do to grow vegetation to feed the local slug population. So did Melanie have a word?' He was grinning. 'I've been moaning that you don't keep in touch enough.'

'She did. But that's not why I'm calling. I've had a bit of a day.'

Matthew tilted his head and then shifted position as if sitting down. 'How so?' There was now a new backdrop, and Amelie could see the trays of cuttings set on a huge old pine table by the windows of the shed.

'I saw my first body today.' Amelie was aware how quiet her voice had become.

'Oh right. So how did that go?' Her father's face betrayed a sweep of concern, his eyes tired. Worried.

'Melanie gave me the option not to go inside. A guy had been suffocated. Bag over his head. Horrid. I was a bit gung-ho. Arrogant, if I'm honest, but it was much worse than I expected.'

'Right. It's never easy. First body. So are you OK now?'

'I am actually. Melanie told me you threw up in a shoe. First time you saw a murder victim.'

'That story gets exaggerated in the telling.' Matthew had raised his eyebrows. 'It was very hot in the room. And I had overeaten at lunch—'

'I nearly gagged,' Amelie said suddenly. 'But I managed to hold it in.'

There was a long pause and she just stared at her father's face, wishing he were there in the room. That she could have a hug. She realised now that the past hours had made her feel so much closer to her father. Facing up to the reality of the job she was chasing. Understanding better now why he had tried to dissuade her, not because he did not have faith in her but because he *knew*. What others didn't. Precisely what it would be like. Bulging eyes. A twisted body in a sad hotel room.

'Anyway. I'm OK now but my head's sort of buzzing. I just feel so angry for the guy. He was only in his twenties and I keep thinking of the people who will have to go out and tell his parents.' She paused. 'Melanie said that seeing a body always makes her really focused on getting justice. That she tries to use the shock to fuel her determination. I understand that now.' Amelie became aware that she was talking very fast. 'I just want to get the bastard who did that.'

'Right. Good. That's good.' Still her father's face looked etched with worry.

'The problem is I'm sort of working on another case too. An unusual road accident, and so I feel stretched. Torn.'

'That's the job, I'm afraid. Always pulled in different directions.'

She changed the subject for a bit, asking after her mother. After his cuttings. And was the neighbour's cat still crapping on his new lawn? And then there was another long pause, during which Melanie's voice was suddenly calling up the stairs. *Amelie? You got a moment? I've had a call. We need to go back to the hospital . . .*

'Just coming down,' Amelie shouted in reply, frowning. Why would they need to go back to the hospital? She thought they were about to have their very late supper.

'You know what that's about?' her father asked.

'No idea. But I'm starting to see how mad the job can be.'

'Don't say I didn't warn you.'

Amelie smiled. Her father smiled back. All those lectures about the frustrations of the job. 'By the way, Melanie is absolutely amazing. She doesn't stay in the office. She's always turning up at crime scenes.'

'Bet that keeps everyone on their toes,' he laughed. 'She's one of a kind, our Mel. And I'm very glad she's looking out for you.'

'Listen. Before I go.' Amelie took a deep breath. 'Do you still hate that I'm going to do this? Become a detective.'

Her father looked down at the ground for a while before lifting his head to reply. 'I'm not going to lie. I'm still worried. But that's a parent's job. To worry. But honestly? Seeing you like this. Hearing you *talk* like this . . .' He paused. 'I'm starting to see why you need to do this. And why you're going to be very good at it.'

'Thank you. That means a lot. Look. I'd better go. Give my love to Mum.'

'I will.'

'I love you, Dad.'

'You too.' He raised a palm to blow her a kiss. 'You keep yourself safe.'

'I will.'

Amelie pressed the button to disconnect the call, and let out a slow breath. Her stomach was grumbling as she rose and headed out the door to the stairs, still wondering why the hell they needed to go back to the hospital.

CHAPTER 37

BEFORE

LAURA

It threw me completely. Ruby walking on to the ward.

Her train from London was held up. Diverted. It meant I had no idea what time she'd turn up and I'd expected to have Clara with me as a bridge between us. An ally to chaperone us through what was always going to be difficult.

But all of a sudden there she was. My Ruby. Walking towards Joe's bed. No Clara as a shock absorber. She was still at home, complaining of IBS, and so I just stood up. Heart pounding. Fighting the powerful urge to rush across the room and hug Ruby tight; instead driving my nails into tightly clenched palms to fight off that urge because I had no idea how she would react.

I held her gaze. I tried to read her face but couldn't, and the agony of that took me right back to that moment standing in the kitchen the day she left us. I had ached for a hug back then too, stretching out my hands, physically begging for that hug goodbye. Ruby had locked eyes in that moment also, but her stare back then had said no way. Instead she'd turned away. Left . . .

What did her stare say this time, at the hospital? I still couldn't tell.

'Ruby,' I said. 'It's so good to see you. Here. Come and sit by your father. You must be exhausted.' I stepped back. She just stood a few strides from the bed, holding my gaze. I so badly wanted to move closer to her. Touch her. Hug her. But still I couldn't read her face and so, dreading the horror of another rejection, I stepped back even further. It was a bit like magnets. As if there were a set distance that needed to be kept between us before the energy went all wrong. I edged even further back and at last she moved, finally and ever so slowly sitting beside Joe.

'How is he?'

Was I imagining that her tone was cold? Was that for me, the coolness? Or was it just the shock and the tiredness from her difficult journey? Worrying about her dad?

'He's still in an induced coma but they will reduce his medication over time as the swelling to his brain eases. They're being careful what they say to us. You know what doctors are like. But he is stable. Doing OK, aren't you, darling? They say the surgery went well and we just have to wait.'

'Has he opened his eyes at all? Can he hear us?' She was now gently taking his hand in her own.

'He hasn't opened his eyes but they say it's possible he may hear and I believe he does. I've been reading bits of the papers to him. Chattering away. Trying to reassure him.' I paused. 'Clara's been here but she needed to pop home. Not feeling great.'

'Yes. I spoke to her.'

'Oh right. Good. That's good. So how was the journey? Delays sounded a nightmare.' I was surprised the journey had taken so long.

'Never mind. Nightmare trains. I'll tell you later.' She lifted her father's hand to her face then, and kissed the back of it incredibly gently before laying his arm back down on the sheet. 'Hey there, you. It's Ruby. So what's all this then? A bit drastic – all this drama – to get me down from Scotland, don't you think? You could have just phoned, you know.'

I felt tears forming in my eyes. Heart still pounding.

'The accident was on Anstey Way,' I said. 'We don't know much about what happened. I've told Joe not to worry about any of it. To just rest.' I paused, thinking of the police. No. There was no real evidence yet to share with Ruby. I'd leave it until we knew more.

'Mum's right,' Ruby said. 'Bet you never thought you'd hear me say that, eh? You need to just rest. Listen to the doctors. Let everything heal.'

She kept his hand in hers and she chattered on, telling him about the journey. The sleeper. How it was a weird experience. The little cabins. The strange sensation, rumbling along through the dark of the night.

She told him more about the food and the staff and how he would have liked the bacon baps for breakfast. And the good selection of malts.

I just stood back, listening, wondering if she was partly sharing all this to answer my own question about the journey. But she did not look up at me again. She kept her gaze fixed on her father's face and so I just took in every inch of her. The longer hair. The warm auburn highlights. The denim jacket and neat white jeans.

She looked as if she had lost weight, and I worried that this was a sign of not eating properly. Working too hard? I could imagine myself saying this out loud and her rolling her eyes and telling me not to fuss.

But we hadn't talked. In nearly a year. And I realised I had no idea how to navigate our reconnection. With Joe like this. Joe listening.

'Would you like me to give you some time with your dad on your own? I can fetch drinks?'

'Great. That would be lovely. Coffee please. Been a very long day.'

Only as I nodded did I realise that I had hoped she would say no. That she wanted us to be together. All three of us. Again I wondered if it would have been any easier if Clara were here.

'I might phone Clara,' I added. 'Get her to make your room up fresh. I'll stay at the hospital overnight again. But you can take turns, getting some rest at home if you like—'

'No need,' she interrupted, lowering her voice. 'I'll be staying with Ned's mother. It's all sorted.'

And there it was. The slice right through my flesh. The slash and then twist of the knife.

I couldn't quite believe it. Nothing was better between us and nothing was fixed. She was here for Joe. Not for any kind of reconciliation with me.

'Fine, darling. Whatever works best for you. It's just so good to have you here. Your dad will be thrilled to hear your voice. Isn't that right, Joe? Isn't it lovely to have Ruby here?' I was speaking faster and faster, almost gabbling as I picked up my handbag from alongside the bed and headed for the door. 'I'll get those drinks.'

Only in the corridor after striding away from the ward did I let it out, the sobbing so sudden that I had to momentarily put my hand on the wall, leaning my head on to my elbow. Afraid of collapsing. Afraid that I had not walked far enough and that Ruby might hear me.

CHAPTER 38

BEFORE

THE POLICE

'This is going to be tricky.' Melanie stared directly ahead, waiting for the traffic lights to change as she spoke.

Amelie sat alongside her in a daze, hardly able to take in the update. They were heading back to the hospital, and the truth was she also felt just a bit sick, having bolted her supper.

'You're really going to arrest her, the daughter? At the bedside?'

Amelie pressed her hand to her stomach, praying it would settle soon. She was imagining travelling to see her own father after an accident and then being pulled away and taken to a police station. The chances of Ruby Harry kicking off on the ward were surely pretty high.

'I'm hoping it won't come to an arrest but we need her down at the station for questioning tonight. And if she's tricky, I'll do what needs to be done. Optics be damned.'

'So talk me through it again. Why is the evidence suddenly pointing to this daughter? To Ruby?' Amelie could still hardly believe it.

'Right. So the inspector we met at the murder scene got into the victim's phone very quickly. Just after we left.'

'How the hell did he do that? I thought it took ages. At college we were told it was one of the big frustrations—'

'Probably best we don't ask. Officially his wife is a technical wizard. She works on tech support. Did him a favour to fast-track it. Unofficially – and by that I mean don't share this – I'm afraid he used the victim's fingerprint to open the phone.'

'You're kidding me? Is that even allowed? Or possible? I thought that wouldn't work. That the finger had to be warm. Have an electrical charge.'

Amelie had read about some teams abroad using the faces and fingers of victims to unlock phones. It made her feel seriously uncomfortable. Word was that fingerprints could be used by technicians who knew what they were doing.

'Like I say. Best we don't ask questions at this stage. The key thing is we have access to the phone and it's dynamite. We've spoken to the hotel he worked for in Scotland and staff said he left in a hurry without permission to follow Ruby south. Word is he had a big crush on her. There's gossip he's been seriously hassling her. There are a number of angry message exchanges on his phone. The most recent suggests he followed her on the sleeper and she was livid. Warned he would regret it if he kept following her to Cornwall.'

Amelie was stunned. It felt incredible. The two cases possibly linked to the Harrys at the hospital. The car accident – which might not have been an accident, given her laser pen theory – and now a young man dead in a hotel room in Truro.

'This all feels a stretch. Like too much of a coincidence to me,' she said, narrowing her eyes.

'Not a coincidence when the geography is so clearly linked,' Melanie replied, pulling away swiftly as the light changed to green.

'They worked together in Scotland. They travelled south at the same time. Fact is he was following the daughter, Ruby Harry, and she was unhappy about that. And now he ends up dead. We have to speak to her.'

'But if he was hassling her, surely she's the potential victim here too. Do we have enough to arrest her?'

'I'm hoping she'll agree to questioning voluntarily. But if she doesn't, I will arrest her if I have to. He's the one who ended up dead. She made threats. We have to get to the bottom of what happened between them.'

Amelie felt shaken. Also still a little bit nauseous, the large portion of slow-cooked chicken sitting heavy. *Eyes bigger than your belly*, her mother always warned. Hand still pressed against her stomach, she was again imagining what might happen on the ward. Joe Harry lying in his coma. The daughter pulled away. She had arrested a few people herself but never for anything serious. Drunk and disorderly. Minor assaults. Criminal damage. No one ever wanted to be arrested, but she'd never had anyone put up a real fight. Just swearing and a few threats.

But this scenario was a whole different ball game. And there was another complication.

'What about the media outside, doing interviews on the alleged cult? What was the name?' Amelie had followed it on socials.

'StarBonders,' Melanie said. 'Far from ideal. Some have moved off but Sky are still there apparently, waiting for an update. It's why I'm handling this one myself. And we have hospital comms involved. The girl's condition is critical, so a few other media are back in the car park, so I hear. We'll try to use the back exit to avoid all that. Like I said, this one has the potential to be controversial so I need to control the optics if I can. And we can't afford to make any mistakes. Comms are going to help pull Ruby Harry away from the bedside. We don't want this kicking off on the ward. Not with phones around.'

Fifteen minutes later and they were in the lift to the wards, Melanie checking her phone and re-reading the preliminary report from the DI about the evidence from the murder victim's phone. She took a couple of screen shots of the message exchange between the victim and Ruby Harry, showed Amelie and then closed her eyes as if rehearsing tactics in her head.

'So what do I do? Do you need me to say anything?' Amelie, in truth, was afraid of saying the wrong thing. Putting her foot in it. She badly needed her stomach to settle. This was no time to need to bolt to the loo.

'No. You're my backup if things get tricky.' Melanie opened her eyes and her expression changed. Determined. 'You watch and you wait. Is that OK?'

'Sure.' Amelie tried to sound more confident than she felt. In her head a nightmare scene was playing out. The daughter refusing to leave the bedside. The mother hysterical. The pair of them calling the media and everything kicking off in front of the phone cameras . . .

CHAPTER 39

BEFORE

RUBY

Sitting alone alongside her father, Ruby very quickly ran out of things to say to him.

Once she'd tried to be amusing, teasing him about all the drama, and had shared all the details of the sleeper trip, she really didn't know what other topics were safe. The truth was it was a shock seeing him there with his bandaged head and his eyes closed. All the machines and the tubes and the nurses trotting to and fro to check his charts.

Ruby suddenly understood why Clara had found it so hard. Scuttled home with her IBS playing up. Or was that just an excuse? Ruby thought about phoning her sister but didn't want their father to overhear. She didn't know whether to believe their mother – the idea that he would be listening. But what if he really *could* hear everything? She needed to be careful.

Her hand was trembling and she wondered if he could feel that. Deep down, a part of her wanted to pour out her heart. About Scott. About the awful time and how everything had spiralled and gone so terribly and darkly wrong. She felt closer to her father than anyone, and so wanted him to know what had happened. How very afraid she was. But that would be selfish, wouldn't it? She had to think of him and not herself. And what if he really *could* hear? She couldn't risk saying anything that would distress him even more. She checked her phone, a sweep of anxiety as she went over the string of messages between her and Scott. In black and white, it all looked so wrong. What had she been thinking? She shouldn't have put her anger in writing.

Ruby put her phone back in her pocket and started to chatter to her father about her job. About the staff shortages and how everyone took the mick out of the manageress. Her catchphrase. *We have a bit of a situation.*

She told him about the good bits too. How glorious the loch looked in different lights. How the morning was her favourite time. Getting up early to set breakfast when all the guests were still in their rooms and the morning sun would shimmer on the water beyond the terrace outside the dining room.

It was a bit rundown, the hotel, she told him, but the location was breathtaking and she liked to take lakeside walks on her breaks between shifts. *You'd love it. When you're better, you should come and visit me.*

And then she fell silent. Was she really ever going back there? After what had happened with Scott? Could she? Dare she?

Ruby felt a chill pass through her again and once more examined her phone. She looked at the final message from Scott.

I'm nearby. Sandy Heights Hotel, Truro. Here for you. Shall I come to the hospital?

She felt all the blood drain from her face. Her neck. And then a shiver right through her whole body as if the blood no longer knew how to work itself around her frame.

165

Ruby felt light-headed. She looked again at her father and was overwhelmed with need. She remembered how he had always been her rock, right through childhood. Her mother was loving but a bit of a drama queen. Forever catastrophising and overreacting. Her father was the solid one. The practical one. Calmly patching her knees when she fell badly after roller skating. How old had she been? Eleven, maybe twelve. She remembered too how quickly he had encouraged her to *get back out there. Don't put it off. Don't be scared . . .*

He had taught her self-belief. Resilience. He had tried to teach the same things to Clara, they all had, but it had always been so much harder for her sister. Ruby felt tears pricking her eyes, thinking of her sister's struggles with anxiety.

And now? It felt all back to front. Her father the one in need. She was supposed to be here to support *him*. She wondered how people managed it. When the tables seemed to be turning. How did a child stop being a child? How did you stop needing your parent? She realised this was the first time she had ever had to think about this. And she just couldn't figure it out.

It was as she was trying to decide what to do next – should she get a newspaper and read the headlines to him? – that the double doors to the ward opened and a woman she didn't recognise appeared, glancing across at her. The woman, tall and with a blonde pixie cut, was clearly hospital staff because she was wearing the familiar turquoise lanyard with her photo ID dangling just above her stomach. Behind her in the corridor were two other women. One older in a blue trouser suit, one a similar age to Ruby, dressed more casually.

Something churned deep in Ruby's stomach. She knew instantly that this was not about her father. They did not look like medical staff, this strange little posse. And for a moment she was surprised to wish that she had not so enthusiastically encouraged her mother to leave her alone on the ward.

Ruby started talking again to her father as if the distraction might deter the trio.

'So – how about I read you some of the sporting headlines from my phone? I'll call up a news site. Find the sports section. Just give me a moment.'

She started scrolling through her phone but it was no good. The three women were now standing close by.

'I'm so sorry to intrude at such a difficult time, but are you Ruby Harry?' The woman wearing the lanyard had stepped right up to the bed. 'My name is Stella and I'm on the hospital communications team. These two women are police officers who would like to have a word with you, please. Would it be OK to step outside the ward? I think that would be best.'

'I'm sorry but it's late. I can't leave my father. No way. The investigation into his accident will have to wait.' Ruby could feel her pulse pounding in her ear as she spoke. It was so loud she wondered if Stella and the two police officers could hear it. Or see a vein pulsing on the side of her head. 'I'm just about to read him some of the sporting headlines. He loves sport.'

'I think we need your father to rest.' It was the older of the two officers talking now. 'This is not about his accident and I'm sure you don't want him to hear.' A pause. '*Do you Ruby?*'

CHAPTER 40

BEFORE

Clara

Clara was still lying on her bed, staring at her wig back on its stand on her dressing table across the room. The wig was reflected in the mirror so that she could see how the hair fell at the back. It surprised her how good it looked and she wondered if people felt the same admiration when they stared at the back of her head, not realising it was a wig, when a message pinged into her phone. She expected it to be her mother. Or the retreat group.

> We need to meet. Can you come to HQ? To the Lighthouse?
> Phoebe x

Clara was shaken. Phoebe hardly ever sent messages directly. Mostly they worked over WhatsApp video. For weeks she'd been asking, practically begging, to visit the StarBonders HQ to see the site for the retreat for herself. But she'd been told this just wasn't possible. The address was being kept top secret until the 'big reveal'. She didn't even know which part of the country it was in. The plan apparently had been to share an album containing lots of photographs with all the retreat participants at the same time. Phoebe was so paranoid about messages and video chats being intercepted by journalists or critics that she used an avatar for her profile. No picture.

So this message, a personal invite, was a big deal. And the last thing Clara had expected. She sat up quickly, shuffling back to use the headboard and pillows to support herself. As she began typing, she felt so conflicted. She *desperately* wanted to see the Lighthouse, and it was just incredible for Phoebe to trust her with a face-to-face meeting, but no way could she leave her father. And what about all the stories in the media? She wanted to believe the blogs; that the media was just stirring. That the mother was just lashing out in her trauma. But it all felt so confusing.

I'm sorry. I can't. Family crisis. I can't get away just now. C x

Clara watched the pulsing three dots for a moment, clenching her left fist and tapping her lower lip. She had worked so hard to win Phoebe's trust and was terrified she would now lose it. Sure enough . . .

Oh, right. I'm sorry to hear that. It's just you said that I could rely on you.

Clara again began typing frantically.

You can. You absolutely can. But just not today. My dad is unwell. In the hospital.

She paused, for some reason feeling uncomfortable sharing her father's situation. But what else could she do? She thought of her father and all the machines and the tubes. How in truth she was a coward and couldn't face all that.

So – are you at the hospital?

No. I'm home at the moment. Needed a break. My sister and mother are with him.

Good. Great they're with him. How about you tell them that you just need a few more hours at home. You can join me and I can explain what help I need. I daren't trust anyone else with this, Clara. The media are trying to find us. They're sharing so many lies about us. It's a complete nightmare. You can go back to the hospital straight afterwards.

So where exactly are you? How far is HQ from me? Is the Lighthouse in Cornwall? I can't be away long . . .

I can't tell you exactly where. Too dangerous to share over messaging. But I promise the geography is very doable for you. I will meet you at this rendezvous café – I can send a link – and drive us on to the Lighthouse in my car from there. To make sure no one follows you.

You seriously think someone might follow me?

Who knows. I have sent two of the staff home as journalists were on to them. Like I said. A nightmare. We can't have this place on the news. I really need your help, Clara. I trust you more than anyone . . .

But I haven't passed my driving test.

Take a taxi. You can charge it to StarBonders later.

Clara felt herself frowning. She thought about the blogs. The explanation that the media were lying. And it was true, wasn't it, that the tabloids often made stories up? Exaggerated. She thought about all the work she had put into the plans for the retreat. The offer of the sponsorship through university.

OK. I can do that. Send the café link. But I must get back to the hospital later. Or first thing in the morning. You sure it won't keep me away too long? A few hours tops?

Trust me, it will be fine. We just need to talk strategy face to face. And decide how to handle the retreat postponement. It will take you away for a few hours at most. While everyone is sleeping. I want to meet you in person so that you can see the place. Keep the faith.

Of course I have faith.

Good. Sending the satnav café coordinates now. I'll be in a black Polo in the café's car park.

And then the three dots were pulsing again.

Clara felt panic rising within her as she waited for the next message to land. She still felt torn. It was as if she were choosing StarBonders over her family. The problem was it had taken so long to win Phoebe's trust. And StarBonders *had* been so good to her. The promise of sponsorship and holiday work throughout her degree was no small thing.

But what if her father's condition changed? What if her mother messaged and needed her? It all felt such a stretch . . .

One last thing. Very important. You need to leave your phone at your house. It may be tracked. The tabloids are trying to hack our records and so they may have your number. I can't risk this unless you promise me . . . Book a taxi. Pay cash. But . . . no . . . phone. Is that agreed?

CHAPTER 41

BEFORE

JOE

Joe was really struggling now. He couldn't understand why Ruby had not returned. She'd kissed him on the forehead and said that she would only be a few minutes. So what on earth had happened?

It was such a long journey from Scotland and it made no sense that she would want to leave him on his own. And who was the woman he'd overheard speaking to her? Hospital staff? Some news about his condition? He hadn't been able to make out the exchange properly.

Joe tried very hard to steady himself, but he must have failed as the machine alongside the bed started bleeping. His heart rate up?

Sure enough two nurses were soon by the bed, checking the machines and the charts. He was well used to this now. Tried again to calm himself.

'Sats down and heart rate up. Do you think we need to call the registrar?' It was the voice of a nurse he didn't recognise. Someone new to the ward?

'I'd give it a minute. A lot going on with the police turning up.'

'You think he heard all that?' It was a deeper voice. An older woman. He recognised this voice; she was often on duty.

'No. I don't see any sign of that. But the activity around the bed might have unsettled him at some deep level.' A pause. 'Everything is fine, Mr Harry.' Her voice raised again. 'Your family will be back with you soon, I'm sure.'

Joe could feel the alarm inside him rising. The police? What the hell were the police doing here? Oh, wait. The accident. Yes. It was probably just a routine inquiry about the accident. But – hang on. Why would they need to speak to Ruby? She didn't know anything about the accident. She was still in Scotland when it happened.

A new and terrible thought landed. The police were probably into his phone, investigating the accident. Checking if he'd been on the phone when it happened. So would they have seen the WhatsApp messages? The awful photo from the awful girl in the nightclub? Was that what this was about?

Joe heard the monitor alarms going off again. He was worrying that the police might speak to Laura. Tell her about the horrible messages. Even show her the horrible messages before he had a chance to explain.

'Right. Think you were right. I'll call the registrar. I don't like the look of this. He's definitely in distress. This doesn't look right.'

CHAPTER 42

BEFORE

LAURA

The queue for the sandwich machine had thrown me. Made me think of all the other families wandering the hospital this late. Pitch-black outside. The cafeteria now closed.

Once it was my turn, I felt ridiculous – standing there, dithering. Torn between tuna mayonnaise and prawn with salad. Which would Ruby prefer? It felt as if everything was a test. So awkward already between me and her. Overthinking. She'd had a spell as a vegetarian in the past. Did she even eat fish still? It felt terrible not to know.

So when the doors to the lift opened, I was worrying about the stupid sandwiches. Distracted. Then genuinely shaken to see Ruby in the corridor, remonstrating with three women. It threw me so badly that I promptly dropped the lot. All the sandwiches and packets of biscuits in my left hand, only just managing to steady my right hand with the cardboard carrier holding two cups of coffee.

'What's going on?' I managed as I leaned down to gather up the food, putting the biscuits in my pocket and struggling to pick up the sandwiches by the cardboard corners of the wrapping.

There was no reply, just a narrowing of the eyes of the hospital member of staff, the only one of the trio facing me and wearing the familiar health trust lanyard. I checked her name. Stella Hawkins. Communications Unit.

Ruby was pale, not wanting to meet my eye. And then the two other women turned and I was shocked to recognise the two police officers who had talked to me before about Joe's accident.

'I asked what's going on. Is this about my husband's accident again?'

'No. This is not about that.' It was the chief inspector talking. 'We need to speak to your daughter on another matter.' A pause. 'Down at the station.'

'Well, I'm sorry but she can't. She's only just arrived to see her father who's very unwell. It's late and she's had a long journey—'

'I told them that, Mum. But they're not listening.' For the first time Ruby met my gaze properly and I could see the panic in her eyes.

'There. My daughter has made it plain that she's not free to talk to you. Not at the moment.'

I could feel my heart quickening. Why the hell were they back here? I didn't like their expressions. The determination on the senior officer's face. I wanted to ask more questions, but stared at Ruby some more, looking for her cue. What was this?

'We are investigating a separate and very serious crime, Mrs Harry. I have already told your daughter that if she does not want to accompany us voluntarily, she will be arrested for questioning.'

'Arrested? What the hell are you talking about? *Arrested?* Ruby. What have they said? What are they talking about?'

'I'm not leaving my father,' Ruby said suddenly. 'I have done nothing wrong and I am not leaving the hospital.'

'This is your final chance to agree to help us with our inquiries voluntarily. If you don't, make no mistake, I will arrest you.' The chief inspector had moved to stand directly facing Ruby, with the much younger woman – assumed to be a second officer – also standing close by.

'Ruby. I don't know what this is but you don't want an arrest on your record. How about we get your sister here and go to the station together and sort whatever this is.' I moved to put the sandwiches down on seating by the wall and took my phone out of my bag. 'I'll phone her to come to be with your father and we'll sort this out.'

CHAPTER 43

BEFORE

The police

Sitting in the back of Melanie's car alongside the mother and daughter, Amelie was surprised not just by the silence but the vibe.

The two women didn't even look at each other. It was a relief that nothing had kicked off on the ward but it felt seriously weird that neither woman had asked any further questions on the drive. Amelie would have expected chatter and quite possibly outrage. *What the hell is all this about? Why the questioning so late?* Blah blah.

Given the stress of the situation, Amelie would also have expected some physical contact between the mother and daughter. Hell – if she had been pulled away from her father in hospital for goodness knows what, she would have been hugging her mother tight or at the very least holding hands for reassurance. But this pair? Nada. Zilch. They had actually opted for Amelie to sit between them in the back.

And so now Mrs Harry was sitting pressed against the door behind Melanie in the driver's seat. She was frowning, constantly checking her phone while Ruby, the daughter, just stared at her feet in the passenger well, eyes so wide that they began to water. Amelie, sitting between them, ended up wondering if there was something on the carpet which had caught Ruby's eye. A spider or a sandwich crumb or something. But no. She checked the well herself and it was completely clean. Just a grey carpet square, recently hoovered by the look of things. She watched the younger woman more closely and tried to weigh up if her strange fixed expression was from guilt over some true connection to what had happened to the man in the hotel room. Or was this just general shock? Upset over the father in hospital?

It could be any of those things, of course – including the possibility that the daughter *was* the killer. But whatever was going on here, it was most odd that the two women did not even exchange a glance. Amelie had been drilled during both her degree and her training as a special not to be too distracted by instincts and 'gut feelings'; that good police work was *always* about evidence. But her father was someone who'd often trusted his gut. *Her* gut was saying right now that there was something seriously odd going on between this mother and daughter. And she sure as hell wanted and needed to know what it was.

At the station Mrs Harry asked to be present during the questioning and Ruby agreed. But again their gazes did not meet. Melanie had touched base with the DI heading the murder inquiry who was on his way to the station, waiting to hear the outcome of the interview. Mel decided to use interview room three. She confided in Amelie that she wanted the starkness and formality of this interview room so that the Harrys would take their situation seriously.

Just before they started, the mother used her phone to leave a message, her tone exasperated. 'Clara. I'm assuming you're sleeping, darling, but I really need you to ring me as soon as you pick this up. Can you do that please? Ring me asap.'

'Darling' suggested this was the other daughter.

They were just about to start the interview when Melanie received a call. 'I'm sorry but I'm going to have to take this.' She left the room for just a couple of minutes, and when she returned was looking at her phone, eyebrows raised. She turned the screen towards Amelie to display a photograph of an evidence bag. It contained a business card and a branded pen, both trumpeting a copywriting agency. *Write Away . . . Laura Harry.*

Now it was Amelie's turn to frown. 'Both items found on our victim's body,' Melanie said quietly. And then she took her seat opposite the mother and daughter and a long, slow breath.

'OK. Thank you for your cooperation. I appreciate this is a difficult time for your family, with the road accident. But something unexpected has happened. I need to question you *both* in connection with the suspected murder of a young man in Truro. But I need now to do that separately, please. I'm happy to continue informally with voluntary interviews. Is that still OK with you both?'

'I have no idea what you're talking about. What young man? And why *both* of us?' The mother glanced at her daughter but Ruby Harry did not move. 'We need to get back to my husband. And I don't understand what any of this has to do with us.' Mrs Harry's voice was now high-pitched. Stressed.

Yet the daughter remained in her zombie-like state. Skin white. Eyes wide. But not a word.

CHAPTER 44

BEFORE

CLARA

The taxi was tatty and smelly. It stank of cigarette smoke, which surprised Clara. She didn't think people were allowed to smoke in taxis.

The driver was a middle-aged man, tall and skinny with long, curly hair which covered his shirt collar at the back. It didn't look particularly clean, his hair, and Clara felt uncomfortable travelling this late, wishing she had been patient enough to insist on a female driver. Her mother had set this rule that whenever she was in a taxi she should message to say where she was going. For safety. Clara felt this growing unease as she thought of being out of touch with her mother. Her phone back at the house.

She'd done as Phoebe had asked and left her mobile in her bedroom on her pillow. This went against every instinct. She felt so twitchy without her phone. Couldn't remember when she had last gone *anywhere* without her phone as a crutch. But she could see there was no choice. Suppose someone really did have some way of tracking their messages and then tracking her phone? She didn't want to be the one to lead a journalist to the StarBonders HQ.

Before she left the house Clara had phoned the hospital ward to do a 'condition check' on her father. They'd been difficult, checking that she really was a relative and finally confirming that he was stable. She knew that only two people were allowed next to each bed in ICU, so staying away was perhaps not as dreadful as it made her feel. Clara had messaged her mother to say that she would have an early night and would text for an update in the morning. She was sure to be back from the StarBonders HQ by then, wherever it was. Her mother would not expect her to be up early.

The all-night café was about thirty miles from their home and Phoebe hadn't said how close it was to the Lighthouse. Clara felt her stomach muscles tighten. The driver reached left to open the glove compartment and Clara noticed a packet of cigarettes. So *he* was the smoker. Yuck.

Years back, when her mother had first launched her copywriting work, she used to freelance for charity campaigns. One was a relatively small organisation, campaigning against the tobacco industry targeting young people. It used the grim health warning pictures that cigarette companies were forced to put on cigarette packets. Her mother had come up with a few slogans for posters used online.

She was all energy with her campaigns back then. All her horses were high. Mrs Soapbox, they called her. Always with some new cause to champion and rant about.

That kind of campaigning work had fallen away as the copywriting agency grew. Now there were more lucrative but duller contracts to promote expensive glass and architecture agencies – even a tool-making factory in Brussels. *It may be dry but it pays for all this*, her mother would say defensively, waving her arms to signal the large kitchen extension.

'How much further?' Clara asked, pushing away the thoughts. It made her feel so much more vulnerable to imagine her mother trying to contact her.

The driver checked his satnav screen. 'About ten minutes.'

'Thank you.'

She didn't want to get sucked into a chat and stared instead out of the right-hand window. She'd deliberately sat directly behind the driver so it was harder for him to catch her gaze in the driver's mirror. Clara hated the thought of him looking at her. She was wearing her best wig again but still worried people would rumble her.

Would Phoebe rumble her? Give her that strange look that always made Clara feel 'found out'.

She checked her watch. It was just past 10 p.m. Pitch-black. Rural roads with few street lights. When Phoebe picked her up, Clara would press her to confirm that the retired lighthouse was not too far away. All she had been told was it was on a headland with adjoining cottages, so quite easy to access. Clara technically had all night to make her way home, but it would make her feel very nervous to be too far from the hospital.

She wondered if the landline at the StarBonders HQ would be safe. Would she be able to ring the hospital again from there? To check on her father without her mother realising she didn't have her phone?

CHAPTER 45

BEFORE

Ruby

Ruby and her mother gave their DNA samples and fingerprints before being taken to different interview rooms.

It was late and dark and there had been this terrible impasse when Ruby wasn't sure if they should point-blank refuse to give samples. I mean, why would the police need samples? Didn't they need a warrant for DNA? Would they lock her in a cell if she didn't cooperate?'

Ruby was trying very hard not to let the police see how stressed she felt. She had asked these questions out loud but her mother had widened her eyes as some kind of warning. She was taking an entirely different conciliatory tack. 'We have done nothing wrong, so of course you can take samples from us,' her mother said finally. 'It will eliminate us, yes?'

'That's right. It's for elimination purposes,' Detective Chief Inspector Melanie Sanders had confirmed. 'You're aware that your daughter knows the murder victim. It turns out they travelled on the same train from Scotland. We are processing the crime scene and just need to get some things straight. We'll explain more during the questioning.'

'OK. So I say – let's get all this nonsense sorted. You take the samples, you eliminate us and then the samples can be removed from records. Is that right?' Her mother had looked steely as she spoke and the strategy made a sort of sense, even though Ruby's heart was pounding in her chest.

'That's right,' the older police officer confirmed. 'So is that all agreed? Ruby? Do you agree with that?'

And so finally she had nodded and they each had their DNA and fingerprint samples taken before being led to separate rooms.

But that was about half an hour ago and *still* Ruby was waiting. She assumed that the police were talking to her mother first, but it was a complete mystery why they would even *want* to talk to her mother. She'd never met Scott. Knew nothing about him.

This room, Ruby's interview room, was much smaller than the one she had shared initially with her mother. It had a small, high window and just one Formica table with three chairs. Her own and two opposite, ready for the detectives.

Ruby found herself wondering about the younger of the two detectives. She looked about the same age as Ruby. Switched on for sure, but surprisingly young. So why were this odd duo working so late? Why couldn't this wait until the morning?

At last the door opened and the pair appeared. Ruby took in their differences in height and age again and remembered her shock when she first saw them in the hospital. She didn't want to give away her sense of panic and so tried very hard to keep her expression neutral. It was still all so difficult. Scott dead. A *murder* investigation.

'This feels surreal,' she said as they took their seats. 'I still can't believe it.' She paused. 'So are you going to tell me now how it happened? How Scott died?'

'We just need to start the recording first.' Melanie Sanders broke off to activate the digital box at the side of the table, confirming who was in the room and the time.

'Why do you need to record this? I thought it was informal? I haven't done anything wrong.'

'It is informal. A voluntary interview for the benefit of the tape. We very much appreciate the cooperation, but we still record these things, Ruby.'

'So do I need a lawyer?'

'It was explained when you arrived that you can request a lawyer to be present. Your mother said it was fine without. You agreed. But you can change your mind. Do you want a lawyer, Ruby?'

Ruby thought. How would it look to request a lawyer now? And how long would it take to *sort* a lawyer? They'd already been in the station for more than an hour. It was like the decision over giving the DNA sample and having her fingerprints taken. What would get them off her back? What would make her look guilty? Would she be arrested and held in a cell overnight? She just wanted this over with.

'I don't need a lawyer. I want to get back to my father as quickly as possible. So – let's get this over with. What do you need to know?'

'We understand that you know the victim of our inquiry – Scott Crawford. Tell us how well you know him. When you last saw him.'

Ruby took a long, slow breath. 'Scott works at the hotel' – she lifted her chin – '*worked* at the same hotel as me in Scotland.'

'How long have you worked there?' The older woman again.

'Nearly a year. I wanted a change of scene. I'd heard Scotland was beautiful.'

'Go on.'

'Scott was kind when I arrived. When I was learning the ropes. We became sort of friends.'

'What do you mean – sort of?'

'Well, at first I was really pleased to have a new friend. But then I realised that he was hoping for something more.'

'A relationship?'

'Yes. And I didn't want that. So it became difficult.'

'Explain *difficult*.'

Ruby paused, weighing up how much to say. Wondering how much they knew already. They clearly somehow knew he'd been on the same train. So how much exactly did the police know? Did they have his phone? The messages?

'OK, so Scott started bothering me. Messaging me a lot. Turning up at the house I shared and at the hotel when I was working and he wasn't. It became uncomfortable.'

'Was he ever violent or threatening towards you?'

'Not physically violent – no. But I felt uneasy about it all and I asked him to leave me alone. There was a row at my shared house when he called round while I was out. One of my housemates thought he was going to hit him. All my housemates decided to bar him. They wanted me to report him to the police.'

'And did you? We haven't found a record of that.' Melanie Sanders looked down at her notes and shook her head.

Ruby looked away to the corner of the room. She was thinking of the moment she'd been told that her mother had reported Ned to the police. The shock that she would do that. The anger and the outrage.

'No, I didn't. I wouldn't do that. I hoped it would blow over. That he would move on.'

'And did he?'

'No. He became very interested in this weird online thing. StarBonders. It's a sort of love cult thing.'

'Cult?'

'Well, they say they're not a cult. But it sounded like one to me. He was paying money to StarBonders every month for readings and study. And StarBonders seemed to be telling him that I was THE ONE. And it made everything worse.'

There was a long pause as if the police officers were waiting for her to volunteer more. Ruby stayed silent.

'Did you discuss all this upset with your mother?'

'No, I didn't. We haven't been close lately.'

'I see. And why's that?'

'It's not relevant.' Ruby felt her face flushing. Again she thought of that moment when they had parted nearly a year back. Her mother's arms outstretched. Ruby turning away.

'Do you carry copies of your mother's card? Her agency card.'

Ruby frowned, no idea where this was going. 'No. Why would I? I told you – we haven't been close lately. I don't go around promoting her business.'

The two police officers exchanged a look which Ruby didn't like, before Melanie Sanders continued. 'OK. So bring us up to date on your last contact with Scott. I should perhaps mention that we have his phone.' The chief inspector had leaned forward now, eyes wide.

Ruby suddenly realised precisely where this was going. *His phone.* She remembered how afraid she'd been when she got off the train. The noise of the wheels of her case as she hurried along the platform, away from Scott.

'You have the messages between us?'

'Yes we do. Can you explain what happened? Why you threatened Scott?'

'I didn't threaten him. I was just trying to get him to leave me alone. He followed me from Scotland when I left to visit my father in hospital.'

'You're sure he followed you? That he didn't have any other reason to be heading south?'

'No. He was supposed to be working. You can check all this with the hotel. He knew that I had to leave in a hurry and suddenly he was on the same sleeper train as me. It really scared me.'

DCI Melanie Sanders then took a sheet of paper and started to read.

'*You come near me, Scott, and I swear to God, I will make you VERY sorry . . .* A few hours after you sent that message, that threat to Scott, he was found dead in his hotel room in Truro, the name of which he had also messaged to you.'

'You're not understanding. I was just warning him off. It was like stalking that he got the same train. It was not OK that he followed me. I didn't want him to follow me to the hospital.'

'So you were afraid and you were angry with him?'

'Sure. Afraid – yes. Angry?' Ruby paused again, thinking of the messages printed off on the table in front of her. 'I suppose so.'

'Angry enough to go to his hotel room and confront him. Angry enough to make *sure* he didn't follow you to the hospital . . .'

CHAPTER 46

BEFORE

LAURA

It was agony waiting. An absolute age before DCI Melanie Sanders and her younger sidekick finally appeared in my room.

I'd expected to be alongside Ruby to support her while she was questioned and felt blindsided when they asked to speak to us separately.

It was a big shock too that they started the tape, like you see on the television, naming everyone in the room. Why so formal?

'I thought this was voluntary? Informal?'

'Just routine.' Melanie Sanders suddenly turned her phone around to show me a picture. 'You recognise this, Mrs Harry?'

'Yes. It's one of my business cards.' I didn't add what I was thinking. Why the hell was it in what looked like a police evidence bag?

'Can you explain how one of your business cards was found at the scene of the murder of Scott Crawford at a hotel in Truro?'

'No, I can't. Someone must have put it there.'

'And why would that happen?'

'I have no idea. But I mean. It's just a business card. I give them out a lot. Anyone could have one.'

'Did you give any cards to your daughter, Ruby?'

'No. I didn't.' I was trying frantically to work out where this was going. It honestly felt as if there was some kind of set-up going on. But who the hell . . . ?

I thought of the terrible year between me and Ruby. The row over Ned. The chasm between us. A terrible thought landed. *No. No. Surely Ruby would never . . .*

I shut down the thought as Melanie Sanders started to ask different questions. But I wasn't listening properly. I was suddenly regretting giving the samples voluntarily. The DNA and the fingerprints. Where the hell was all this going? And why did I let them interview my daughter on her own?

'I'm sorry but I have no idea where this is going and I don't feel comfortable with this. I want a lawyer. And I want a lawyer for my daughter too.'

CHAPTER 47

BEFORE

Clara

As the taxi pulled into the car park to the left of the café, Clara strained her head, looking out for Phoebe's Polo. Nothing. Clara didn't move.

'This is the place,' the driver said.

'Oh right. Yes. It's just I'm supposed to be picked up by someone else. I can't see them yet.'

Clara felt uneasy sharing this detail but she also felt a rising panic, not sure what to do. It was so dark. It was only a small car park – just four cars visible. She continued to cast her head left and right as if repeating the search might change the outcome. But no. Definitely no black Polo.

'Sorry. We don't do waiting. You could maybe wait inside?' The driver nodded towards the café entrance as Clara paid in cash. 'Do you want a receipt?'

'Oh, there's no need for that. I don't need a receipt.' Clara felt a new panic, wanting no record of this journey.

'Whatever.' The driver sounded even more hurried. 'You OK? You want me to take you back? There will be a double charge. It's just I have another ride waiting.'

'OK. Sure. No. This is fine. Thank you.'

Clara undid her seat belt, hooked her small cross-body bag over her neck and shoulder and finally left the car. The driver pulled away incredibly fast and Clara felt an almost ridiculous sense of abandonment, instinctively pressing her palm against her jeans pocket. No phone. Still no black Polo.

She strode to the café entrance, relieved to see a sign confirming 24-hour opening. She imagined it was a pit stop for lorries, and yet there were none in the car park. There was just one server, a boy. Late teens at most. He looked bored, sitting on a stool behind the counter even though there were a number of tables that were strewn with cups and plates. Clara could imagine her mother alongside her, whispering in her ear that he should be clearing up. *He should at least be wiping down the tables.* And again she felt the guilt behind her lie to her mother. The lie that she was at home sleeping.

At least there were a few customers. A middle-aged couple, sipping what looked like cappuccinos. A guy on his own, maybe late fifties, just staring at his phone; and another young woman, maybe mid-twenties, also on her phone.

Clara normally used Apple Pay, and so felt in her bag for her small purse, relieved she had remembered to bring a bank card as well as cash. She selected a small bottle of sparkling water from the shelves alongside the counter, quickly paid and then found a seat near the front window where she would be able to see any arriving vehicles.

Ten minutes. Twenty. No black Polo. No new cars at all. The middle-aged couple left, followed by the young woman.

Clara started to wonder what the hell she was supposed to do if Phoebe didn't turn up at all. When she'd left the house without her phone, she had never factored in this possibility – that Phoebe wouldn't be waiting where she'd said. What if she'd been in an accident like her father? Or a journalist was following her and Phoebe had to abort?

With no phone, how the hell was Clara supposed to know what was happening?

Or what to do next?

CHAPTER 48

BEFORE

JOE

The next time Joe surfaced, he strained immediately for Laura's voice. Or Ruby's. Or Clara's.

But there was nothing. He wondered for a time if one of them might be reading beside his bed. Ruby had sounded a bit nervous when she was talking to him about the hotel in Scotland. Self-conscious. He felt this terrible pang inside as he thought of how long it had been since they last saw Ruby.

She was forever changing her hair, Ruby. Colouring it and cutting it in different styles. Each time he persuaded her to FaceTime, he wondered what new look she would be wearing.

Laura always quizzed him after a call, wanting to know all the details that mothers need. *How did she look? Did she look as if she's eating alright? Getting enough sleep? Looking after herself?*

Joe thought next of their lovely Clara. Her very different hair issues. The *awful* time of it all. The special appointments and the counselling, none of which had seemed to come up with any answers. Or solutions. For himself, he couldn't care less if his beautiful younger daughter went bald, but it broke him to see her fiddling with her hairbands and her wig. He so wished he could take that hurt on himself and he knew that Laura felt the same.

He listened some more. Still nothing. And then finally after five, maybe ten minutes, there were two nurses alongside the bed. Younger nurses prone to gossiping as they checked the machine. Filled out their charts.

'You see the media still outside when you turned up?'

'Yes. The girl's doing better, they say. Two of the TV vans have gone, but the mother's still giving interviews and radio updates left, right and centre. Wants a public inquiry. Says the StarBonders thing is a cult. You heard her on the radio lately?'

'I switched it off. Fed up with them taking up so many car parking spaces. It's hard enough to park. I think the hospital should move them all off site, don't you?'

'Think they're scared of a backlash. Waiting it out. My husband says journalists normally move on pretty fast to the next big story.'

'So why's this one not got visitors? I thought his wife was always here?'

'Didn't you hear?'

'No.'

'Police turned up. Took the daughter away for questioning and the mother went along too. One of the porters saw them taking the lift to the rear entrance.'

'So what's that all about?'

'Word is she might have killed someone.'

'You're *kidding* me?'

'I'm not. To be honest, working in this place, nothing surprises me anymore. It's always the people you least suspect.'

That was the point the bleeping started. One of the alarms from his wretched machines. Joe tried so hard to calm himself. He wanted to hear more. Listen in some more. But his heart started pounding again. And the machines struck up their matching moan.

And no matter how hard he tried, he could not slow his pulse. Or quieten the stream of questions pounding inside his brain.

Someone dead?

Ruby with the police?

What new hell is this . . . ?

CHAPTER 49

NOW

LAURA

'And you gave DNA and fingerprints voluntarily?'

Across the chipped table, my lawyer looks confused. The official arrest 'on suspicion of murder' and the summary of the evidence against me has thrown both of us.

'I thought it would eliminate us.'

'So how do you explain it? Your DNA was at the scene of a murder. Strands of your hair. A definite match.'

I close my eyes and scan through the nightmare since they suddenly arrested me. At first it had seemed so ludicrous – over a business card at the scene of the murder. For heaven's sake – anyone could have put that there. Or the victim could have picked it up somewhere. I'd expected it all to be cleared up quickly. And I knew there were rules around how long they could hold me.

But then they discovered that only *my* fingerprints were on the business card. Not the victim's. So they were granted permission to keep me longer in custody. Under official arrest now. Let Ruby go, 'pending inquiries'.

My solicitor said that was probably because they had something else.

And now we know. Worse and more confusing than I ever imagined. The tests fast-tracked. My DNA at the scene. How? How?

'Someone must have planted my DNA,' I blurt suddenly. 'I swear to God, I've never heard of this boy. This Scott Crawford. I have never met him. I have no idea why he had my business card. And I swear I've never been at that hotel.'

'And why would someone plant your DNA?' My lawyer's eyes look disbelieving. 'You must see that is going to sound highly unlikely. If there's a formal charge, I have to brief someone now, a barrister, to take this case forward. Someone experienced. And I need to ask – if there is something you need to tell me. Now is the time.' He pauses. 'Did you have anything at all to do with the young man? With his death?'

'I've told you already. Of course I didn't. I swear to God. I have done absolutely nothing wrong.'

'And your daughter. I understand there has been a rift with Ruby. I'm sorry but I have to ask. Do you think there is any way that Ruby could have anything to do—'

'No, no. I didn't mean that I suspect Ruby of planting evidence. Or having anything to do with this. Absolutely not.' A pause in which I cannot bear the terrible sinking feeling deep inside me. 'She wouldn't.'

'OK. So this is where we're at. They will have to make a decision on charges very soon. If that happens, you'll be taken to the magistrates' court first, where the murder charge will be put to you formally and the case then referred to the Crown court.'

I can't believe what I'm hearing. 'But I'll get bail?'

'We will try for bail, but I need to warn you it's rarely given in murder cases.'

'You seriously mean I have to stay locked up? But I can't. I need to be with Joe. Oh dear God.' Still I can't believe this is happening to me. 'My daughters. They'll be so scared. And so shocked. They need me. I simply cannot stay locked up.' I was allowed to try a phone call to Clara, but it just went to voicemail.

My lawyer tilts his head. 'There's overcrowding in all the prisons. Chances are they'll probably keep you in custody locally for now. I suspect you may even stay at this police station. But if they take the charge to the magistrates' court, you may be transferred to prison while on remand.'

'*Prison?*'

'This is worst-case scenario. I just want you to understand the gravity of where we are. Murder cases take a long time and there's a backlog. As I said, I'll need to instruct counsel if and when a charge is confirmed. We'll visit you as soon as we can to take further instructions.'

I find myself thinking again of all those postmasters and postmistresses who did nothing wrong and yet were locked up. Some for years.

'Can I ring my daughter again?'

I mean Ruby this time. I've spoken to her once but it was all a blur. She said that Clara was not at the house and she was going to stay with Ned's mother because she had things she needed to discuss with her. It was like a slap to the face. Why would Ruby not want to stay at home with all this going on? She sounded very confused and very scared and we didn't have long to talk. *Why have they arrested you but let me go? What the hell?* We left it that she would ring Clara and divide her time between visiting Joe and Ned's mother until I can sort out this misunderstanding. I told her it would all be resolved soon. I couldn't bear to say that I was just as scared as she was.

'Can I ask Ruby to visit me? Or get my mobile back to ring her?'

'We can request a call and we can request a visit, but it will be up to the custody officer. They won't give you your phone back.'

My mind starts bouncing between the two possibilities like a manic game of table tennis. If I'm allowed another call, should it be Clara or Ruby?

Clara is so young. And stressed. No. I won't ask to speak to her as it will put her anxiety through the roof.

I'm assuming she was on the way back to the hospital when I tried to get hold of her. But she'll be beside herself with worry, not being able to get hold of me. So I need to find out from Ruby how they're both doing. To try to reassure them that I will sort this all out. Somehow.

I think of Joe lying in his hospital bed. Is he alone or are the two girls with him?

'I must speak to my daughter Ruby again. My husband's in hospital. I don't even know how he is.' My voice falters and I can feel tears brimming.

'OK. I will do my best to arrange that and to see if we can get a condition check on your husband.' He looks genuinely concerned. 'This is a lot for you.'

'It is. It's a nightmare.'

CHAPTER 50

NOW

Clara

When Clara comes to properly, she's still woozy. Disorientated. The back of her head is extremely painful and there's blood on her shoulders and stickiness on the back of her neck. Dried blood?

She is aware that she's opened her eyes before. Recognises the brick wall opposite but she must have passed out again. She has no idea how long she's been like this, drifting in and out of consciousness.

She listens out but there's no sound from upstairs.

The room is a basement but there's a tiny stream of daylight now, stealing in through a gap in a rough blanket pegged to a piece of rope across the top of a very narrow window. That outlet must be at ground level outside. It's a small relief to have this chink of contact with the early morning light, but it's still gloomy enough for her to have to wait for her eyes to adjust.

She tries again to fight the panic, remembering now that the last time she surfaced she was so terrified of suffocation. She has a gag, fairly loosely tied but still uncomfortable. She felt sick when she first came round and was terribly afraid of not being able to breathe. She tried to scream through the gag but it was hopeless. In the end it exhausted her, draining every ounce of energy. Her head was pounding and the blood at the back of her head was still gushing a little. She could feel it trailing down on to her shoulder. She must have just lost consciousness again.

Clara wonders how deep the wound in her head is. Will it get infected? How the hell is she going to get help?

She tries again to call out through the gag for Phoebe, terrified that she too is unconscious upstairs. Or worse.

But her attempts sound like unintelligible mumbling.

There's no reply. Just her own groaning through the gag echoing back in the grim, dark space.

She can just see the stairs up to the ground floor. She pulls again at the cuffs on her wrists but they are attached to a second set of cuffs linked to a pipe skirting the floor of the room. The pipe won't budge. She yanks harder and harder but it's no good. The pipe is thick and firmly attached to the brick wall by a number of brackets.

The room smells damp and she thinks again of arriving here. The blur of what happened so very quickly. They were supposed to be inside the place only for a few minutes to pick up diesel from the basement for a generator for the retreat. Phoebe was too worried to get diesel from a garage in case they were picked up on CCTV. She said the Lighthouse and adjoining cottages were vulnerable to power cuts and she was worried about that with the retreat. So she'd hired a generator and just needed fuel as a backup. This place was owned by a mate who had offered diesel. But neither of them liked the look of the place. They both agreed – *in and out as fast as we can*. Phoebe was urging her to hurry when they were taken by surprise. From behind.

The blow to Clara's head was so sudden, she struggles to even remember falling. She thought she was on the stairs when she was hit. So was she carried down to the bottom? Or did she fall all the way down the stairs? Her body feels bruised and weak so she probably fell.

She looks around the basement and tries to piece together how the hell this happened.

Was it her fault? Someone must have followed them. Yes. Someone must have watched her get in Phoebe's car. Maybe someone from the café or even the taxi driver. She should never have told him she was meeting someone. *Stupid. Stupid. Stupid.*

Or maybe it was one of the trolls targeting StarBonders. Maybe Phoebe was right and one of them had somehow managed to trace her. And follow her. Is that what this is about? That mother blaming StarBonders for her daughter's suicide attempt?

She thinks of her own mother. Aches for her.

Clara tries to call out for her mother but again the gag makes her cry unintelligible.

Nothing. Not a sound. Her biggest fear now is whoever hit her hard on the back of the head may have attacked Phoebe even more fiercely. Clara blacked out so immediately that she has no way of knowing what happened. Maybe Phoebe as the leader of StarBonders was the main target.

Oh Jeez.

Maybe Phoebe is dead.

Clara pulls her knees up and hugs them tight. She feels the pounding in her head from the wounds and the increase in her heartbeat.

She thinks of her father in his hospital bed. Her mother, who will be frantic with worry.

And Ruby.

And at last the fear and the panic overwhelm her. She starts to cry, sobbing so hard that her shoulders roll. Worrying, as a wave of pure despair moves through her whole body, that she will never see her family again.

CHAPTER 51

NOW

RUBY

Ruby is in the orangery of Ned's family home – his mother busying herself in the kitchen, making coffee and toast.

Ruby's heart is racing, wondering what the hell is going on with her mother. Why hasn't she phoned? Why are the police still holding her? And why is Clara not answering her bloody phone?

She looks around the grand extension of wood and glass and impossibly impractical sofas with plump, cream linen cushions, and remembers the first time Ned brought her here.

That debut visit she was stressed too. Ned had warned his mother could be 'a handful', though Ruby had no real idea what that meant. Her own mother could be a handful, after all. Couldn't all mothers?

They had met briefly in the hall and his mother waved them through to the orangery while she went to fetch a tray of drinks. En route Ruby teased Ned. '*Orangery?* I think you'll find the rest of us call it a conservatory.'

He sighed. 'Wait until you see it.'

His tone was almost embarrassed as he led the way through a wide hall with a stunning terracotta floor of reclaimed tiles boasting a myriad of colours with little pitted treasures. The imprint of a leaf. The wear of a thousand footsteps across a hundred years or more. And then suddenly they turned a corner into blinding sunlight. And Ruby stood very still, awestruck. The orangery was huge. Like a National Trust café space.

And now here she is again in the same room, with its view of the lawn stretching like a perfect puzzle picture framed by bushes and trees; at the far end a greenhouse in which she and Ned once made love on a blanket on the floor, staring up at the stars through the panes of glass.

Ruby's family home was impressive in its own way too. A five-bedroomed red-brick house with a large and very pretty garden. It had often wowed her friends when she brought them home. But Ned's home was in another league. *Proper* money. She'd understood a lot about Ned from that first visit. She'd sat in the orangery, immediately starting to better understand the suffocating tension between him and his mother over money. How much was at stake. *Big* numbers.

Why his mother didn't know how to play it. She had wanted him to 'make his own way' but didn't quite know how to get that right. There were mixed messages and a lack of continuity. It was like ping pong. Spoiling him one minute, then raging the next over his recklessness and his laziness. And the drugs. Oh my goodness. The horror of the meltdowns when Ned's mother found out about the drugs . . . Paying for rehab one moment. Cutting him off the next.

'Here we are.' Ned's mother appears suddenly with a large tray sporting beautiful turquoise ceramic mugs and a cafetière of coffee. A jug for milk and a matching bowl with sugar lumps.

Ruby's hand is trembling and so she plunges it into her pocket. She's not told the truth about what happened overnight. The time at the police station. The awful situation with her own mother, aware of how very much Ned's mother dislikes her. Blames her.

'It was good of you to invite me to stay. I'm so very sorry about turning up so late.' Ruby still doesn't know what to call Ned's mother. 'Mrs Summer' feels too formal. 'Barbara' would sound too chummy. And they aren't chums. Since she arrived at the house from the police station, Ruby has avoided calling her anything at all.

She's tried to contact Clara. No answer. And she's tried to get more information from the police, who are saying very little. She needs to get back to the hospital but is desperate to hear from her mother about what the hell is going on.

'I'm glad you agreed to stay here.' Ned's mother clears her throat. 'I know it's difficult – with things still strained between you and your mother. Anyway. Like I told you already. I wanted to put things right between us. It was very wrong of me to ask you to stay away from Ned's funeral.' She pauses as she slowly pushes the cafetière plunger down through the coffee. Ruby watches, mesmerised. The hotel in Scotland uses small cafetières for its breakfast service and all the staff hate them. The stock is unpredictable. Some of the older cafetières have plungers that get stuck, spraying coffee everywhere. It is as random as landing the supermarket trolley with the wonky wheels. Staff can never know when they will land the cafetière with the tricky plunger.

'I've been too afraid to ask how it went. The funeral. I didn't want to upset you.' Ruby takes the coffee cup and adds just a dash of milk, shaking her head to the offer of sugar.

'Toast?' Ned's mother lifts a plate and the smart, ceramic toast rack.

Ruby shakes her head and asks again. 'The funeral? It must have been terrible for you.'

'To be perfectly honest, I don't remember it well. I asked the doctor to up my antidepressants, which was probably a mistake. I felt quite out of it.'

Ruby doesn't know what to say next. Ned had told her his mother had been on antidepressants for some time. She'd blamed him. The drug use. He'd claimed she was constantly using that against him. *You see what you've done to me?*

'Was Isabella a support?' Ruby glances to a picture on a side table of Ned and Isabella as children. Brother and sister were sitting by a large sandcastle, the sea visible behind them. Beaming. Arms around each other's shoulders.

'Isabella wasn't able to make the funeral.'

'She *missed the funeral?*' Ruby is shocked. It was no secret that Ned was his mother's favourite – the reason she was so overwhelmed by his drug issues. Mother and daughter were apparently often falling out over the favouritism. Isabella had always loved travelling and moved to Canada with a job promotion just before Ruby started dating Ned. He never went into detail but said his mother and sister just didn't get on.

But she'd never imagined Isabella wouldn't fly back after Ned's death. The brother and sister were always in touch.

'I'm so sorry. I didn't know. So is Isabella still abroad?'

'Yes. As far as I know. She's not in touch much. Too busy for family these days. We don't really talk.' A pause. 'Just like you and your mother. Ironic, some might say.' She takes a long, slow breath. 'Did your mother tell you I bumped into her in town? In a coffee shop?'

'No. We haven't had much time to talk. At the hospital, it's been difficult. And Clara's gone AWOL now, which is the last thing we need.'

'Is she still not answering your messages?'

'No. The thing is she gets stressed, Clara. She's gone to ground before – stayed with a friend when she felt low. I'm assuming that's what this is again. The stress of the hospital.' Ruby feels her heart quickening. It's been a nightmare, trying to juggle everything without being totally honest.

She's afraid that if Mrs Summer finds out her mother is under arrest, she will release her name to the media. Several outlets have reported that a woman is being held in connection with a murder in Truro but no name has been confirmed yet.

Ruby thinks of her father alone at the hospital and feels a terrible weight of responsibility. She needs to visit him but first needs to track down Clara. She doesn't want to have to tell her mother that Clara is suddenly out of touch.

Though she still feels so horribly conflicted over her mother – what happened with Ned – Ruby doesn't feel what Ned's mother feels towards her. She doesn't *hate* her. The truth? She thinks of her mother at the hospital. With her packets of sandwiches. At the police station, trying to reassure. To step up. Ruby realises that she doesn't quite know *what* to feel towards her mother anymore.

'Have you tried Clara's friends?'

'A couple. I'm going to ring round today. Her phone goes straight to voicemail. She may just be out of battery somewhere.'

Before she can say anything further, Ruby's phone buzzes with a message. It's from the solicitor helping her mother. She feels a stirring deep in the pit of her stomach as she reads. At first just shock. Then real gut-wrenching fear.

'I'm really sorry, but I'm going to have to make a call.'

CHAPTER 52

NOW

THE POLICE

'So you don't mind if I stay on a few more days? Come to Devon later? You understand?'

Amelie watches her father's face framed alongside her own on her phone. He's not a big fan of FaceTime and Amelie believes that's because he knows she can read him. Right now she notes the sweep of disappointment. He scratches his nose. Doesn't immediately answer.

Amelie's already updated him on the murder case, including the shock of the Harry family's apparent involvement. He's asked a lot of questions. Right on point. She can tell that he's intrigued by the case himself and hopes he'll understand why she wants to see it through with Mel.

'It's just your mother,' he says at last. 'She really misses you.'

'I know. And I'm sorry. I don't mean to upset her. Do you think I should speak to her now?'

'No. She's having a lie-in. Let me prepare her gently and you ring her later, when she's had time to adjust.'

'OK. Thanks, Dad,' Amelie adds, lifting the phone higher to improve the picture – the sun getting brighter through the curtains behind her.

'But you promise me you will come home as soon as you can? Yes? I miss you too, you know.'

'Course. I've got to go but I love you both.'

'You too.'

She ends the call and heads down to the kitchen where Mel has been speaking to the DI on the murder case again. She's jangling her car keys in her left hand, and as soon as she finishes the call, she marches towards the front door.

'So are you OK to stay on?'

'Yes. All squared with the fam.'

'Good. Let's get going then.'

'No Tom and George?' Amelie glances around.

'Left already. Tom's giving him a lift to work.'

On the drive to the office, Mel brings her up to date. They already know that only Laura Harry's fingerprints are on the business card. Not the victim's. Or anyone else's. That's why they formally arrested her. In theory this puts her in the hotel room. Now the fast-tracked DNA has confirmed hair samples on the victim's clothing. A new twist. A full match not to Ruby, whose row with the victim made her the mostly likely suspect of the two . . . but to her mother. Laura Harry.

'So we charge the mother today?'

'In theory. We were all set to get CPS approval. But we have . . .' A pause. 'An *anomaly.*'

Amelie frowns.

'More a great big gaping hole in our case, actually,' Mel adds, letting out a sigh, her tone one of extreme frustration.

'So – something new?'

'Yes. A new witness back at the hotel. A guy on the housekeeping team. He'd gone off shift when we did the earlier interviews and we couldn't get hold of him. He's now just confirmed that he got a request from our victim for extra towels. He delivered them to the room and saw the victim very much alive and well at five o'clock. He remembers the time exactly as he was about to leave for home. End of his shift.'

'And the victim was found at six p.m.?' Amelie remembers their rush to the scene with the hotpot supper forgotten. He was found by a chambermaid doing the turn-down service.

'Yes. So we now have just a one-hour window for the attack. We have some CCTV from the hotel lift but nothing pointing to our attacker. They must have used the stairs. Problem is we now also have CCTV from the hospital.'

Amelie frowns again. 'And?'

'Hospital CCTV very clearly shows Laura Harry on the ward with her husband between five o'clock and six o'clock. No gaps, other than a quick trip to the canteen where she was picked up on all the other cameras.'

'But that's not possible. If we have her DNA at the scene.'

'Exactly. I was all ready to press for a murder charge but now we can't quite square the circle.'

'Could there be a fault with the time-stamping on the hospital CCTV?'

'I'm told not. Also the hospital nurses confirm Laura Harry was at the bedside, bar a few minutes. The CPS won't like it. Because we'll have to release this to the defence if we go to trial. And technically it's a watertight alibi.'

Amelie feels her stomach churning. She thought DNA was foolproof. If Mrs Harry's hair samples – presumably including roots to give her DNA – were on the victim, she must have been in the room. Or at least been with him at some point, despite claiming she'd never met him. She was the prime suspect. There was no DNA at all at the hotel from the daughter.

'So what are we going to do?'

'I haven't a hundred per cent decided yet. We have a bit of time in hand. Probably interview Laura Harry again. She's asked to speak to her daughter Ruby while in custody.'

'Are we going to allow that?'

'Given this conflicting evidence, yes, I think we will *have* to.'

'So what are we supposed to think? That we can't trust the DNA?'

'I always trust the DNA. I'm saying there's something not right in this case, that's all. And I want to speak to Laura Harry again to try to figure this out. *Before* we get egg all over our face with the CPS and commit to the first magistrates' hearing.'

'OK. Bottom line. Do you really think this mother, Laura Harry, would be capable of killing this guy?' Amelie is remembering the shock of the body. Twisted and struggling for air.

'If she knew he was stalking her daughter, who knows? I gave up being surprised what people are capable of a long time ago. All I do know for certain is that Laura Harry couldn't be in two places at the same time.'

CHAPTER 53

NOW

JOE

Joe feels himself surfacing again. Suddenly he can hear noises in the room. The familiar bleeping of machines and distant whispering. The nurses? Or maybe visitors.

He is so used to being trapped in limbo, even when rousing from sleep or whatever this is, that at first he does not try to move or open his eyes, so very fed up with the frustration when his body just won't work.

But after a few minutes, he's suddenly aware of glare. Too much brightness. He is so disorientated that he cannot register quite what is happening. Joe winces at the brightness of the light above him as his brain adjusts. He closes his eyes.

And only then does he realise. If he's just closed his eyes . . . they must have been open. He waits for a moment, struggling to take this in. He tries to open his eyes again and, sure enough, there again is the blinding light, and slowly the ceiling with its big square panels and strip lights comes into focus.

Joe can't quite believe it. He tries turning his head to the side and feels the pillow on his cheek. He clenches his right fist and feels the fingers touch his palm. He tries the left and that too responds.

I can turn my head. I can move . . .

Still, he can hardly believe what is happening as relief sweeps through his whole body. He tries to call out for a nurse but only a croak leaves his mouth, his throat parched.

He tries again to speak and a strange noise leaves his mouth, but louder this time.

'Oh look. Mr Harry is waking up.' A nurse strides across the ward to the side of his bed, pressing some kind of alarm button. 'Hello there. Welcome back, Mr Harry. Try to stay calm. I promise you everything is going to be OK. You're in the hospital after a road accident but you're going to be just fine. I'm Judy and we've been taking good care of you. You've had an operation so you need to take it very slowly.' She reaches to the cabinet beside the bed and holds a beaker with a straw just in front of his face. 'Sip this. Can you sip this for me?'

Joe nods and sips on the straw. It's heaven. The water so soothing to his throat, as if he's never had a drink before. He pauses to enjoy the extremity of the relief to his parched mouth and then sips again.

'Thank you.' His voice is still croaky but the words are at least intelligible now. 'I need to see my family. Where are they?' He turns his head to look across the room.

The nurse frowns as if unsure what to say.

'I heard that the police were here,' Joe says. 'I've been able to hear everything, except when I've been sort of sleeping.'

'Oh, right. Well, we need to get the doctor to check you over first and then we will reach out to your family . . . You're right. The police were here. That's routine after a road accident. I don't have information on what's happened but I will look into it for you.'

Joe closes his eyes momentarily and thinks about the accident. The pictures on his phone. The messages. The blinding light suddenly filling his windscreen.

'What day is it?'

'It's Friday. You've been with us since Wednesday evening—'

'Good grief. I need my phone.'

'I think the police may have it. That's routine too after an accident. There was no phone when you were brought in.'

'In that case I need to speak to the police.' Joe opens his eyes and clears his throat. 'Could you call them, please? Say that it's urgent.'

CHAPTER 54

NOW

CLARA

Clara has given up trying to scream for help through the gag. The cottage, which belongs to one of Phoebe's friends, is remote. She remembers the drive here. The long and bumpy track. However much noise she makes, no one will hear.

When they detoured here for the diesel for the emergency generator, Phoebe apologised and admitted the place gave her the creeps. But she didn't want to use a garage with CCTV in case they were tracked. There was no electricity at the cottage so Phoebe had to use the torch on her phone. And the place smelled. To lift their mood, Phoebe showed Clara pictures on her phone of the renovated Lighthouse and the adjoining accommodation for the retreat. It was magical. So stylish. So beautiful. Phoebe explained that StarBonders had agreed a five-year rental on the whole lot. Income from StarBonders members had helped to fund the renovation of four adjoining cottages. Fourteen en-suite rooms initially, with more in the pipeline for future retreats if the first one went well.

Phoebe said the renovations were top quality. But they had to have a generator as backup in case they lost power during the retreat. Belt and braces.

Now suddenly there is a noise from above. Creaks of the floorboards. Clara takes a sharp breath in. Spins her head to the right so she can see part of the staircase. It must be their attacker. If it were Phoebe, she'd surely call out to her. But maybe she's gagged too?

Clara shuffles back to position herself against the wall and the pipe. She suddenly desperately needs the toilet and is worried about an accident.

There is the creak of a door opening. She now remembers that, yes, there was a door off the hall to the basement staircase. Next she hears footsteps and finally a figure comes into view.

Clara is so shocked that it is as if time has frozen. She stops breathing. Widens her eyes.

'Hello again, Clara.'

It's *Phoebe*. And yet it isn't Phoebe. How can it be Phoebe?

Phoebe has dark short hair. This new version is blonde. Long-haired.

It takes Clara a moment to realise the awful truth. In the disorientation from her pounding head and the blood running down her neck to her shoulder, she had not taken in the extra humiliation. The lightness around her head.

The fact she is no long wearing her wig.

'Oh, dear God. What is this? Why are you wearing my wig?' Clara mumbles the questions through the gag but the words come out muted. Unintelligible.

'Sorry but I can't understand you. But if it's about my new look, I am open to compliments. Rather suits me, don't you think?' Phoebe sits on the second step, running her right hand through the length of the hair. 'I can see why you picked it.' A pause. 'Especially looking the way you do. *Without* it, I mean.'

Clara feels a sweep of shame and anger. And complete confusion.

Again she blurts out more questions. All still unintelligible.

'Oh dear. Has our little empath really not figured it all out yet?'

What on earth does she mean? *Our little empath?* Why is she being so horribly cruel? Why isn't she setting Clara free? They need to go straight to the police. Never mind the Lighthouse. Never mind the retreat.

And then Phoebe begins to laugh. And the full and terrible truth dawns.

Phoebe slow-claps and finally stops laughing. 'Oh, Clara. Catching up at last, are you? So here's the deal.'

She pulls a white crumpled cloth from her pocket.

'This has chloroform on it. I'm not sure about doses so let's just say that I've been generous. I'm going to remove your gag because we need to talk. Sort out how we're going to get your mother and your sister here. But if you scream or shout out in any way at all, chloroform it is.'

Clara feels a new wave of fear. The dread of being unconscious again.

'So do we have a deal? No screaming? No one can hear you out here anyway, but I can't face the noise.'

Clara nods.

And finally Phoebe stands and moves across the space, the white cloth still in her right hand, pulling the gag down so it sits around Clara's neck, away from her lips.

Clara coughs for a moment, her mouth parched.

'I need the toilet.'

'Oh, don't worry, I've thought of everything.' Phoebe marches across the basement to a curtain over what Clara assumed was storage boxes or something similar. But when she removes it, there's a commode with a lid. Like you'd see camping. Or for someone recovering from an accident. It's low-level, old and also dirty.

'Been down here years. The place has been abandoned for a long time. The commode must have been for the grandmother. Don't worry, it's empty. No chemicals. But better than going on the floor, don't you think? If you shuffle across, sliding the cuffs along the pipe, you can use this.'

'You are insane. I'm not using that. You need to let me go.'

And then Phoebe's expression changes. Hardens. She narrows her eyes and moves closer, lifting the white cloth in her hand and at last removing the wig which she tosses to one side.

'So you choose the chloroform?' Phoebe tilts her head. Her tone is chilling, sickeningly childlike, like a taunt. Clara takes in her face, so menacing and unreal, and feels that she is going to be sick.

CHAPTER 55

NOW

LAURA

'I'm so sorry about all this, Ruby.' I sit across from my daughter in the same small meeting room where I talked to my solicitor. 'I really have no idea what's going on.' She doesn't answer. I check the clock on the wall. Only a few hours before they must charge me or get another extension to hold me for longer.

What to say to her? What to say to her?

Ruby's still staring at her lap and won't meet my eyes. I think of that awful car ride to the police station when she wouldn't look at me either. I just can't believe this nightmare. I've lain in bed so often this past year, imagining our first meeting after what happened with Ned. Me apologising and begging for forgiveness. A hug. Some kind of tearful reunion.

Never in a million years could I have imagined *this*.

'I asked to see you because I can't bear what you must be thinking. And I want to say again, very clearly, that I had absolutely nothing to do with the death of this man. This Scott or whoever he is. *Was*. It must be some terrible mistake. A mix-up in the lab or something; this evidence they say they have. Like I say, I just don't understand it.' I clear my throat. Still she won't look up. 'Please look at me.'

She remains frozen.

'You don't really think I could ever hurt someone, do you?' I reach out to touch her arm but she pulls back.

'I can't do this, Mum.' At last she lifts her head. Tears in her eyes. 'The only reason I agreed to come was because of Clara.' She stands as if to leave. I assume she means to report back to Clara. Poor Clara all alone out there, dealing with her dad at the hospital. Precisely why I need to make Ruby see. To step up and help. To understand that this nightmare is some kind of huge mistake. I can't bear this look on her face; the awful possibility that she may think I actually had something to do with this.

'Please sit down. *Please.* I wouldn't put you through this if I had any other choice. But with Dad in the hospital and Clara so young and so vulnerable—'

'What do you mean *vulnerable?*'

'You know she's always been vulnerable. Finds pressure difficult.' I think of Clara's hair problems. All the therapy and the trials and the awful worry. How she's begged me not to tell her older sister because she loves her and fears Ruby will blame herself for leaving home the way she did.

This thought takes me back to that awful day. When Ruby left. So much hate in her eyes . . .

'Look. I've never really had the chance since you came to the hospital to say again how desperately sorry I am. What happened with Ned—'

'Oh no, no, no,' she interrupts. 'We're not going there. We're not talking about Ned. Not today.'

'OK. OK. Not now. But down the line, we do need to talk about it—'

'What? You seriously think I want a conversation with you about how men who come near me suddenly end up *dead?*' Her eyes are flashing with anger and confusion.

'What do you mean by that? The police said you knew this Scott. They told me he was stalking you. But I didn't know if they were making that up. Or exaggerating or trying to trick me or something. I told them I've never heard of him. Never met him. Had absolutely no idea he was hassling you—'

'Well, he was hassling me. He works at my hotel. *Worked* at my hotel. And he followed me on the sleeper. I had a row with him.'

'Oh right. Goodness. That sounds awful.'

So the police *were* right. This was about Ruby?

'And now *your* DNA is at the scene of his death.' Ruby pauses. 'His murder.' There are tears in her eyes now and I see that her left hand is trembling. She notices me glancing and moves her hand swiftly to her lap. 'I just don't know what to think.'

'And nor do I. Like I said, I have no idea how that has happened. It's as much a shock to me as it is to you. It must be some kind of mistake. Or someone must be *framing* me.'

'Framing you? Can you hear yourself? You seriously think the police will buy that?'

'Oh, come on, Ruby. I know how angry you are with me. But you know I could never harm anyone deliberately. You know that.'

She starts to cry now and I reach across the table again to try to put my hand on her arm. I fear that she will shrug me away once more but she doesn't. It's as if this is a surprise to her too and she continues crying.

'Clara's gone missing, Mum, and I'm so afraid. I just can't handle all of this on my own. It's too much.'

'*Missing?* What do you mean – missing? Is she not at the hospital with your father? What have you told her about what's going on?'

I'd been imagining poor Clara frantic with worry but at least in the dark about my arrest. At the hospital with her dad, sending me messages while the police are holding my phone.

'I haven't been able to get hold of her. She isn't answering her phone. At first I thought she was out of battery. Or upset or something. I assumed she'd gone to the hospital to see Dad but I phoned the ward and she's not there. So I went to the house. You know that I've been staying at Ned's mother's overnight?'

I nod. It hurts me so much that she chose to go there.

'I went home. The police have been there – they wanted to do a search, apparently. Put up one of those white tents in the garden. One of the neighbours told me. They thought it was about a break-in or about Dad's accident. But the point is Clara isn't there. And her phone is on her bed.'

'But she never goes anywhere without her phone.'

'I know. That's why I came straight here when the solicitor called me. I just don't know what to think or what to do.'

'Oh, dear God. Have you tried her friends?' I feel a new sweep of complete and utter panic.

'Yes. I've tried some of her friends. No joy. So what do we do?'

'We need to tell the police.'

It feels so obvious. Was how I was brought up. *Go to the police.* The thing you do when something is up. Something wrong. A crime. A worry. A crisis.

And yet, as the words leave my mouth, I see the change in Ruby's expression and I hear the echo around the room and inside my head too. The irony. Me in police custody. The police hardly likely to believe me. And worse? Yes. This terrible change in Ruby's expression as I mention the police, so that I'm sucked right back to that awful day. Over Ned. Ruby shouting at me . . .

Why did you go to the police? Why couldn't you just leave it alone? Why did you have to go to the bloody police?

CHAPTER 56

BEFORE

Laura

It was a Thursday I reported Ned to the police. By Friday evening he was dead.

Often at night, I lie in bed unable to sleep and imagine a time machine to take me back to that morning. Undo it. The truth? It wasn't black and white and I don't wholly blame myself in the way that Ruby and Ned's mother do, but I do have big regrets. And yes – I would do it all differently if I could have that second chance. Of course I would.

But hindsight is not a wonderful thing. It is a cruel trick that can break up families.

That dreadful Thursday started for me very early. I remember that I woke just after 5 a.m., aware of torrential rain hammering on the roof. Any woman navigating their early fifties – the dreaded 'change' so widely debated but never quite solved these days – will know what I mean when I describe staring at my clock. Just past 5 a.m.? *Really? So we are doing this again?*

You start to sleep differently from your late forties. Feel differently in your skin. Your moods suddenly start to swing, as does the needle on your scales. It is all baffling at first because it doesn't feel as if you are doing anything differently per se. You are working the same. Exercising the same. And eating the same. And yet suddenly your clothes feel tight and you don't have the same energy anymore, and along creep all these other unwelcome changes too.

So yes – I remember feeling dread, lying awake from just after 5 a.m., knowing that I would be tired all day. Was that a factor in what happened? The tiredness? I hope not but I will never know.

It was nearing the end of the autumn term. Clara had finished some mock exams – I can't remember what for – and Ruby was home after her first term at university. She wasn't liking it as much as she'd hoped, mostly because she was missing Ned. In all honesty, I'd rather hoped they would take a break in the relationship so that she could give university a proper chance, but Ruby was still besotted with Ned. And that made me afraid for her.

I knew about the drugs because Clara had told me. Also, it had become rather obvious. Ned's problem had spiralled to the point where he didn't seem to care about turning up at our house stoned. Some visits his eyes were on stalks and he was borderline incoherent. Ruby always made excuses. She tried to say he was unwell. *Going down with a virus.* We all knew different.

I checked websites for advice. And I challenged Ruby directly once. At first she swore to me that it was just a bit of cannabis. She promised she was not taking drugs herself. When it became clear other drugs were involved, she admitted that Ned had been to rehab, paid for by his mother, and was still working hard to stay clean. That was why he was struggling some days. I didn't believe a word of it. He didn't look to me like someone who was clean.

I knew via Clara, who was still very tight with her sister, that Ned's mother had long since cut off Ned's allowance. She had done this to his sister too, apparently, wanting them to make their own way in the world. To get jobs and not to take the family money as an excuse to dilute personal ambition. I approved of this strategy. And it certainly worked for his younger sister, Isabella. She got herself a decent job and eventually moved abroad – a company transfer on good money and with a fancy flat thrown in. Ned was incredibly proud of her.

But his was a very different outcome. The 'tough love' financial strategy backfired big-time with Ned.

He tried a few jobs – working in a café and a bakery. But only half-heartedly. He had trouble getting up in the mornings and got himself fired very quickly. Increasingly he became angry with his mother, blaming her for his unhappiness. The truth was he needed money for drugs and was struggling with withdrawal symptoms when he was broke.

We guessed he must be stealing, because I was convinced he was still using despite the stint in rehab. Ruby's story that he was clean just didn't wash. I never believed it personally. His eyes just looked too odd. Too often. I imagined he must be shoplifting or something to pay for his addiction. Clara had told me once in the past that she'd caught Ned taking money from our holiday fund – the big china money pot on the windowsill in which I collected coins all year. It appalled me, though I couldn't imagine he'd been able to take more than a hundred pounds. I had a big row with Ruby over this, who fell out with Clara for 'stirring things'. Ruby swore that Ned had just been taking a few coins for parking. Ridiculous that she believed him.

One of the trickiest things we had to navigate was Ned staying over at ours. I wasn't comfortable with this at all. It's a big departure to let your child have their partner sleep over in any circumstances but I was worried that he would bring drugs into the house.

Joe was also worried, but he argued it was better to know where Ruby was. Safe with us. So in the end I let the pattern continue.

Of course, my biggest fear was that Ruby would get sucked into the world of drugs. Become a user herself. She swore over and over in rows between us that this would never happen, but it was at the root of everything that happened that Thursday. My fear.

That dreadful Thursday, I lasted in bed until just after 6 a.m., got up and set the table for a nice breakfast so everyone could help themselves. Croissants that I'd bought the previous evening. Jam and butter. Fruit and yoghurt.

I then retreated to my office and did some early work for a new client who wanted a website update and social media push to launch a new product. Routine stuff, but it was nice to get ahead, given I couldn't sleep.

It was probably about half past eight when I ventured back into the kitchen for some more coffee to find Ned standing by the breakfast bar. There was no sign of Ruby and he was clearly surprised to see me. He seemed startled and sort of jumped back to stand nearer the cooker, fidgeting with his pockets and then his hair.

'Everything OK, Ned?'

I couldn't help but notice that my handbag was on the breakfast counter. I looked at it. He looked at it. There was this really awkward meeting of eyes and then a moment when neither of us knew what to say.

'I didn't know you were up,' he said eventually. 'I'm just getting us tea.'

'Fine. Help yourself. Tell Ruby there are croissants. She loves croissants.'

'I know.'

Did I imagine the edge to his voice as he said that? Ned always liked to pontificate that no one knew Ruby the way he knew Ruby.

He turned away from me to switch on the kettle and I took the opportunity to grab my bag.

'I'm in my study if you need anything.'

And my big mistake? I didn't check my valuables carefully enough. I glanced into my bag, fearing the purse would be gone. But it was still there. I opened it to see that the cash, around a hundred and fifty pounds drawn out the previous day, was still in place. I counted the notes and felt a pang of guilt for thinking the worst of Ned. But foolishly I didn't check my cards. I felt sort of guilty for doubting him. With the cash still in place, my brain concluded that Ned had not stolen from me.

Ruby and Ned went out and Ruby returned later, saying Ned had job interviews and she wanted to watch a film in her bedroom.

It was about 3 p.m., just as I was wrapping up my day's work, that I had a call from my bank, reporting some suspicious behaviour on my account. I'm always wary of scammers and at first suspected it was a hoax call. I hung up and rang my bank from a different line. They asked me if I had been making a number of cash withdrawals from different ATMs that day. I said that I had been working from home and had not been out at all. I said I would check my banking app and call them back. *Please block any further withdrawals until I get back to you.*

I checked my purse more thoroughly to find that my business bank card had gone. It allows higher cash withdrawals than my personal account and so I started to go cold.

Of course, I do most business payments by card, but just occasionally I need cash to pay freelance staff for events and promotions. I felt another chill as I held up my phone for face recognition.

The app opened.

I went into the business account to find nearly two thousand pounds withdrawn across five different locations. My first thought was it wasn't possible. Withdrawals needed my pin. And why had the bank allowed several large cash withdrawals before ringing me?

My next thought. *This was Ned.* He and Ruby were often with me when I paid for things. Maybe he'd watched me to note and remember my pin?

Ruby was up in her room. I did think about calling her down but I knew she would hit the roof. She would say I was making this up to get at Ned. She would say that Ned would never do something like that.

And so I did what I thought was right. I phoned my bank again to report card theft and fraud. The woman on the line said that I had to make an official complaint to the police. Get a case number. And so, without thinking, I did just that; I phoned the police.

My big mistake – and I will always regret it – is I told them I suspected Ned had taken the card. I stressed that I had no proof and asked them to investigate. I gave his name and his home address.

I knew, even as I did this, that it was dangerous. That it would threaten my relationship with Ruby. But my head was swimming. I had no idea what else to do and I also had no clue how it would turn out. I was convinced that Ned was lying about being clean.

Let the police handle it, is what I thought. *This is a crime. I can't just let this go. The woman said I had to report it.*

Later, when that dramatic Thursday evolved into the tragedy of Friday, Joe asked me if I had hoped that by reporting Ned to the police, it would break them up. Ned and Ruby.

I see now, looking back, that maybe he was right. All I remember is that I was very afraid for her. My Ruby on the fringes of a world of drugs and stealing. So yes, I was relieved when the bank told me to report the case to the police. A big part of reporting Ned – misguided or not – was trying to keep Ruby safe.

I guessed she would not see that. But I hoped she would understand my reasoning.

I did not guess how it might turn out. And that my daughter would *never* forgive me.

CHAPTER 57

NOW

Ruby

The first Ruby knew of Ned's arrest was his mother screaming at her down the phone.

What the hell has your mother done? Why did she report him to the police? WHY?

Ruby went straight to the police station where Ned's mother was causing a scene in reception. Ned had apparently kicked off when he was arrested and was being held in a cell, point blank refusing to see anyone.

I am his MOTHER. You have to let me see him. This is my family. My right!

Ruby did her best to calm Ned's mother down, afraid that they would both be asked to leave. It was extremely difficult. Turned out *no one* had the right to see Ned if he didn't want to be seen. He was an adult with rights himself.

Eventually, by trying charm at the front desk instead of shouting, Ruby was able to piece together at least most of the facts.

Ned's mother summoned the family lawyer and mercifully Ned agreed to see him briefly. What they discovered was that Ned had been found in possession of Ruby's mother's bank card, which he'd allegedly used to withdraw large amounts of cash. He had got aggressive with the arresting officers and so was being held overnight, pending charges for theft and possibly assault too. It was expected he would appear at the magistrates' court the next morning. CCTV was yet to be checked at the various cash machines.

Ruby waited and waited, praying that Ned would change his mind and agree to see her. He didn't. Still he refused to see anyone beyond the brief chat with the lawyer. His mother waited for a few hours and eventually left to consult further with the lawyer. She told Ruby that Ned was not welcome back home but that she would pick him up from the police station on his release, take him to court and then take him straight back to rehab, which she would happily fund until he was truly clean. She asked the front desk to alert her the moment he was released.

But none of that happened.

The CCTV confirmed it was Ned at the cashpoints. He was charged and released on bail, pending a court appearance a few days later due to a backlog. He refused to have any family informed of his release. Not his mother. And not Ruby either.

No one knew where he went until it was too late. Some ten hours after his release he was found in a coma at a notorious squat used by drug users on the outskirts of the town. He had taken heroin from a supplier unknown to him. Ambulance crews tried resuscitation, but it failed. He was pronounced dead in hospital, late on Friday. His inquest later confirmed that several drug users had collapsed and the batch of heroin was found to have been cut with a synthetic opioid called nitazenes. Witnesses from the squat said Ned was depressed by his arrest and did not want to go back to rehab. He was tired of the ordeal of withdrawal symptoms and did not care what happened to him.

His mother blamed Laura. *Why didn't you come to me? Why the police? I could have taken him straight back to rehab. Repaid you the money . . .*

Ruby, in her shock and grief, blamed her mother too.

In the police interview room Ruby opens her eyes, coming to as if from a daydream. She looks down at her hands, aware suddenly that they are shaking.

'You seriously think I'm going to let you report Clara missing to the *police?*'

Everything that happened with Ned is still replaying in her head. His mother collapsed on the floor at the hospital outside the ward. Ruby herself wailing in disbelief. *He can't be gone. He can't be . . .*

'This is not like with Ned,' her mother says.

'Don't say his name. You don't say his name.' Ruby withdraws her arm, shaking her mother off. 'What if Clara just needs some space? What if she's just taking some time out before visiting Dad in hospital? We have to respect her privacy. Give her some space.'

'Without her phone? Clara never goes anywhere without her phone.'

'But that could just be a mistake. And if the police go after her, she'll be horrified. And afraid.' Ruby stands. 'You have no way of knowing how she'll react. We need to wait. We can't say anything to the police. Not yet. We just need to wait and see if she turns up at the hospital.'

'Ruby, I'm sorry but Clara is more vulnerable than you realise. She's just eighteen and we don't know where she is. I'm her mother and this is my decision, not yours.'

CHAPTER 58

NOW

CLARA

When Clara next comes to, her head is spinning. She's aware of a sweet smell to the gag which is back in place. Also another very different smell. She looks down at her trousers which confirm her worst fears.

She closes her eyes to the pounding in her head for a moment. She thinks of how she must look. No wig. Wet trousers like a toddler. She starts to cry but keeps her mouth clamped shut beneath the gag so that it's a muffled sobbing. If Phoebe is still in the house upstairs, she doesn't want her to know that she is this low. This weak.

And then, as the stifled weeping at last starts to subside, she begins to replay the encounter with Phoebe.

Why oh why didn't she see it before? Why was she so *stupid, stupid, stupid*? When those poor girls harmed themselves. When the mother went to the media. Why did she just suck up the excuses? Why didn't she see what was right there in front of her eyes all along?

She had thought that StarBonders understood her. That it was a place she could be heard. A place where a girl with hardly any hair and a stomach full of nerves could fit in. A girl who, for all her flaws and insecurities, might actually find true love one day.

And now this awful truth. That StarBonders was a scam. An illusion. That it was never about happiness. Or love. Or being heard and understood. It was all fake. And cruel. It was about money and manipulation and bullying. It wasn't helping vulnerable people. It was *targeting* vulnerable people, just as the mother had warned in her interviews.

At last, tired and still terribly afraid, Clara feels the silence. And the stillness. Her weeping over. She lets out a final huff of air. She steadies her breathing and realises that she needs to stop feeling sorry for herself. To pull herself together. She opens her eyes to take in her surroundings. She needs to clear her head. Try to make some kind of plan. There's still light creeping in through the makeshift curtain over the small window. So it's still daytime. Still Friday? She glances around the basement to see if there is anything she can reach. Anything that might help her to escape.

There's an old bookshelf in the corner of the room. It has some boxes on its shelves. Could something inside be useful? She shuffles along the floor, easing her handcuffs along the pipe. If she gets closer, maybe she can kick one of the boxes with her foot?

But as she moves, the metal of the handcuffs makes a horrid scratching noise along the pipe, and there's the dreadful squeak of the upstairs door to the basement stairway.

Clara feels her eyes widen. Her heart pumping. At last Phoebe appears again. This time there is mercifully no wig but her cocky face and tilted head as she sits on one of the lower steps is torture.

'Ah, good. I wondered when you would come to.' Phoebe suddenly screws up her nose. 'But no offence. Not a good smell. You should have used the commode, like I suggested.'

Clara feels her face flush and hates that Phoebe will see this. Her humiliation. Her fear. She pauses and is surprised to feel something stirring. Not strength, not quite that. But the beginnings of a defiance that is as welcome as it is surprising. Also a sweep of true hatred and disbelief that someone could be this evil. This cruel.

'So this is where we are.' Phoebe straightens her back. 'It's not like the movies – chloroform. Not an exact science. It takes quite a lot to knock someone out and, according to Google, there's a grey area between anaesthesia and – well, death. Probably why they stopped using it for surgery all those years ago.' A pause. 'Anyway. What I'm saying – warning actually – is that I need you to cooperate. I will take the gag off again but I need you to do as I say because if I have to use more chloroform I really don't know what will happen. Understood?'

Clara stares at her torturer. She thinks again with shame of her own stupidity. She thinks how she allowed herself to be led here, truly believing that they were picking up diesel from a friend's abandoned cottage. How could she have been so stupid? How could she ever have believed there was a lighthouse?

'So if I take off the gag again, are you going to cooperate this time because we need to talk?'

Clara narrows her eyes and finally nods. Phoebe lets out her own long breath, as if exasperated, and moves across the room to again pull down the gag to hang around Clara's neck. Then Phoebe steps back.

'So what's your real name and what do you want?' Clara stares at Phoebe as she speaks.

'Now this I like. Clara finally catching up. You don't need to know my name. That's part of the fun. But we do need to talk turkey. Get on with things.'

'Money. You want money, yes?'

Clara spits the question, thinking of all the members of the WhatsApp group and how they've all been tricked. Cheated. It has to be about money. That's what the mother said to the media. That StarBonders was all about money.

Phoebe begins to slow-clap and again Clara feels her eyes narrowing with something between despair and shame and fear. She thinks of her father in the hospital. Her mother who will be frantic, unable to contact her. And Ruby. Clara feels tears pricking her eyes and tries again to pull herself up, not wanting Phoebe to read her.

'At last the penny drops. Yes. It's about money. Of course it's about money. Life is about money. Now that StarBonders is going pear-shaped, I need a change of scene. I fancy somewhere warmer. Abroad. And for that I need a fund.' She runs her fingers through her hair and tilts up her chin, her tone almost childlike again, as if she were discussing something perfectly normal.

You are insane, Clara is thinking. Which makes her feel even more afraid. Because how can you reason with someone this mad? And what will Phoebe do next to her even if she does cooperate? Clara feels a shudder pass right through her.

'So your mummy has quite a lot of money, doesn't she? Successful business and all that.'

Clara now feels suddenly cold. So there is going to be some kind of ransom? A kidnap demand? Is that the plan here? For a moment and for the first time, Clara wonders if there might actually be some way of surviving this. Her mother will pay up. Of course her mother will pay up.

'Yes. My mother is successful. She will pay for me to be released. But only if I am unharmed. If you make the demand to the police, she will—'

'The police? And there I was thinking that you had some brain cells.' Phoebe is shaking her head and then tutting. 'No one is going anywhere near the police. What we need, my dear and ridiculous Clara, is to get your family here. Your mother and your sister too. Nice and cosy. All of us together so we can have a nice chat and work this out.'

Clara cannot believe what she is hearing. Why would Phoebe want that? How could that possibly work out?

'No, no, no. You keep my family out of this. Away from here. You let me call them and they can deliver money somewhere isolated. Or transfer it to your account. No police. And then you can let me go.'

There is a pause and Phoebe begins to laugh. Another mad and misplaced laugh which echoes around the basement. And echoes inside Clara's head too.

'No wonder you have no friends,' Phoebe says finally. Clara feels as if she has been slapped, remembering and regretting all the personal things she has shared with Phoebe. When she thought that StarBonders was real. When she thought it was a safe place. A place where people cared. Understood. She thinks of the other people who have been duped. The poor girl on the motorway bridge? The girl in the hospital? She remembers with another pang of guilt and confusion all the messages she sent out herself, encouraging people to join the retreat. How was she so easily sucked into this dark tunnel? A new despair passes through her and she's again fighting the tears pricking her eyes.

Because suddenly she feels not just duped herself. But complicit.

'I'm disappointed in you,' Phoebe adds, standing up. 'You really are no fun at all.'

CHAPTER 59

NOW

JOE

For Joe everything seems to take too long. Waiting for the doctor. Then waiting for the police.

His head is pounding. The medical staff say this is to be expected. The machines and the monitors say he's doing OK. He tries to sip more water, hoping this will help his headache. It doesn't.

Pictures keep exploding in his brain, taking him right back to the crash. The beam of light. The screech of the brakes. The picture on his phone of the woman in the nightclub.

He needs to speak to the police. And Laura. And he needs his phone . . .

'Why are the police taking so long?' he says to the nurse who comes to his bedside with painkillers in a little plastic pot. She has a trolley and is ticking off the medication from her list. 'And my family? I need to speak to my family too.'

'I don't know about all of that. I'm sorry. I'm just doing the drugs round at the minute.' She hands him the little cup and waits until he takes the dose. 'But I promise that I'll ask for you. Do try to just rest.'

Joe closes his eyes with frustration, so tired of being told to rest. How can he rest? It is a ridiculous expectation. He feels as if he has lost days of his life, stuck down at the bottom of a pool waiting to surface. And now he is finally back on dry land, he's still helpless. He feels not just disorientated but abandoned. He stares at the empty chair next to his bed and frowns. Has Laura found out about the picture? Is that why she isn't here? He should have spoken to her right when it happened. He should never have imagined it would all go away. He should never have got so short-tempered with Laura over the pendants turning up. Her health. And the bloody dry-cleaning . . .

He closes his eyes, feeling the pulse of his headache intensify. He is wondering how long it will take for the painkillers to kick in when there is a rustle beside the bed.

'Mr Harry?'

He opens his eyes to see a woman in a navy skirt and cream blouse. No hospital lanyard. 'Are you with the police?'

'Yes. I'm Detective Chief Inspector Melanie Sanders. I'm overseeing the investigation into your accident.'

'A detective chief inspector investigating a road accident?' He's pleased to see her but surprised at the rank.

'It's untypical.' She smiles. 'But we suspect your accident may involve foul play. And may even be part of something wider, so let's just say I'm taking an overview.'

'Well, that's good. Very good. Because that's why I need to speak to you. And why I urgently need my phone back.'

'Your phone?' She pauses. 'It will have been held as part of the inquiry. But I have no record that we've accessed it yet.'

'Well I need it urgently because I have something that I need to show you.' Joe pauses, unsure how to explain himself. *Oh damn it.*

'There was this woman in a nightclub. Who was trying to blackmail me before my accident.'

Melanie Sanders' expression changes completely. He cannot figure if it is just surprise or disapproval.

'I swear to you, I did nothing wrong. I'm in sales. I have to entertain clients. I went to a nightclub, which is rare for me. Much too old for all of that. Anyway, these girls joined us. Young girls. I didn't encourage them and I was very uncomfortable. I'm a father of young women who go to clubs, for goodness' sake. But my colleagues let the women join us in a taxi to another venue. I made my excuses and left them to it, but later that night I was sent pictures by one of the girls. A colleague must have given her my number. I certainly didn't. The pictures were topless. She claimed I asked for them. I swear that I didn't.'

Melanie Sanders takes in a slow breath.

'I know what you're thinking. You've heard it all before. But I swear to you. I'm not that sort of man. I've been married a long time and I don't fool around. I blocked the girl's number. Ignored her. But a few days later she started to send the same pictures from a different number. And then she started asking for money, not to tell my wife.'

'Blackmail?'

'Yes. She wanted cash – fifty thousand pounds – transferred to an account. I said I would go to the police and was keeping the evidence on my phone. She replied that the price had gone up to a hundred thousand. I ignored that message and decided that I needed to tell Laura what was going on and then report it to the police. I was in a panic about it all. The next thing, driving home there was this blinding light shone into my windscreen. And I had the accident.'

Melanie Sanders is now standing up and taking out her mobile phone from her pocket. 'You're saying your accident was caused deliberately? And you suspect this blackmailer?'

Joe nods.

'I have to tell you, Mr Harry, that what you're alleging regarding the accident might, under any other circumstances, sound like a stretch. By which I mean, difficult to believe. But I need to be straight myself and say that it is not entirely a surprise to us.'

'Really?'

'Well, not the blackmail. We obviously didn't know about that. But one of my colleagues has been working on the same theory about a light, possibly a powerful laser pen, causing your accident. I'll get your phone as quickly as I can and we'll go from there.'

CHAPTER 60

NOW

THE POLICE

Amelie is back at the station when the call comes in from Melanie. It's dynamite. It confirms Amelie's theory, backed up by the doorbell footage and witnesses on the street. That someone really did shine a light at Joe Harry's car. Maybe that very laser pen she picked up from the boy.

But it all feels so confusing. Is the whole Harry family in the middle of some kind of whirlpool that they can't quite understand? Or is this just Laura Harry? An unlikely killer, granted, but maybe secretly unhinged? Maybe she tried to kill her husband for playing away? And did she kill Scott Crawford for targeting her daughter? Is that even possible?

'So what are we going to do about Laura Harry? Charge her?' Amelie has her mobile pinned to her left ear, the DI staring at her. He's already complained to anyone who will listen about the DCI stomping all over his case. And he's furious that Melanie is keeping Amelie in the picture before him.

'Is that the chief inspector on the phone?' he asks, sidling up to her desk.

'Er, yes. She wants me to tell you that she's on her way back,' she lies.

Melanie is silent for a moment, then guesses. 'Is that the DI getting tricky?'

'Yes. Sort of.'

'OK. Put him on.'

Amelie hands the mobile to the DI, who gives her a look of complete disdain. He listens for a time, then looks surprised. 'Are you sure that's the right course, boss?' He pauses some more. 'OK. Understood. I'll sort the release of that mobile and I'll wait for you here.'

He hands the phone back to Amelie. 'Apparently we are to let Laura Harry go. *Pending further inquiries.*'

Amelie can't quite believe what she's hearing. The DI is looking simultaneously puzzled and then smug. 'Be it on Melanie Sanders' head. Not a decision I would have made. And not a decision I will be endorsing on the files. But what do I know, eh? Just the DI on the case.'

He marches back to the front of the office, shaking his head as a text message pings in from Mel.

Is he livid?

More perplexed.

Amelie sends her reply then pauses to add:

. . . tbh feeling confused myself.

Three dots and finally another reply from Mel.

Will explain when I get back.

CHAPTER 61

NOW

LAURA

I am back in reception at the police station in complete shock.

I fully expected the next step to be the worst. A charge. A committal at the magistrates' court and then prison custody, awaiting trial. I had pictured more white tents all over my lawn. And my picture all over the news.

Instead I am back in the waiting area, my phone and other personal belongings returned with no real explanation for the U-turn. My solicitor seems none the wiser either. All he could say at our brief meeting was that the police ran out of time. And there must have been some new doubt cast over the evidence, otherwise they would have sought another extension on my detention.

'What doubt?' I asked him.

'I don't yet know,' he said, shaking his head. He'd clearly been fully expecting a charge too. That's why he turned up to support me as the deadline for holding me ran out. 'But I will be doing my best to find out. Because this isn't over. There is still a risk they will re-arrest you and a charge will come very soon. We're not out of the woods.'

My solicitor has gone now, promising to be in touch. And the young man in uniform on reception seems surprised that I have not bolted too.

'You're free to go, you know,' he says, eyebrows raised.

'I'm waiting for Detective Chief Inspector Melanie Sanders,' I say, lifting my chin. Even I realise this is the last thing anyone expects. But I feel it's *time*. My cards on the table.

Everything has been building up in my mind while in custody, and I feel it's time to share. *Everything.*

I phone Ruby who picks up immediately. 'What's happening, Mum?'

'They've released me. I'm in reception at the station.'

There is a very long pause.

'I told you. I didn't do anything, Ruby. They must believe me. But the most immediate thing is Clara. Any news? Has she turned up?'

'No. No sign of her at home still, and I've just spoken again to the hospital. No sign of her there either.'

'Right. Well, I'm waiting for the senior officer and I'm going to report her missing. I know that's not what you want but it's my call. She may be an adult but this is not like her. And I'm very worried.'

She doesn't reply and so I continue. 'Can you go to the hospital to see Dad? I'll meet you there.'

'That's the thing,' she says. 'I've just had a call to say he's come out of the coma.'

'Oh my God.' I genuinely can't believe it. A sweep of emotion passes through me, so powerful that I have to sit down. Relief and then conflicting feelings. Because I want to be with him. 'So – is he OK? What are they saying?'

'He's talking apparently. So I assume he's doing fine. I'm going straight there.'

'Right. Good. Good.' I put my left hand up to my mouth, patting my lips with the frustration. And the shock. And the relief. My eyes close now as I try to weigh up what to do for the best. Go straight to the hospital? Or report Clara missing first? Along with my other suspicion . . .

'OK. Tell Dad I'll be there just as soon as I can. But don't tell him about all this nonsense with the police. And about Clara. He'll be frantic.'

Again, she doesn't reply.

'*Please* don't tell him. Not yet. I know it's a mess and all very confusing for you, but wait until I get there.' And then, when she again stays silent, I hang up.

Which is when the text comes in. An unknown number.

Re Clara. Ring this number in precisely half an hour. DO NOT SPEAK TO THE POLICE. I will know if you do. And Clara . . . will . . . pay.

CHAPTER 62

NOW

Ruby

When she turned twelve, Ruby thought that she had killed her sister.

It happened in a wood. In a blur. In the rain.

Back then, Ruby was in that confusing lull between childhood and the longing to be all grown-up. Part of her wanted to wear make-up and the latest clothes, while another part was still very much the tomboy who loved nothing better than to climb trees and push the boundaries. Clara in contrast was young for her age. She was no tree climber. Afraid of heights. Afraid of rather a lot of things.

Ruby loved her sister very much, but once they were allowed to play out together unsupervised for short spells, she tired of being responsible for her. Having her own wings clipped by Clara's nervous nature.

It had been a long and frustrating struggle for Ruby to persuade their very protective parents to let them out at all. Their house was a mile from the village centre and Ruby wasn't allowed a mobile phone until secondary school. From the age of ten she was driven to friends' houses to 'hang out' during the holidays but she still wasn't allowed to just walk off from the house on her own to meet up with her friends.

We can't have a young girl just wandering around on her own. It's too remote.

Ruby found this ridiculous and suffocating and it caused a lot of arguments. So Ruby was both surprised and relieved, once Clara hit ten, by her parents' idea that the two girls could perhaps head out together occasionally. *So long as you tell us where you are and look out for each other.* At first they were allowed to walk into the village to use the park and the shops. And later to pack picnics to take to a wood near a stream that a lot of local families used in the holidays.

One part of Ruby was cross that Clara was getting this privilege aged just ten while she'd had to wait so much longer. But there was one fast road to cross and her parents argued that they had to wait for Ruby to be older, hence safe enough to oversee the crossing of that road. And for Clara to be old enough for the sisters to play out together. Safety in numbers . . .

You have to hold Clara's hand to cross. No argument. And you stick together. Yes?

The day of the near-death experience, the sisters had sandwiches and drinks packed into a small rucksack and were forced into raincoats with hoods by their mother.

We look ridiculous. It's hardly raining.

OK, so you choose, Ruby. You look ridiculous and have some freedom or feel free to stay home and wear what you like.

Why did parents always play their trump cards over freedom? Life just wasn't fair, Ruby reckoned.

And so reluctantly they set off in their ridiculous coats, their mood only lifting as they began to debate what Ruby might buy with the money gifted for her recent birthday. Make-up? Or would she get her nails done at a proper salon? Clara thought the prices at nail salons sounded ridiculous. A waste of money, as Ruby would be told at school to get the nails removed. Make-up was safer.

At first they followed the official path through the wooded area, but Ruby became bored by having to regularly overtake the slowcoach mums with toddlers and also having to step aside for cyclists ringing their bells to pass. After about half an hour, there was a sign to the left for the 'Foragers' Way'. It was supposed to be a good route for mushroom gathering but Clara and Ruby were strictly forbidden from foraging in case they picked something poisonous by mistake.

'Let's go this way,' Ruby said casually, guessing that Clara would kick back.

'No. Mum said we have to stick to the main path. With all the other people around.'

'Well, Mum isn't here so she's not going to know, is she?'

Ruby was remembering that on a walk with one of her friends (they were supposed to hang out at her friend's house but her parents were more liberal), she had discovered a fallen tree along Foragers' Way. It had landed across a deep hollow, creating the effect of a sort of bridge across a dry moat. All too soon workers would no doubt turn up with chainsaws to cut up the tree for logs. Meantime it was an obvious challenge for some fun.

'I'm not walking along that,' Clara said firmly when they reached the tree.

'It's perfectly safe. I've done it before.'

'How have you been here before?'

'Never mind. It's plenty wide enough. Much easier than the bar in gymnastics. I'll go first.'

Ruby promptly set off across the tree trunk, holding out her hands for balance. It was, to be fair, just a little bit trickier than she remembered. But not truly dangerous. Just a nice challenge.

By going first and closing down any debate, she left Clara with no real option but to follow. There was no other way to cross to the hill on the other side of the hollow.

'You're going to have to come back. I can't do it.'

'Don't be silly. It's easy. Come on.'

And so finally Clara set off, her face bright red – whether with rage or fear, Ruby couldn't tell.

Clara moved very gingerly. She made it to the middle of the tree before she suddenly stopped and started to cry.

I can't do it. I can't do it.

Ruby shouted encouragement but Clara's mood spiralled. She tried to edge backwards, but as she did so, her left foot slipped on the damp bark. The more nervous she became, the more unsteady she became. She waved her hands frantically, trying to recover her balance, but it was no good. Clara ended up stomach down on the trunk with an alarming slap. She reached out her hands, trying to get a grip around the trunk, but the wood was too slippery.

Within seconds she was suddenly falling. Ruby couldn't believe it. She watched as time seemed to freeze. Clara suspended in the air, arms flailing and screaming, and then flat on her back on the ground beneath the fallen tree. Silent. And completely still.

Those next minutes were the time that Ruby really believed she had killed her sister. No sound and no movement from Clara as she lay on the ground below while Ruby drew out her mobile phone to ring her mother, and then an ambulance. As they waited, two concerned mums turned up, following the screaming to try to console Ruby while shouting encouragement to Clara.

Keep still. Help is coming. You're not on your own.

It all came good, of course, thanks largely to the season. Autumn had provided a reasonable bed of leaves to break Clara's fall. She suffered a concussion and had to go to A&E, but the only real damage was hurt pride plus a twisted ankle which required an ugly plastic boot for a while.

But through all the ensuing drama, Ruby had never been so afraid. Or in so much trouble . . .

What were you thinking? her mother said. *You're grounded.*

And now, as she travels by taxi to the hospital, it is those scenes that haunt her, streaming so vividly like a film she knows too well. Clara in trouble. Clara out there on her own. Is her mother right that they should alert the police? Or is Clara just being Clara, needing some time out? Away from all the stress? Is Ruby calling it wrong again?

'Here alright?' the driver asks. He has a soft Irish accent. A nice voice. Ruby lifts her head and is sucked from her daydream, back into the moment.

'Sorry. Yes. This is fine. Thank you.'

She checks the fare and taps her phone against the card machine. It takes a while to ping a confirmation. She worries that she has not added a tip and has no change, but is in too much of a hurry to fix this.

She takes the lift to the third floor and finally up on the ward Ruby rushes to her father's side, to be swept into a hug.

'Oh, dear God. We've been so worried. How are you? How are you?'

'Pounding head but fine otherwise. Doctor says I'll be OK, though they're keeping me in a few more days. I've been wondering where you've all been. Your mother? Is she not with you?'

'On her way,' Ruby lies, not at all sure what to share. 'Actually, can you just give me one minute? I need to leave a message with the nurses.'

Her father looks puzzled as she bolts across the room to the nurses' station, where she asks if her sister has been in at all. The nurses say no but mention that Clara did phone in to check on their father's condition. It was just before he woke up.

Ruby feels relief. So Clara is OK. She's phoned the hospital. Probably just wants some space, just as she suspected.

She quickly messages her mother to say that Clara has been in touch with the hospital so must be OK. Then she marches back to her father's bed.

'What was all that about?' His face looks very anxious.

'Oh nothing. Sorry. I just promised to pass on a message from Mum.'

'What message?'

And then her phone vibrates with a new text. Not from her mother. From an unknown number.

CHAPTER 63

NOW

CLARA

Clara watches Phoebe staring at her mobile phone. She's been typing and there has been the ping of a return message. Phoebe is still sitting on one of the lower steps to the basement. Her phone has a red-and-white marbled case and Clara thinks of all the messages she sent to that very phone and all the naive and faux-positive WhatsApp video calls she joined, with no idea of the black hole she was digging.

For herself. And for so many others too.

Clara's stomach grumbles with fear. She doesn't want her mother and sister brought anywhere near Phoebe. This cruel and twisted excuse for a human. This person who can so easily fake charm and compassion but in truth has ice running through her veins.

No. Clara feels shame that she has been the conduit. The fool. But how on earth to *end* all this without her family coming to harm?

'Just send my mother the bank details. She'll transfer the money you need and you can let me go. No need for the police to know. We won't say anything.'

'Like I said, there's no fun in that,' Phoebe says suddenly, standing up. 'And in any case, your mother is being prickly. She wants proof you're OK. So let's send a little picture, shall we?'

Phoebe surprises her by taking a picture immediately. Clara is mortified, imagining her mother's shock to see her in this awful place. Without her wig and with the dried blood on her neck.

A minute passes as Phoebe sends the picture. They wait. Phoebe begins to hum – a fake, mickey-taking hum as if this is all some big joke. At last there's the ping of another message.

'Goodness. Your mother really is a pain. When you said she was full-on and very particular, I thought you were exaggerating. But no. Mummy wants to *talk* to you. To prove the picture isn't old.' Phoebe lets out a long sigh of apparent exasperation. She looks to the ceiling and then directly at Clara, narrowing her eyes. 'OK. So this is what is going to happen.' She walks across the basement. 'You're going to tell your mother she needs to do exactly as I say or things will go south. Understood?' A pause. 'All you say is – *I am OK. But I only get to stay OK if you do what she says.*'

Clara nods. She feels bile in her throat. Coughs to try to clear it.

Phoebe stands an arm's length away, her phone in her right hand. Clara has a moment when she wonders if she might slide her leg to trip Phoebe up and maybe grab her. Hit her? But the handcuffs are tight, the moment is lost, and to Clara's horror, Phoebe draws something from her pocket.

There is a click and it takes Clara a moment to realise that it is a large penknife.

'It's very sharp, in case you're wondering. And I'm not at all queasy about these things. Blood, I mean. So don't make the mistake of thinking I won't use this. God, you really do smell, you know.' A pause. 'Are you ready?'

Phoebe presses the call button; waits a few moments. 'Here she is.'

She moves the phone to hold it against Clara's ear and mouth. Clara has only a moment to decide. She thinks of the strange tone Phoebe uses when she speaks. And the knife.

'Don't come here. Whatever you do, don't come here—'

Phoebe snatches the phone away from her head and puts it against her own ear, stepping back and then turning away.

'Your daughter is a very foolish girl. But you will know better. I will send you the postcode and you come here as quickly as you can. We are inside the property. Down the steps to the basement. If you call the police, I will know straight away. Believe me, I am not bluffing. I have a contact on the force. A very good contact. I *will* know. And you will not see your daughter again.'

CHAPTER 64

NOW

THE POLICE

After racing back to the police station from the hospital, Mel Sanders is baffled. Laura Harry, who made such a surprise song and dance about needing to speak to her again urgently, has all of a sudden disappeared.

'So she just left?' Mel asks the sergeant on reception.

'Yes. All very odd. She was released from custody but refused to leave the station. Don't get that very often, do we, boss? Anyway. Sat there waiting for you for ages. She wouldn't speak to anyone else on the team. The DI came down but she refused to say what it was about to him. And then she got a message on her phone and suddenly legged it.'

'Right.' Mel frowns. 'Thank you.'

It makes no sense. Letting Laura Harry go was a calculated risk but unavoidable, given the conflicting evidence. Mel needs to get the team to review everything again and figure out how the hell Laura Harry has been, evidence wise, in two places at once.

Upstairs in the murder incident room, she quickly reviews the next big push. Two sergeants are already busy interviewing all the hotel staff in Truro again and also reviewing all the CCTV once more. Both at the hotel and the hospital. Footage from the hotel stairwell shows someone in a hoody, clearly aware of the camera and turning away from it to conceal their face during the one-hour window that Scott Crawford was killed. It doesn't look like Laura Harry. Too slight. It does look rather like the figure on the doorbell camera that seemed to fire a laser beam at Joe Harry's car, causing his accident. The hoody has a similar-looking large logo on the right side of the chest but it is blurred. Mel asks for the two pieces of footage to be enhanced and compared by the techies, especially that logo. *Is it the same person?*

She has words in her office privately with the DI who clearly disagreed with letting Laura Harry go. His nose is very obviously out of joint and it gets heated so she decides to do the team update herself, fearing he might undermine her.

'OK. So quick update, everyone.' She stands at the front of the room with the digital board behind her, the DI standing to one side, hands in pockets. Jaw set. Openly pissed off.

'Today is all about detail. Putting everything together. I've just spoken to Joe Harry, who says he was being blackmailed ahead of his accident. He also confirms that a bright light, possibly a laser pen, was deliberately shone at his car. So that confirms the work done by Special Constable Amelie Hill. Good shout, Amelie.' She stares at Amelie, who's at the back of the room and promptly blushes as several members of the team turn their heads.

'So let's get all that on the digital file officially. Because we have to see if there's a link between the murder in the hotel and the attack on Joe Harry. Unusual to have several members of the same family on our books. I'm not buying into coincidence. It's a tricky one and an interesting one, which is why I'm still overseeing. So today – let's look for evidence to explain any links. Yes? Dan.' Melanie turns her gaze to one of the sergeants at the front of the room. 'I want Joe Harry's phone returned to him and any blackmail evidence downloaded and a copy sent straight to me and the DI. Soon as, please.'

'On it,' comes the reply.

'And I want us to find Laura Harry and bring her to me.'

'But you just let her go, boss. Are we re-arresting her?' The DI has his eyebrows raised as he speaks. A clear challenge. Mel strains to keep her face calm in front of the team.

'She said she wanted to speak to me urgently then disappeared. That's the issue. We need to know why she changed her mind. And what she wanted to speak to me about.'

'And what about the daughter – Ruby Harry? That text exchange. And the new information from the sleeper steward that there was a rumpus on the platform. Is she no longer a suspect?' It's one of the younger detectives on the team. A promising young man on attachment. Melanie finds a smile for him.

'Both Ruby and Laura Harry remain suspects in the murder of Scott Crawford until evidence to the contrary. But there's no forensics pointing to Ruby. Only Laura's DNA. And the CCTV placing Laura Harry at the hospital at the time of the attack is problematic for the CPS, as you all know. We check and we double-check everything. We have to figure this out. *Today.*'

Melanie then thanks the team and marches through the room, heading for her own office.

'With me, please Amelie,' she adds as she passes the back of the room.

In her office finally, she asks Amelie to close the door before leaning against her desk.

'I want you to go straight back to the hospital, please, to speak to Joe Harry again. Be with him when his phone is returned. I want you to check what's on that phone and report to me directly.'

'I thought Dan was handling that.'

'He is. But Dan is also a very close buddy of the DI and I need another pair of eyes. To be sure I'm kept in the loop on *everything*.'

Amelie frowns. Her father once warned her that office politics and rivalries could cause all manner of problems on live cases. She is only just beginning to see what he meant.

CHAPTER 65

NOW

Laura

In the car, my heart's pounding non-stop. At first I drive too fast. Who cares about speeding tickets? But then I start to worry about patrol cars. What if I get unlucky? I can't afford to be stopped for speeding.

I've agonised about whether Clara's abductor is bluffing about having someone inside the police. It's an easy lie and I really need the police support. Twice I've held my mobile in my palm, ready to dial 999. But the problem is you do hear about it. Dodgy cops. And the truth is I just can't *risk* it.

. . . and you will not see your daughter again.

I think of the awful picture of Clara. Her voice on the phone.

I feel totally overwhelmed, thinking next about Joe in the hospital. His accident. I check the dashboard. Nearly 2 p.m., Friday. He's been awake for a few hours and he'll be wondering why I'm not there. And Ruby. Good grief. Ruby must be worrying what the hell is going on *now*. As if my arrest wasn't bad enough for her. Me in a cell.

It's pure agony. It all feels too much. But – no. Joe and Ruby will be worried and confused but at least they're safe. I have to keep my focus on *Clara.* My poor sweet Clara. The picture I was sent of her looked so terrible. Her wig taken from her. Eyes so frightened. What looked like blood on her neck. What cruel maniac would do that to a young and clearly vulnerable woman? I feel my chest tighten as I worry that I should have ignored the threats and phoned the police immediately. Too late. I start to think about tactics.

This will be about money. I have money. I can give them money. *Sort* this. But I have to make them let Clara go first.

I check the satnav. Ten minutes to go. The route is getting more rural. Narrow lanes with passing places. Tall and overgrown hedges. Visibility is poor and I keep having to pull in to let other cars pass. It's so frustrating, and at one point a tractor appears. I bash the steering wheel and feel tears pricking my eyes. *Come on. Come on.* The tractor driver points to the entrance to a field partly blocked by my car. Just my luck. I reverse to let him forward, and while I wait for the driver to open the gate and then turn the tractor into the field, I check my phone again. No new messages.

I think again about the police team who arrested me. I frown, remembering all the dramas I've seen about bent coppers taking money. Have I made the right call?

I have a contact on the force. A very good contact. I will *know . . .*

I glance at the speedometer and touch the brake. Was she bluffing? The voice on the end of the telephone sounded quite young. It's pure agony, the weight of this decision.

I take a long, slow breath, checking the satnav again. Five minutes. Good. I have a plan in my head now and I'm going to keep it very simple. I will agree to pay whatever money they need, but only if they let Clara go. Yes. I will offer to stay in her place. Whatever it takes. But getting Clara *out of there* is all I can think about.

The only issue is how much money this person wants. I can only transfer £25,000 inside twenty-four hours on my banking app. If she wants more, I'll need access to other savings and it gets complicated.

I have a big chunk of money in an online savings account, but there's no app and I'm ashamed to say I don't know the password off the top of my head. I keep all those details in a locked filing cabinet in my office. It's hidden under a rogue file that no one would guess. *Pet insurance.* (We don't have a pet.) I feel stressed, trying to figure out how this will go. How I can transfer money quickly.

Let's hope she'll be reasonable. Take an easy £25,000 and disappear.

OK. For the final few minutes, I'm directed off a B road along what feels like a farm track. Certainly an unmade road. Narrow and potholed and with deep ridges at the sides between the old and very worn tarmac and the earth of a wide bank running up to low hedges. I start to get more anxious again, worrying that if a wheel falls into that dip, I'll be stuck.

Concentrate, Laura. Concentrate.

At last the satnav says this is it. The road swings a sharp left, and ahead is what I imagine was once a front garden but is now just a mess of brambles, nettles and cow parsley. There is a small stone building, presumably an old cottage but clearly long abandoned. And by all accounts uninhabitable. The roof has big chunks of tiling missing. There's a lean-to on the left with a flat corrugated metal roof, half of which has slid off and is lying on the ground.

I think that the place can't possibly be waterproof. I imagine Clara cold and damp inside somewhere.

My heart is pounding even faster as I get out of the car and hurry to the front door. It's pushed to but doesn't close properly so I kick it with my foot.

'Hello? It's Laura Harry. Are you there?'

There's the sound of heels on steps, the creak of a door. And then she appears in the small hallway, framed by the dated and peeling wallpaper behind her.

'It's *you*,' I say, utterly astonished.

And then the shock sweeps through me, replaced by a strange sense of knowing. And only in this second do I realise that for quite a while I have deep down suspected it would be her.

CHAPTER 66

NOW

Clara

When Clara hears her mother's voice calling out from upstairs, she's tempted to shout out a warning to her, but Phoebe puts her finger to her lips. She still has the penknife in her right hand and so Clara freezes, the sound of her heartbeat pounding. *Pounding.*

Phoebe heads back up the steps into the hall. Words are exchanged but Clara can't make out much, other than her mother saying 'It's you,' which makes no sense. How could she know Phoebe? Recognise Phoebe?

Very quickly Phoebe is back on the staircase. She hurries down and bolts across the basement to grab Clara's head by her chin, tilting it backwards and holding the knife to her throat so that when Clara's mother starts to descend the stairs, she gasps in shock.

'No, no. Don't hurt her. *Please* don't hurt her.'

'No one is getting hurt if you do exactly what I say.' Phoebe then reaches into her pocket and removes a second set of handcuffs. She slides them across the floor towards Laura. 'Put these on and attach the other end to the far end of the pipe. Beyond that central clasp attaching it to the wall.'

She still has the knife to Clara's neck, the blade pressing into the skin. Clara strains her head backwards, trying to pull away from the blade, terrified.

'I need to sit next to Clara,' her mother says. 'We won't do anything. You can put the knife down. I would just rather—'

'You seem to be misunderstanding who's in charge here. You do exactly as I say. The far end. And I need to hear the click of both ends of the handcuffs. I will check.'

Slowly Clara's mother does as she's asked. She puts one end of the handcuffs around her left wrist. *Click.* Next she stares at Clara, her eyes terrified but then softening as if trying to offer reassurance. And then she moves to the far end of the wall to attach the other end of the cuffs to the far end of the pipe. *Click.* Clara watches her, thinking that maybe their combined weight will be able to pull the pipe from the wall once Phoebe leaves.

Please leave, Clara thinks. *Take your wretched money and leave us.*

Still she can feel the tip of the blade against her neck. Her mind in overdrive with fear – *one slip.* She's afraid she will have another accident. But then Phoebe does something unexpected. She takes a third set of handcuffs from her pocket and moves away from Clara and across the basement to clasp one end around a metal ring set in concrete in the wall, about three feet above the floor. Clara frowns. She wonders what the ring in the wall is for. And why a third set of cuffs? Is she going to be moved even further from her mother?

'What's that for?' Clara's mother's voice is both direct and angry, and Clara is shocked at how bold she is. 'You have me here now. You can let Clara go. I'll sort the money for you. I can do a transfer on my banking app.'

'Like I said to Clara, your family really is no fun.' Phoebe starts to laugh. 'What's life without a bit of fun?' And then her face changes, becoming more serious as she glances between the two prisoners. 'Slide your phone across the floor,' Phoebe says, signalling to Laura.

'No, I won't.'

Phoebe moves back quickly to press the knife once more against Clara's throat, this time piercing the skin.

'Ow. Ow!' Clara's neck is really hurting now. She's terrified how deep the knife will go.

'Stop it! Stop it. I need the phone to transfer money. You leave her alone.'

'You slide the phone to me right now or I slit your daughter's throat. Don't believe I won't.'

Clara pulls her head back as far as she can but still the blade is piercing the skin. She can feel a trickle of blood.

'OK. OK. You can have the phone, but you don't hurt her. You hurt her and I won't cooperate. I won't help you with the banking app.'

At last Laura takes her phone with her free hand from her right pocket, puts it on the concrete floor and pushes it gingerly in Phoebe's direction. 'This is hardly wise. If that phone breaks, I can't do the transfer.'

Phoebe bends down to pick up the phone, which she checks before putting it in her jacket pocket. Then she moves back to Clara's side, placing the knife to her throat yet again. Terror once more courses through Clara. She tries to tell herself Phoebe won't hurt her now, because she needs the money. But this doesn't work. Phoebe seems so volatile. So unhinged. What if she loses it completely? What if her fuse blows?

'So let's play a game,' Phoebe says suddenly. 'Clara. You first. How about you tell your mother who I am.'

CHAPTER 67

NOW

RUBY

Ruby puts her key in the door and realises that it has never occurred to her to return it. The key.

Thank heavens, she thinks. She has no idea if her mother still keeps a spare key in a flowerpot in the greenhouse.

She thought about doing the whole journey to Clara by Uber but has no idea how far it will be. How much money it would cost. Also – she feels nervous at the thought of travelling alone by Uber out into the countryside. After everything with Scott.

In the end, she decided on a taxi home from the hospital to pick up Clara's car. It is used rarely and has the embarrassment of L plates front and back, but who cares. Clara apparently shelved the driving lessons for a while, having failed her test twice. The old silver Polo has just been sitting on the drive since Ruby moved to Scotland and she is worried it might not start.

The keys are thankfully where they have always hung. On a hook just inside the utility room. She races back outside and fires the unlock button. The driver's seat is pushed too far back and she curses as she adjusts it into position. To her amazement, the car starts first time.

But there is no time for relief. Ruby feels a wave of unease and is still feeling completely overwhelmed as she taps the satnav code into her phone and places it near the handbrake. Her phone case is getting bulky with all manner of cards. Cafés and shops are loyalty mad these days. Ruby stares at the case and thinks of the most recent one she'd added. A contact card from Special Constable Amelie Hill, who took Ruby aside when she was released from the police station.

If you need to get in touch. If anything occurs to you . . .

As if. She should have binned the card. No way will she phone the police after what happened to Ned. And the trauma of being grilled herself.

It still genuinely puzzles her why someone like Amelie Hill, someone young and at university with so many options, would choose the police.

Ruby resolves to ditch the Amelie card along with all the surplus cards when she gets home. She takes a deep breath and glances around. The familiarity of the car is a shock to her system. She learned to drive in this car, just like Clara, though Ruby was luckier and passed her test first time. She stares at the handbrake, remembering her panic during her first few lessons. None of her friends' cars even had handbrakes.

It felt a million years ago. Learning to drive in this car. A different life and a whole different Ruby.

At last she pulls away, heart pumping hard, and starts to follow the directions.

Her phone predicts a thirty-five-minute journey. The route guide shows a destination in the middle of nowhere.

She thinks again of the text message.

This is Clara. I've borrowed a phone. I'm in big, BIG trouble and you need to come and get me. This is the address. Don't tell mum and dad, please. I've messed up. They'll freak.

The message came in while Ruby was with her father at the hospital. She tried ringing the unfamiliar number but there was no answer. And no voicemail either.

She wonders what kind of pickle Clara has gotten herself into. Drinking? Hooking up with the wrong guy? She feels a little afraid about what lies ahead, but more for Clara than herself. She feels so protective of her sister. Everyone messes up at Clara's age. Ruby certainly did, several times. She needs to find out what the hell is going on. Get Clara out of her scrape and home quickly.

She did feel sufficiently afraid to think of telling her father, but he still looked so ill and so vulnerable on the ward. It wouldn't be fair. And her mother is God knows where – out of the picture and still, shockingly and unbelievably, the main suspect in Scott's murder. It's system overload. Ruby isn't at all sure what the right thing is to do but she simply has no one else to turn to. She thinks again of the card in her phone case. No. Ruby doesn't trust the police. Will never involve the police, not after Ned. So she has no choice but to set off and sort this out for Clara by herself.

The drive takes longer than estimated. Nearer forty minutes. She keeps checking her phone, hoping for a new message from Clara with an update and an explanation of what is going on. But there's nothing.

The road becomes more and more rural until finally a perilous unmade track takes her further and further from civilisation then swings to the left. Suddenly there, right in front of her, is some kind of derelict cottage. And her *mother's* car.

Ruby can't take this in.

How the hell is her mother here too?

CHAPTER 68

NOW

LAURA

'This is all my fault. All my fault.' Clara is weeping as she speaks, her shoulders rolling. Still she has a knife to her throat.

'No, darling,' I say. 'This is not your fault. It's mine. This is Jade. The young woman I shared my room with at the airport hotel. You know. The story I kept telling. I don't know why she's doing this. But it's *my* fault, not yours.'

I turn to Jade, shuffling along the floor and moving my manacled hand as far along the pipe as I can, desperately trying to get closer to Clara. 'You leave her alone. You take that knife away from her neck. You will get your money. But not if you hurt her. You hear me? You touch her and you get nothing.'

To my surprise, Jade moves the knife away from Clara's neck, but she keeps it held upright.

'You look surprised, Clara. Aren't you listening to your mother?' And then Jade starts to laugh. A truly horrible, mocking laugh.

'Jade?' Clara turns the word over as if utterly baffled. 'She's not called *Jade*. I told you. She's called Phoebe. She's in charge of StarBonders.'

'*StarBonders?* You run StarBonders?'

I'm staring directly at Jade now, thinking of those poor girls. The young woman who lost her life on the bridge. The one wired to all those machines in hospital. So she's behind all that too? Dear God. I thought from her pendant that she was a follower. Someone who'd been sucked in. I can't quite take this in. So Jade is actually behind it all.

'I don't understand,' I say. 'How do you even know her, Clara? I just don't understand.'

'I've been doing all the online techy stuff for StarBonders.' Still Clara's weeping. 'I'm sorry. I thought it was all real. Kind. Good. She said I could have an internship. That I would be paid. And that StarBonders would find my one true love. She said it didn't matter. My anxiety. My hair. And I *believed* it all. I didn't know it was a trick. I'm so, so sorry, Mum.'

'Hey. Hey. You have nothing to be sorry about.' I hate that I can't reach Clara. Touch Clara.

I turn my gaze back to Jade. 'So what is this? You get some kind of kick out of playing games. Changing your name. Play-acting and preying on vulnerable young people. Is that it?'

'I told you. I like fun.'

'This isn't fun. This is cruel. And evil. You're insane.'

She laughs again.

I feel myself frowning. So this woman, this Jade or whatever her real name is, latched on to me after I tried to help her out. Got hold of my details and then targeted my own daughter somehow. But why? Money probably. That's what StarBonders clearly is. Some scam. But why not just blackmail me directly?

I feel a sweep of cold passing through me. It still makes no sense but I start to see that my utter folly in France, my wretched Good Samaritan act, has brought all this to our door. I think of all the times I told the story, the anecdote of me sharing that hotel room. I felt so pleased with myself. Smug even. And now I see the truth of it and die inside. *Stupid, stupid, stupid . . .*

'This is absolutely my fault, Clara. But I am going to sort this out. OK? So how much money do you want?' I'm again looking straight at Jade. 'I can raise money and transfer it straight to your account. But only if you let Clara go first. No money unless you let my daughter go.'

'But we're not even all here yet,' Jade says suddenly.

CHAPTER 69

NOW

JOE

Joe is frantic. Still no word from Laura and now Ruby's disappeared. She said she had to leave the ward for just a moment but hasn't come back.

By the time the police turn up – a sergeant and a young special constable called Amelie – he's highly agitated. The nurse, alarmed by the numbers on the machines he's wired to, strides across to warn that he needs to calm himself.

'You're not quite out of the woods yet, Mr Harry. We can't have you working yourself up like this. You need to take it easy.'

She offers him water to drink and he sips at it to pacify her, then reaches out eagerly as the sergeant hands over his phone.

'It's charged,' the man says. 'We need to see the material you mentioned, please. The blackmail messages.'

Joe uses the face recognition for access. The front screen is awash with messages and notifications from his time in the coma. He ignores them all, swiping straight through to WhatsApp. He deleted the first message from the girl in the club but kept the final messages and pictures sent from a different phone number, fearing he might need evidence.

'Here it is,' he says, calling up the later messages. 'I blocked the first number, then this came in from this different phone.' He feels himself blushing at the thought of the topless picture. 'I swear to God I did NOT ask for any pictures from this woman. She just wanted money. As you see. She asks for money not to tell my wife.'

The sergeant uses his own phone to take pictures of the message stream. Also the topless photo. The sergeant shows the copies of the photo and messages to the young special constable and Joe feels mortified. False shame.

The younger officer frowns and zooms in on the photograph, taking a copy on her own mobile.

'You'd definitely never seen this woman before?' She sounds puzzled. 'It's just she looks familiar somehow.' She looks away to the wall and then back at the photograph, as if she can't figure it out.

'No. I'd definitely never seen her before. Or since.' Still Joe feels embarrassed. The whole thing a nightmare. Maybe the nightclub woman had been recognised because she's in the police's files. Has a record for blackmail?

'Right. So we'll do what we can to trace this phone, but they probably know what they're doing.' It's the sergeant stepping up again. 'Might be hard to track it. I see you didn't reply.'

'No. I decided that I needed to tell Laura what had happened and then go to you lot. The police. But I didn't get the chance. I had the accident on the way home to speak to my wife.' Joe pauses. 'So can I keep the phone now? I need to try my wife and my daughters again. I'm getting worried. I don't understand why they're not here.'

'OK. How about we go through that in more detail. When they left. Where they might have gone. Why you're worried.'

It's the younger officer again. Her colleague is still standing, checking his watch as if impatient to leave, but the special constable takes out her notebook and sits alongside the bed. Joe feels a sweep of relief. He needs them to listen. And to help him find out why his family has suddenly disappeared.

CHAPTER 70

NOW

RUBY

'Natalie! What the hell are you doing here? And where's my mother? Her car's outside.'

'It's complicated. A lot to explain. Your mother was in touch in a panic. She's down there. The steps. You need to be quick. It's *Clara*.'

'But what's happened? You're supposed to be in London—'

'Seriously. There's no time to explain. They need you down there, quickly. I don't know what to do.'

Natalie pushes a door open and Ruby sees steps beyond, leading down to a lower floor. None of this makes sense but she's every bit as worried as she is confused. Has there been some big row between Clara and their mother? Did one of them contact Natalie somehow? She's mentioned her friend to Clara often, but how would they even know how to contact her? A Facebook message maybe?

She starts down the stairs to be greeted by the shock of her life. Her sister and her mother both handcuffed, sitting on the floor of some kind of basement.

Ruby feels fear cascade through her.

They both call her name. 'Ruby! You need to run!' Her mother's voice the loudest of the two. 'Run! Try to get help!'

She swings round instantly but too late. There's a whooshing sound and then terrible pain. And next, blackness.

The next thing Ruby is aware of is a dreadful pounding from *inside* her head. She comes to very slowly. Distant sounds at first. Her name being called. Then her vision returns, blurry initially, then clearing like a picture coming into focus. She is aware of wetness and coldness on the right side of her face and realises she is slumped on the floor. Her left arm is stretched upwards. Hurting. She turns her head to see that her left wrist is in a set of handcuffs, linked to a ring on the wall. It's a few feet up the wall and the metal of the cuff is cutting into her wrist. She shuffles her position backwards to ease the stretch of her arm so that the metal feels a little less tight.

'Oh dear God. Are you OK, Ruby?' Her mother has moved her own position along the pipe she's chained to and stretches out her hand. But she can't quite reach her.

'I don't understand. What the hell is going on here?' Ruby can't believe this. A dream surely. A nightmare. She closes her eyes and pinches her leg with her free hand. But no. Nothing changes. She opens her eyes to feel her face, which is wet with blood. Next she gently touches the back of her head, which is terribly sore. But the wound is smaller than she feared.

'She hit you with a piece of wood,' Clara says. 'She hit me too.'

'Natalie hit us?'

Ruby turns her head to take in Natalie coming back down the steps.

'Ah good. You're back with us.' Natalie seats herself on the third step from the bottom, eyebrows raised. Smug expression.

'Why are you calling her Natalie?' Ruby's mother asks.

'She works with me in the hotel in Scotland. She's been visiting her mother in London. At least that's what she said.'

At this, Natalie bites into her bottom lip and then laughs. 'Isn't this the best fun, guys?'

'We don't know who she really is,' her mother cuts in quickly. 'She uses different identities. God knows why. I shared a room with her in a hotel in Paris. As a favour, more fool me. She called herself Jade that time. And she tricked Clara into working for some cult called StarBonders. Called herself Phoebe for that.'

'But *why?* And why StarBonders?' Ruby turns to stare at their tormentor directly. 'Who the hell are you really and what's this about?' She can't take it in. Natalie seemed so genuine. She actually worked at the hotel. Did real shifts. Why would she go to all that trouble? Involving her whole family. It is beyond madness.

'Money,' Clara says. 'It's all about money.' A pause. 'And playing games. She's sick in the head. Enjoys playing people.'

CHAPTER 71

NOW

LAURA

I glance between us, and what feels most surreal are the odds. Three against one and yet *we* are the ones trapped. And afraid.

How did we let this happen?

I look at the woman sitting on the steps. Jade or Phoebe or Natalie. What the hell does it matter? She's not right in the head; Clara is correct about that. But she's also spot on that the motive here is money. Our tormentor is greedy so I have to find a way to use that. To get my daughters *out.*

'OK. So this is what's going to happen. I can pay you. I can transfer money – £25,000 immediately – but if you want more I need the girls to get a password from the house. To access my online savings.'

'You really think I'm going to fall for that?' Our captor has this awful sing-song tone, as if this is all some hilarious game.

I turn my head to take in Ruby, worrying about her wound. It seems to have stopped bleeding, which is good. But she fell, and Jade, or whoever she is, dragged her very roughly across the cement floor. She could have a concussion. And dirt in that wound. I need to get both her and Clara out of this.

'I'm serious. How much do you want? Because the only way you are getting anything is if you release my daughters.'

'So they can try to attack me? And go to the police?'

'They won't do that.'

There is a long pause.

'Just transfer the money on your phone,' she says finally. 'Six figures. As much as you have.'

'I can't transfer more than twenty-five thousand pounds in a single transaction by phone. So is that OK?' I know she won't like that. Not enough money.

'No. That's not enough.' She's looking right at me, eyes steely. Cold. Both my girls are silent. Good. I need them to follow my lead on this.

'How much do you want?' I stare, unblinking.

'What's the maximum you can raise today?'

'Two hundred thousand, but only if someone gets that password.'

'You're lying. You must know the password—'

'I don't. I seriously don't. My savings are in a separate online account with a different provider. For safety and for the interest. I just leave the money there to grow. I only check the figures once a year for my tax return so I don't need to know the password. It's in a file at home.'

'For any burglar to find. I don't believe you.' She has cocked her head again.

'OK. So it's twenty-five thousand maximum. That's all I can do on my banking app.'

'I told you that isn't enough. I want a quarter of a million. You must be good for that.'

'If we get access to the savings account, I can request that. They'll send a verification code and ask extra security questions but we can manage that. But you need to let my daughters go back to the house. The password is in a fake file marked *Pet insurance*.' I turn to Ruby. 'You get the file and password. You log into the savings website. And you can transfer the money to any account. They will send a security code to my phone for approval. That's all.'

'What about limits?' Jade or whoever looks sceptical. 'Aren't there limits on your saving transfers as well? How long will this all take?'

I can't tell her the truth. That it will take twenty-four hours minimum for a big transfer to land. And with the weekend coming, it could be *days*.

'It can take a few hours. Ruby can handle it at the house. But she will need her phone back. To liaise with us for verification codes and to update once it's sorted.'

Our captor now looks uncertain, narrowing her eyes. I wonder if she is swallowing my bluff.

She takes the knife from her pocket again and opens the blade, then she moves across to hold the knife to my throat this time. I tilt my head back but not quite far enough. The blade just pierces the skin and I can feel first the pain and then drops of blood dripping on my neck.

Clara starts screaming. 'Stop it. *Stop it!*'

Jade or whoever she is moves the knife so that it is no longer piercing the skin.

'OK. Just Ruby goes. Clara stays here.'

'No,' I say. She presses the knife closer but I am determined. 'Both of them go or you get nothing. You can cut my throat. I really don't care.'

There is a long and terrible pause. I am terrified she will use the knife properly and dig deeper into the skin, but I know that I must not blink first. She will get no money without me.

'OK,' she says finally. 'I mean it when I say that I have a contact in the force. If I let them get the password, transfer the money and then message us, I will know if they ring the police.' She is looking at me as she says this. Then she turns her gaze to the girls.

'Do you both understand me? You do exactly as I say. I will give you two hours tops to get all this done. And if you get silly, you will never see your mother again. Understood?'

I feel a sweep of relief. I'm surprised she is going for this, but she's greedy, just as I hoped. Once she realises the money won't transfer as quickly as I said, she is going to be furious. And even more dangerous. I suddenly realise in this moment what this means.

I find that I worry most of all how painful it will be, so I push that thought away and fight as hard as I can to keep my face calm. And not to look at Clara or Ruby. 'OK. Your choice now. You let my daughters go, and you get a quarter of a million pounds to go abroad or whatever it is you have planned.' I try to forget the pain of the cut to my neck and what lies ahead for me. I turn my head to stare right at her. This cruel and so very twisted young woman.

'You hurt either one of them or you refuse to let them go, you get *nothing*.'

CHAPTER 72

NOW

THE POLICE

Amelie waits until Dan, the sergeant, heads out to the corridor to update the DI. She remains by Joe Harry's bedside as he frowns deeply, working through the messages to his phone since he's been in the coma.

'Anything else showing up that could be important?' She tries to keep her tone friendly as he focuses on the phone. He still looks so unwell. Weak. Worried.

'I don't know.'

Still Mr Harry keeps swiping from page to page, occasionally clicking through to an apparent email or message. Then he puts his phone up to his ear.

'Clara. It's Dad. I need to speak to you, please. Phone me soon as you get this.'

He hangs up and repeats the sequence to his elder daughter, Ruby. Then his wife. Finally he puts the phone down on the sheet in front of him.

Amelie still has her notebook ready, pen poised. 'You really don't know where they are? Your wife and daughters?' Amelie feels a sweep of unease. Joe seems credible. And the daughters seem genuinely close to him – Ruby travelling all the way from Scotland immediately. So why aren't they here?

'No. I don't know where they are. I know they've been interviewed about a crime. The nurses told me that, and I know there is no way they would be involved in anything bad. They just wouldn't. I swear. I know them.'

'Sometimes we think we know people and the truth can be—'

'I tell you, I know my family. They are not without faults. Who isn't? But they are all good people. I don't understand what's going on. But I do feel very worried.'

'What do you mean?'

'Someone caused my accident deliberately. That's frightening enough. But I know that one of my family would be here, if they could. This doesn't make sense to me. No word from my wife or Clara since I came round. And the way Ruby just took off.'

'What exactly do you mean – *took off?*'

CHAPTER 73

NOW

Laura

It is chilling. A shock. Just her and me now.

The girls didn't want to leave me. They were both crying but I told them it was the only way to save me. *No police. Don't ring anyone at all. Do you hear me? Just transfer the money and then text my phone when it's done.*

The truth is I just wanted them away from her. Away from here. Because I know now how this is going to end. It's so obvious this is about me. And there's no way she is going to let me live. Why would she?

It was so hard to lie to the girls. *I will be OK. You need to go.*

Broke me to watch them climb those stairs. Weak, and each with wounds. To say goodbye to them in my head but not out loud.

'So. Just you and me. Like in Paris,' she says.

Again, she's sitting on the third step. 'I thought they might at least try to attack me before they left,' she adds with that tilt of the head that is both familiar now and incredibly chilling. Weirdly childlike. 'But nothing.' She sounds disappointed. 'No fight in them, your daughters.'

I don't rise to the bait. She had the knife back at my throat so of course they didn't try anything. Still they wouldn't leave me. And then she took a plastic bag from her pocket and said the terrible, awful thing.

She told us that she was the one who killed Scott in the hotel in Truro. Put a bag over his head and suffocated him. And that she would do exactly the same to me if they phoned the police. Because her contact in the force would tell her. Both girls broke down at that and promised to do exactly what she said. *No police. We promise. We promise.*

I close my eyes and think of what a complete fool I've been. That it must have been her all along. All of the darkness. She must have taken my phone from under the pillow in Paris. Accessed details somehow. Did she watch over my shoulder for my pin?

And the dry-cleaning stunt, just to wind me up. She must have copied my keys. Let herself into the house.

'But why the pendants?' I ask, opening my eyes and thinking aloud, realising that even as I work some of it out, there are other things I still don't understand.

She laughs. 'I kinda hoped it would stir the pot. Spook you and spook Clara too. I liked the idea of you discussing them together. The pendants. You in the dark about Clara working for me.' She pauses. 'So *did* you discuss them? Bet it caused a row.'

I don't answer, furious that she's right. I shut my eyes again, trying not to think of the argument with Joe before his accident. Longing to shut out her voice. I try to think of something else. To take my mind back in time. Happier times. I try to picture a photograph, framed in the dining room. The girls when they were little, playing in the garden. The memory of summers when I would set up a hose pipe on the slide outside. The girls laughing . . .

288

'You do know that both your daughters run you down something awful behind your back,' she adds suddenly, pulling me back into the room. This terrible room. 'Oh my goodness . . . the *moaning about you.* To Natalie. And to Phoebe.' She uses her fingers to put air quotes around her fake names.

Again, I try not to let it show on my face what I'm thinking. The hurt. The fear. The anger at her cruelty.

It's so awful to imagine it. Her posing as Natalie in Scotland and building a fake friendship with Ruby. Posing as some guru to suck Clara into the StarBonders universe.

'Why all the theatricals?' I ask, tired of this. Resigned now to what is coming and exhausted by the drama. And the knot of fear in my stomach. 'Why not come straight for my money after Paris? Why all this nonsense?'

Again she starts to laugh. That awful, throaty and mocking laugh she has. 'You really think that's where this started? *Paris.*'

This throws me. Of course Paris must be where this started. Our chance meeting.

Where else?

I assume she looked me up after Paris, worked out I was worth a few quid and decided to go big with her scheming.

I feel my heart rate increasing and take a few breaths to try to quieten it.

I don't want her to see how confused I now feel. What does she mean?

'I was in prison once,' she says suddenly. 'That's where this started.' She checks her watch and lets out a long breath. 'They've been gone fifteen minutes. I'll give them another hour tops. Clock ticking.'

'You said two hours all up. There could be traffic—'

'Spoiler alert, momma bear. Sometimes I don't tell the truth.'

289

'Spoiler alert. An hour and a half is too tight,' I say. Angry and defiant now. 'They need to get to the house. To log in on my laptop. Sort the transfer. The savings provider will send a code to my phone. You'll need to look out for that and message Ruby so she can get through the security. It will all take time.'

She takes my phone from her pocket and moves across the basement to hold it in front of my face to open it. I watch it light up. Next she scrolls through a couple of pages.

'Let's just transfer the money your banking app allows. The first twenty-five thousand. To get things going. I take it banking is on face recognition?'

'Yes.'

She holds the phone to my face again and I see the banking app load. She sits back on one of the steps and begins typing. I imagine she is setting up a transfer to her own account. I realise it will need Face ID again to confirm the transaction, and sure enough, she moves to hold the phone in front of me.

Finally, she sits back down. 'Well, that's a start. But it's not enough. So let's hope your girlies don't get silly out there.'

I close my eyes, remembering again how afraid they were as they left. Her telling us so coldly how she'd killed Scott. I don't think they will go to the police. Ruby would never do that. Not after Ned. So this is done. Decided.

I try not to think of how angry my tormentor is going to be. When the big money doesn't come through . . .

'Prison, you said. What was that for?' I try to keep myself steady. She seems to enjoy fear. And so I push away the thoughts of that poor man. His awful death. The picture the police showed me when they interviewed me. Found my DNA at the scene.

Something starts whirring in my brain. My DNA. I think of my hairbrush going missing in Paris. Did she take it? Plant my hair at the murder scene?

'*Damn the Scam*,' she says, grinning. 'Remember that?'

I go cold. Haven't heard that catchphrase in a long time. It was a project I worked on for a charity, helping pensioners avoid cons. In the days when I did a lot of charity work. Before my business took off.

'Oh, so you do remember it?' She's watching my face. 'You and your clever little catchphrases all over socials. You and your charity on your pathetic soapbox.'

I don't reply. There's a sinking feeling inside as I try to turn everything over in my brain. Trying to put together this awful puzzle. What does it all mean? My Damn the Scam campaign was quite a while back.

'Of course, prison has some advantages,' she says letting out a long, slow breath. 'You make good contacts, for instance. But it's not a nice place, as you might imagine. It gave me a lot of thinking time. And planning time.'

'So all this is because—'

'Oh goodness me, no. It's not *all* because of Damn the bloody Scam. That was just salt on an open wound. An extra thing to wind me up, so to speak. I didn't even realise it was you for a long time.'

I frown, still not understanding. So she was jailed for some scam that my campaign helped to expose? But how does that fit with all of this? It makes no sense to me.

'You still haven't figured it out, have you?' she says. 'Do you really not see the similarity?' She turns her head to the side. 'A lot of people say we have the same profile.' A pause. 'I was surprised Ruby didn't clock it. Do you really not see it either, Laura?'

CHAPTER 74

NOW

RUBY

Ruby's head is aching inside and out as she indicates to overtake the white car in front.

'You need to slow down!' Clara alongside her is still crying uncontrollably as she speaks, clutching on to the plastic of the dashboard. 'You're frightening me. You're driving too fast.'

'No choice. We have to get home as fast as we can. You heard her. Natalie or Phoebe or whoever she is. She's not giving us long enough.' Ruby feels her heartbeat racing to match her acceleration. She puts her left hand up to her sore head, wondering if the pounding inside is from the wound. Or the stress.

'I mean it. This is too fast,' Clara repeats. 'I'm not even sure you should be driving. What if you have a concussion—?'

'Well, you can't drive. You keep failing your bloody test.' Ruby spits her reply. Angry. Overwhelmed. Clara's sobbing crescendos and Ruby feels momentary guilt mingled within the maelstrom of emotions. Frustration. Fear. *Mostly fear*. 'Sorry. Sorry. I shouldn't have said that, Clara.' She changes down a gear to take a corner and checks the speedometer, realising that she is indeed pushing their luck. She presses the brake but only very gently.

She wishes in this moment that Clara were stronger. That this was not all on her shoulders. She checks her watch. *Not enough time.*

All the while she is thinking of their mother back in that disgusting basement. She is thinking of the terrible picture she was shown in the police station of Scott's body when she was being interviewed. When they were treating her as a suspect. And then she is thinking of the plastic bag that Natalie took out of her pocket to threaten them – the warning that she would do the same to their mother.

Ruby finds that she is crying too now. Completely overwhelmed. Still, she is doing the maths. Working out how long to get home and get on the computer. How long to get the password to transfer the money.

And then there is this sudden explosion in her brain. Like a firework. Like that flash when you suddenly remember the answer in a quiz. *Oh no.* She frowns. Horrified. *Oh dear God, no.*

Ruby narrows her eyes, trying to understand exactly what this means. She is remembering that once, when her mother was sorting funding for her university rent, she told her that the money in the savings account took twenty-four hours minimum to transfer to the bank. Sometimes longer. She frowns more deeply, travelling back in time to picture them chatting in the kitchen. Yes. She was sure her mother said it was one day minimum. And working days only. It is now nearly the weekend. Which means . . .

'What are you doing? Why are you pulling in?' Clara's tone is incredulous.

Ruby finishes the manoeuvre into the lay-by and brakes so sharply that they are both thrown forward.

'We have to phone the police,' she says, shocked to hear the words leave her own mouth.

'What do you mean? What are you talking about? Phoebe said she has a contact inside the police. She'll know. She'll hurt Mum.' A pause. 'It will be horrible. And it will be *our fault*.'

Ruby turns her head to face her sister, tears now dripping down her own cheeks as she takes her mobile from her right pocket.

'Clara. I think she's going to hurt Mum whatever we do. We can't get the money transferred in time.'

'Don't say that. You mustn't say that.'

'I'm sorry. But I remember Mum telling me once that the savings account takes a day or two to clear. More at weekends. So it's not possible to do this transfer quickly enough. Natalie will get really mad.'

'So why did Mum say that we should do this—?'

'Don't you see?' Ruby is sobbing now. 'Mum was just trying to *save us*. To trick Natalie, or Phoebe or whoever she is. To get us out.'

Clara gasps. And then they are still for a moment, the enormity of the realisation sinking in.

'How about we just tell Phoebe it will take longer?' Clara's eyes widen as she clutches at the straw.

'She won't believe us. She'll know it's a trick.'

'But we can't phone the police, Ruby. What if she really does have a contact on the force—?'

'Clara. I'm sorry. But I don't think it will make any difference. It could well be bullshit about the police contact. What if getting police help is Mum's only chance?'

Ruby feels inside the pocket of her bulging phone case for the card she was given at the hospital. She looks at the name.

Special Constable Amelie Hill

'No, no. I don't like this.' Clara is sobbing again, her words barely intelligible. 'What if this is the wrong thing? What if it's our fault now – what happens to Mum?'

Ruby opens her phone, her hand shaking and her head still pounding. *What to do? What to do?* She is still thinking of her rage when she found out that her mother had phoned the police over Ned.

Technically, Ruby hates the police. Technically, Ruby does not trust the police.

But looking at the card still, she is frowning and thinking of Amelie at the hospital. Similar age. The shock that someone her age, someone so clearly bright and with a million options in life, would choose to join the force. She'd asked Amelie outright. *Why the police?* There was this story about being saved as a child by the police. Few details, but this extraordinary look in the young woman's eyes. Serious and grateful and determined all at once. *I need to put something back. I wouldn't even be here were it not for Melanie Sanders.*

Other pictures are also tumbling through Ruby's brain. Her mother in the kitchen, begging for a reconciliation before she left for Scotland. Her mother in the audience of a school play a million years before. Her face beaming with pride. Her mother in that basement now, making up some story about a big money transfer to save them.

Sacrificing herself . . . *to save them.*

Ruby dials.

It rings three times.

'Special Constable Amelie Hill.'

'This is Ruby Harry. My mother has been kidnapped. We were taken too – me and Clara – but we've been released. The kidnapper says she has a contact on your team. I'm scared to talk to you – she says she'll kill Mum – but I don't know what else to do—!'

'OK, OK. Take a breath. Slow down. You've done the right thing and we're going to help you. First. Are you safe? You and your sister?'

'Yes. We're both hurt but we're safe. In the car, heading home. I've pulled into a lay-by.'

'Right. You stay put. I'm going to send an ambulance straight to you and a police team. But you need to give me the address where your mother is being held. Do you have that? Do you have a postcode you can send me?'

CHAPTER 75

NOW

LAURA

Another half an hour at least has passed and we are sitting in silence. Me crippled with fear. That bag in her pocket . . .

I used to worry about dying young and leaving the girls, and now I realise what a waste of time that was. Futile catastrophising when I should have just been living for the day.

I look at her. There is a rustling and now the plastic bag is back in her hand and I realise that I am a coward; that I am terribly afraid now, not of death per se but knowing precisely how I am going to die. And how much it is going to hurt.

I keep thinking of that police photo. The twisted face of the man she killed. How much he must have suffered. And I am afraid of the same suffering. The straining for breath.

I simply cannot believe that someone so young and capable of seeming so ordinary could be so cruel. And filled with such utter darkness.

I feel a whimper of fear rising in my throat and don't want to let it out. Clear my throat to try to shut it down. I don't want her to know how afraid I am. She enjoys fear. All these horrible games. And I don't want to beg.

I close my eyes and think of my girls. *They are safe.* They have the best father in the world. And *they are safe.*

It is the only thing I have left to hang on to. That I got them out . . .

'So, have you figured it all out yet?' she asks.

I don't answer. I'm guessing around an hour in total has passed with no word yet from the girls. Whatever happens, she is going to be livid when she realises she's not going to get the money quickly. She has two phones on the step beside her. Mine and another basic model. Some kind of burner phone, I assume.

'You tried to frame me. Scott's death,' I say, thinking of the police again. *How do you explain it, Mrs Harry? Your DNA at the scene of the murder?*

She starts a slow clap.

'Yes. It didn't go quite as I planned, sadly. I thought they'd charge you straight away. Put you up before the magistrates. I've had to pivot. Plan A was you in jail, awaiting trial. And I would then blackmail your girls somehow.'

'But why?' I blurt.

Why all this trouble? Was it really to pay me back for Damn the Scam? Surely not?

She glances at the phones again and then takes something from her other pocket. She looks at me intently with that awful, smug smile and moves across the room to place a photograph on the floor in front of me.

Two children. A boy and a girl. The boy has his arms around the girl.

I frown. They're young. Friends or brother and sister, I can't tell. But the boy has these saucer brown eyes and he looks strangely familiar. I keep staring at the photograph, trying to figure this out.

'You still don't see it?' she asks. 'The resemblance.'

I keep staring at the boy. Those eyes. And suddenly a new thought lands. I picture those eyes in an older face, their pupils dilated . . .

'Ah. The penny finally drops,' she says, watching my expression closely. 'Ned was my brother.'

A huff of breath leaves my body. Utter shock. So she is Isabella? The *sister*. Ned's sister.

'But Ruby said you lived in Canada.'

Again she laughs, then shakes her head as if exasperated. 'That was a little cover story my pathetic mother came up with through shame. When they sent me to prison.' She stares right at me. 'She couldn't bear it. Her precious boy a drug addict and me the black sheep. In prison. She cut me off after the pensioner scam stuff. The trial and the prison sentence. And she told everyone I went to Canada. Lovely mother, eh? Loyal to the last.'

I am frowning again, struggling to take all this in. So Damn the Scam was just a part of it. An extra grudge. This is all really because of Ned.

'I am very sorry that Ned died—'

'Oh, don't misunderstand,' she cuts in. 'Don't get all sentimental on me, like my bloody mother. People live and people die. Ned was an addict and a fool. He was always going to end up in the same place. But your interference – you going to the police – hurried things up. Blew it all for me before I had everything in place. I thought I had more time.'

'What do you mean?'

Her expression is distant suddenly. 'My mother, who you probably know is loaded, took me out of the will – the bitch. After prison. Left everything to Ned, on the condition he got clean. He felt bad about that and he was very easy to, how shall we say, *influence*. He agreed it wasn't fair. So I got him to promise to split the inheritance with me, regardless of the will. Even got a legal agreement drawn up.

'Strictly between you and me, I didn't plan to wait until the old girl kicked the bucket naturally. She has good genes. Could motor on for years. So I planned to speed things up.' She sniffs and glances at the two phones again. 'Felt my mother was the kind of woman who might have a road accident. Blinded while driving or something like that.' She pauses, staring right into my face. 'A light shone into the windscreen. Yes. Something like that.'

Cold shoots through me. *Joe.* I think of the beam of light in the garden. His sudden accident. So Joe's crash was her too?

'So was that you at the house? The night before Joe was hurt?' I think again of the beam of light in the garden. Why would she do that? Risk that?

'Yes. That was me. I rather hoped Joe would come outside and investigate. He was being very uncooperative.' She sniffs. 'My funds were running low and I asked him to help me out financially. Perfectly reasonable. I needed a little fund boost to keep all these plans on track. Except he wasn't reasonable.' She pauses. 'You can blind someone with a laser if you fire it right into their eyes. So I hear.' Another pause. 'Only he didn't come outside. So I had to improvise the next day. I think I did rather well.'

I close my eyes, thinking of Joe in the hospital. For the first time I feel true relief that he is there. Away from this apology for a human being. That he will *survive* her.

'My . . . whole . . . family?' I whisper in disbelief, my brain and my insides twisted with rage.

'Only fair for you to suffer. Like I have suffered. When you reported Ned to the police and the silly boy went to that squat, I lost my inheritance. Or rather the new route I'd worked out to bypass my mother cutting me off. You *made me lose everything.*'

I look at her face. Cold. Angry. So she didn't even care about Ned. Her own brother. This isn't about loss. Or grief. This isn't about sadness at losing her brother. This is about losing *money*.

All this twisted young woman cares about is herself. And money.

I close my eyes, wanting all this to be over. I don't care how much it hurts. The girls are safe, which is the only thing that matters. I just want this done now.

CHAPTER 76

NOW

THE POLICE

Amelie watches the cottage alongside Melanie Sanders.

Their control position is set back behind an outbuilding at the rear of the property. Everything is in place. The firearms team are spread out, front and back. All hidden.

But it's not looking good. There's no line of sight. No view into the basement. Just a narrow, frosted window with some kind of makeshift covering. The daughters – Clara and Ruby – are being kept informed but are now in hospital. Traumatised and being treated for their injuries.

Amelie thinks of how awful it must be for them. Waiting. And how dreadful it must have been for her own parents. Waiting. When *she* was taken . . . all those years ago. Just eight years old . . .

'If you get a shot, you *take* the shot,' Mel says into her radio.

'Roger that. But no direct line of sight. No sign of target.'

They're waiting for the negotiator but Melanie is not hopeful.

'You really don't think negotiating will work?' Amelie repeats.

'The kidnapper knows she's going down for Scott Crawford's murder. You heard the daughters. She's ruthless. Once this kidnapper knows we're here, I'm *very* worried for Laura Harry.'

'So what do we do?' Amelie feels desperate. Helpless.

'Our only real hope is that she moves upstairs. Or visits her car for some reason,' Mel says.

And then suddenly Amelie has an idea. She frowns. When she recognised the photograph on Joe's phone, she couldn't quite place who it was. The blackmailer from the nightclub. Or how it might help. Facial matching had not yet found anything on the general police files. But Amelie pushed for a double-check across the case file and the team had just this morning found an inexplicable match to a photograph on Ruby's phone. Her screensaver when they interviewed her as a suspect. They'd taken a copy. It was of Ruby and a friend by a beautiful loch near their hotel in Scotland. Which was now confusing, because it meant Ruby had somehow spent time with the blackmailer. So was that under a different identity?

Amelie takes out her phone. 'I need to make a call,' she whispers and then retreats from the position alongside Mel.

Ruby picks up straight away.

'Are you OK? You and Clara?'

'Yes, yes. We're fine. But what about Mum? You *have to save her*. You have to. I should never have been so stubborn with her.' Ruby is distraught. Crying as she speaks.

'I'm sorry. No news yet, but we have a great team. We're doing everything we can. Listen. Something just came up when we cross-matched photographs. Has the kidnapper been using different identities? Have you met her before?'

'Yes. Yes. There wasn't time to explain to you earlier. She's completely *nuts*. She posed as a friend to me in Scotland. Natalie, she called herself. And she runs StarBonders, pretending to be someone called Phoebe. She's insane. She sucked Clara into that. It's all so complicated. And I still can't quite believe it. I've been telling it all to the policeman here. He's going to call you any moment—'

'OK, good. That extra detail will all come through to us. So when you were together in Scotland. When she was pretending to be Natalie. What was she like?'

'What do you mean?'

'I don't know. I'm just wondering if there's anything, any small detail that might help us.'

'I don't know. I mean, she was being fake. It was all a lie.'

Amelie frowns. *Thinking. Thinking.*

'Yeah. I get that. But was there anything odd ever? Like – a weird habit. Or was she afraid of anything for instance? A phobia or, I don't know, a weakness. Something she couldn't cover up.' Amelie looks around her, taking in the firearms team, all hiding in different positions.

With no line of sight to the basement, the situation feels so hopeless. Mel's right. It's unlikely this kidnapper will give herself up.

'I don't know. I can't think.' Ruby pauses. 'She was afraid of the dark, I remember that.'

Amelie sighs. It won't be dark for hours. And that could go against them. She could become even more volatile.

'Oh, and birds,' Ruby says suddenly.

Amelie presses the phone tighter to her ear and turns. Earlier there were pigeons on the grass outside the back of the cottage. Yes. They're still there.

'What about birds?' she whispers, edging back towards Mel's position.

'She's frightened of birds. Like *really* scared. One got into her house share once. Into the conservatory. She went completely nuts. She couldn't have faked that. I had to chase it out for her. She was terrified.'

'OK, thanks. That's really helpful. Try to stay strong. I've got to go now. We'll call as soon as there's news.'

Amelie ends the call and marches back to stand alongside Mel. Five pigeons still in position near the kitchen. Two thin. Three fat.

It's a long shot. Will probably get her into big trouble. But what is there to lose?

'Tell them not to shoot me,' she says to Mel, moving forward slowly while taking off her jacket.

'What the hell? Get *back here*, Amelie!'

Mel spit-whispers her warning, but Amelie is not listening. She is thinking of her time living in France. The farmer next door. His beautiful *pigeonnier*. He kept the birds as pets. Not for food. And she loved to help him with them. Learned to catch them with a blanket when they needed treatment from the vet.

'Special Constable Amelie Hill approaching the building. Hold fire.' Melanie sounds furious as she speaks into her radio.

Amelie eyes the broken windows of the rear kitchen to the cottage, her mind in overdrive. She glances from pigeon to pigeon. The thin ones will be too fast. She approaches, and sure enough they fly off. But the three fatter birds continue to waddle. Pecking greedily at the ground, seemingly oblivious.

Amelie keeps to the right side of the cottage so her shadow won't be seen in the basement. She moves quickly now, throwing her jacket around the fattest pigeon. *Got you.*

The remaining birds fly off as she runs across the grass with the captured pigeon to the back of the kitchen and gently pushes its body through one of the broken windows. She is careful not to hurt it and retreats quickly, running back to rejoin Mel, turning to note that, just as she hoped, the bird is already causing a rumpus inside. Flying and flapping from counter to table and up to the light fitting.

'What the *hell* are you playing at? Have you completely lost your mind?' Mel's tone is every bit as incredulous as it is angry.

CHAPTER 77

NOW

LAURA

Suddenly there is a commotion from upstairs. Crashing sounds.

'What the hell is that?' Isabella, for the first time, sounds genuinely panicked. I'm shocked too. Is it help? Is it a neighbour?

I consider calling out, but she draws her knife again and stands, pointing the weapon at me, her right forefinger to her lips to command silence.

The door to the landing is open. We both listen. More crashing. And then a sort of flapping sound. A pause. And then cooing, followed by yet more crashing.

'Oh Christ, it's a bird upstairs. A *bloody bird*.' Her left hand is still holding the knife, her right arm now stretched out straight by her side, the hand clenched into a tight fist. Knuckles white.

I feel this sinking inside. So it's not help. Not a person at all. *Just a bird*. But the change in my tormentor escalates. Her eyes wild with alarm. It's the first time I've seen her stressed and my heart is racing, worried what this new volatility will mean for me.

'It's fine,' I try. 'It's just a bird.'

'It's *not* fine. We need to get it out. *You're* going to need to get it out.' She's speaking very quickly, her tone high-pitched. I watch her eyes widen further, her head darting from left to right, and I realise that she is genuinely afraid.

I have no idea what to do. I watch and I wait as the crashing sounds continue upstairs and then slowly it dawns that this could be good for me, rather than bad. Yes. I can *use* this.

'It's OK. I can get it out. I've done it before,' I say. 'You're right. It must be in the kitchen.'

My mind's now whirring. She will need to release me from the pipe.

She stares at me and then at the stairs. There is yet more crashing from upstairs which seems to make up her mind.

'Right. You get it out, but no silliness.' Still she is pointing the knife at me as a warning.

She darts across the basement and takes a key from her pocket with her free hand. I consider trying to floor her immediately but she's too fast, clipping the cuffs back around my spare wrist so that I'm free of the pipe but unable to move properly.

'I can't get the bird with my hands cuffed.'

'You'll have to think of something. Now get up!'

I stand and she backs away, knife in her hand. 'You go first. Up the stairs. You keep ahead of me.'

She hangs back and I realise it's fear. Which I need to use. *Think, Laura. Think.*

At the top of the stairs, I can see into the kitchen. It's a pigeon, up on the light fitting. Obviously in a panic itself.

I move gently forward. The bird starts flying around the room. But it's a plump pigeon and it can't fly very well in the restricted space. Keeps landing and crashing into things.

'You need to *get it out!*' she screams from behind me.

'I need something to shoo it to the window,' I say, my gaze darting around the room. 'I can't do it cuffed like this.'

'Well I'm not releasing you. I'm not stupid.'

My gaze settles on an old broom in the corner, covered in cobwebs.

'I could use that. I could shoo it out with that. Is it OK if I use the broom?'

'Whatever. But do it quickly.' Her face is highly coloured. Eyes still wide with alarm, knife pointing at me. 'We need to get back downstairs. You need to do it quickly.'

I move forward with my cuffed hands and get hold of the broom as she stands in the doorway behind me. I make a few gestures towards the bird to pretend that I'm serious, trying to shoo it towards the broken window, and then I pause. I can't quite see where she is behind me, so I have to take a guess, swinging the broom around as hard as I possibly can to *smash* it into her.

She screams. Is on the floor.

I smash the broom into her a second time and then hurl it to the side and run past her through the hall. The front door is difficult to open with my cuffed hands but at last I am through it, running and running.

'You absolute bitch!' she screams from behind me.

Terror courses through me as I run. I'm so shocked that she's able to shout. I should have hit her *harder*. Next, and far worse, I hear her footsteps on the gravel as she runs after me.

And then I trip, my right knee and palms on fire as they slap on to the gravel. I try to get up, but can't, and so bow my head, terrified that any second there will be a knife in my back.

I brace for the pain. But instead there is this sudden crack of thunder.

I don't understand. I cower, eyes closed, still waiting for the knife.

And the rain from the thunder.

But the rain doesn't come.

CHAPTER 78

NOW

THE POLICE

Amelie cannot quite believe it as it all unfolds. Like a film. Somehow too fast and yet also too slow . . .

The figure emerging into the kitchen. The bird in panic, flapping from counter to table to light fitting.

'What the hell! Do we have the target in sight?' Mel barking into her radio. 'Is that our target?'

'No clear shot.'

'What the *hell* did you think you were doing, Amelie?'

'Sorry. But she's afraid of birds. I just thought it might. I don't know. Draw her out . . .'

A pause. Amelie holding her breath. And then the figure in the kitchen, swinging something in the air. More flapping and the bird at last finding the window. Fluttering out and making it to a nearby tree.

'Still no clean shot.' A male voice on the radio. One of the armed team.

They wait. The figure from the kitchen disappears. Amelie and Melanie turn to each other. No idea what is happening. Was it the kidnapper or Laura Harry?

There is the sound of a door banging against a wall. Distant crunching against gravel. Someone running? Another pause and then the sound of a single shot.

'Target down.' A young male voice over the radio. It must be from the front of the house. 'ID confirmed. Kidnapper down.'

'Status of the hostage?' Mel is speaking into her radio. 'Update please.'

'Injured but safe. Laura Harry confirmed safe.'

'Oh, thank God.' Mel lets out a long breath. 'Good work.' And then she turns suddenly to Amelie.

'I don't know what to say to you. That was completely insane, Amelie. Do you know how insane that was—?'

'Sorry.'

'You frightened the *life* out of me.' Mel's voice is cracking and then she surprises Amelie by pulling her into a tight hug. The first time she has ever shown her affection in front of the team. 'That was bonkers. Utterly *bonker*s.' A pause. 'And also just a little bit genius, by the way.' She hugs her even tighter and then pulls back to stare right into her face. 'I had no idea you could be this infuriating.' Another pause. A cough to clear her throat. 'And so *ridiculously* like your father.'

Amelie cannot answer. She feels almost faint with the relief cascading through her. She closes her eyes tightly and for a moment she is right back there.

Eight years old. In the wood where she was held. Gagged in the boot of the car with everyone calling out for her. The day Melanie Sanders saved her life.

Male voices shouting her name. Melanie Sanders calling her name. And cutting through the chaos, her father's voice too.

Amelie! Where are you Amelie?

EPILOGUE

EIGHTEEN MONTHS LATER

I stare out of the kitchen window and I see them.

They have their pink tent set up on the lawn and Ruby has gathered sticks for a pretend campfire. Clara has a bright red toy kettle which she stands on the pile of dry wood.

They wait ever so patiently, and then Ruby pours imaginary coffee into their picnic cups and they sip, mimicking the way I drink, blowing first on the hot liquid. Then sipping. Wincing at the heat but trying again too soon. Impatient. *Sip. Blow. Sip. Blow.* They meet each other's gaze and laugh at their 'in' joke, teasing their mother, and then turn to the kitchen window to catch my eye, raising their cups in a toast to me. They wave. They smile . . .

The image so strong that I am smiling too and move my hand as if to wave back.

I know that it's a memory. Not real. But in this moment, in this daydream, it *feels* real. And I cherish the sliding doors. This trick of the light or the brain or both that lets me travel back to their childhood when my only worries were cut knees and tantrums. And *do they have enough friends? Are they happy in school?*

I feel my wave dissolve, my hand awkward. My fingers fold back in. I let my hand fall to my side. I check my watch, and when I look back up, they are gone. The lawn stretching green and lush and empty, the grass shimmering with autumn dew. No tent. No footprints. No little girls playing make-believe.

The doorbell rings. A rush of nerves. All morning I have worried she would not come. And now I worry that she has. *What to say?*

I want to shout up the stairs – *I'll get it* – but there's no one to hear. And I feel the ache of my empty house.

I open the door slowly, my stomach twisted with nerves. My head spinning with pictures I don't want to revisit. *Is this a mistake?*

It's a shock to see her. This new and diminished version of her. She's lost even more weight since the trial.

I think of her in the coffee shop all that time ago when we bumped into each other. Sad then too, but somehow stronger-looking. Me the diminished one. Misplaced guilt transferred now like a backpack filled with boulders.

'Barbara. Is it OK to call you Barbara?' My voice sounds as nervous as I feel. 'I'm so glad you came. Come in. Come in.'

She doesn't say anything, just walks past me as I shut the door and then we hover in the hall. Awkward. She fidgets with the strap of her handbag, which falls from her tiny shoulders. Skin and bones.

'Let's go into the kitchen, shall we? Would you like a drink? Coffee? Tea?' I am talking too quickly. 'Shall I take your coat?'

She frowns. Is not wearing a coat.

'Sorry. Sorry. I'm a bit all over the place. Come through.'

I think again of my girls in the garden. My daydream. My empty nest.

Her nest empty forever.

'Just a glass of water,' she says, sitting on one of the breakfast stools. Still awkward. 'I nearly didn't come. I was very surprised to hear from you.'

She watches me as I open a cupboard for a glass and fill it from the tap. 'Sorry. Would you rather have sparkling? I have some in the fridge—'

'Tap water is fine.'

I move to the kettle and flick the switch, readying the cafetière, my back to her as I try to regroup. Keen for something to do with my hands.

'I wanted to know how you're doing,' I say, turning. 'The trial. It was awful.' I pause. 'For all of us. I wanted to reach out to you straight after. But it felt too soon.'

She came every day to the trial. She listened while Isabella tried to blame her. For cutting her off. Barbara sat, back straight, through all of it. Isabella, so obviously mad and bad, trying to pin the murder and all the mayhem on her own mother.

I remember the hush in the room as the prosecution explained what had happened at the end. How Special Constable Amelie Hill so madly but brilliantly saved the day. *The bird.* The long shot that made the jury gasp.

'I'm not sure there's really anything more to say.' Barbara sips the water. 'Except that I'm so sorry. What Isabella put your family through.'

'Not your fault,' I say, picking up the kettle as it clicks off to pour the steaming water into the cafetière.

'Isn't it?'

I spin round, frowning, kettle still in hand.

I was shocked that it was Ruby of all people who'd called the police. Ruby who so hated the police. Or rather hated that I'd called the police on Ned.

Isabella was shot in the shoulder when she ran after me. Apparently, she's always hated birds. Feathers. Flapping of any kind.

I won't tell Barbara that I wake often at the sound of that single shot. In my dreams. Mistaking it for thunder.

'It really wasn't your fault,' I repeat quietly, finally putting the kettle down.

Four months since the trial and I overhear from whispering – in the library, in the coffee shops and in the pharmacy – that she doesn't leave the house. Hardly ever.

'He *was* my favourite. Ned. What she said in court. About him being my favourite. I'm ashamed to admit it. But that was true.'

She frowns as I heat milk in the microwave, then take the other stool at the breakfast bar. Steam rising from my coffee. The milk far too hot.

'That doesn't make any of what she did *your* fault,' I say again, feeling tears brimming. Out of my depth. That backpack full of boulders. My shoulders. Her shoulders.

'The truth is she was very difficult, even as a child. Cold. *Different*.' She draws a long, slow breath. 'Hard to love, if I'm honest. But I did love her. Or at least I tried my best. She was unkind to her friends. Unkind to me. Always scheming. And telling lies. But I swear I had no idea what she really was. What she'd become, I mean. I was just afraid for her.'

I know all of this already. It came out in sentencing. Isabella's very troubled life. Expelled from school. In trouble with the police. *Sociopathic tendencies from a young age.* Why a maximum-security prison was recommended by the judge.

Barbara tells me that she gave Isabella some money after she was released from jail for ripping off pensioners. A fake investment fund for grandchildren. It had a fancy website with fancy fake charts and testimonials. But it didn't exist. Isabella pocketed all the money.

'When she was released, I removed her from my will but I gave her a lump sum. Not a lot. But enough to regroup. She wanted to go to Canada for real and I said it was a final, one-off payment. One last chance to make something of herself. I thought she really had gone abroad. But turns out she used that fund to set up the StarBonders scam and to fund her campaign against your whole family. So – yes. I do feel to blame. She wouldn't have been able to afford all that travelling – Scotland and Paris – without that money I gave her.'

She pauses, releasing a long sigh, and I don't know what to say.

'It's so hard when you have a big inheritance. Trying to get it right with the kids. You want to help them but not to spoil them. I take full responsibility for getting it wrong. With Isabella and with Ned too. Oh – he could be lazy. I know that. But he was a good person at his core. Smiley. Open book.' Her turn to pause. 'Until the drugs. They changed his personality. Changed everything. I was told to try tough love. Cut his allowance to try to cut off the drugs. Didn't work out how I hoped.'

We sit in silence for a while and given this was my idea, I feel embarrassed to be so ill prepared. I think of how lonely it must have been for her, handling all the challenges without a partner. Her husband died young. A heart attack in his forties. I couldn't imagine life without Joe. All the decisions without Joe. So lucky that he came back to us. Made such a good recovery.

'So how are your girls? Are they here?' She glances around as if looking for the debris of family life.

I feel a pang at the tidiness.

'No. They're both giving university another shot.'

'Oh, good. That's good.' She looks surprised.

'Yes. We're all a bit nervous about it. Them and me. But they have good support. Counsellors and so on. And Amelie has been really kind to them. The young special constable at the trial. Do you remember her?'

'I do.'

'Turns out she was taken as a child. Held hostage herself. Just eight years old.' I clear my throat. Sip my coffee. Burn my lips. Rush to the sink for a glass of water.

'Goodness. I had no idea.'

'It's why she decided to join the force, apparently.' I turn, my bottom pressed against the sink. 'Put something back after being saved herself. She's been talking to Clara a lot. Helping her. And I'm so grateful because Clara is slowly doing better. So much stronger these days.'

I sip the water to soothe my lips and think of Clara's joy at the hair growing back at last. She wears it short now and it really suits her. No more wigs. She sent me a picture just this morning of the back of her head. *Look. It's getting so much thicker, Mum . . .*

'And you're working with charities again, I hear?' Her eyebrows are raised.

She must have seen the press coverage. I've managed to get our work in the local papers and on socials. Even a few features in the nationals. I'm working with suicide prevention charities with the mother of Zoe. The girl who *survived.* They're doing mother–daughter workshops in schools, warning about scammers and negative social media. And urging people in crisis to look to their loved ones for support. And helplines and professionals. *Talk to someone. You must talk to someone . . .*

'Yes. I'm enjoying it. Good to use my skillset for something positive again,' I say.

'Is that why I'm here? You want me to help with your campaigns. Because I'm sorry but I really don't feel strong enough to talk about—'

'No, no. I would never expect that. I messaged you because I wanted to say that we're doing OK. And to ask how *you're* coping?' I move back across to the breakfast counter, thinking now not of Isabella but of Ned. 'I find it satisfying, the campaign work. But I've found it very difficult. The whole empty nest thing. And it made me think how much harder it must be—'

'It is what it is,' she interrupts. 'I cope. Keep myself to myself. Don't go out much.' Again she sips at her water.

'Yes. I heard that.'

'So people are still talking about me?'

'Sorry. I didn't mean to imply that. To say the wrong thing. It's just I heard about the vandalism.'

It was in the newspaper last week. All the windows of her huge orangery broken. Paint sprayed on her garage. *StarBonders killer.* It all came out in the trial and in the press. How Isabella had pressured StarBonders followers for money. Preyed on young and vulnerable people; on their weaknesses. Tricked them. Emails were read out, showing how she drove one young woman to take her life. And the second girl, who nearly succeeded. StarBonders took money for 'readings' and star mapping, but when the girls ran out of money, the emails became bullying. And cruel. Warning that if they did not find more money, they would be destined to be forever lonely. Failures in love.

It was awful to hear and some families are now trying to sue. But StarBonders is bankrupt.

'Yes. It's been very difficult. I thought it might blow over. But that was naive of me. I'm setting up a fund, to offer money to the victims. Voluntarily. My lawyer's handling it but it's very complicated. I doubt it will ever be enough.' Her voice sounds terribly tired. She looks at me very directly. 'I may have to move. I don't know yet. I've had extra security installed. Cameras and so on.'

She narrows her eyes and leans forward. 'Look. It's kind of you to ask how I am. But I still don't understand why I'm here.' She pauses. 'Is it about money? Compensation for your daughters? Because I do sympathise, but it might be better if we let my lawyer handle—'

'Goodness, no. No.' I'm shaken. 'This is not about money. No. Definitely not.'

I'm appalled she would think that. I take in her haunted eyes and the truth is I don't have the words. To explain.

That I've never really thought about it before. The *mothers*. When you see a crime report on the television, you think of the victims. Rage at the guilty. But when I saw the story about the orangery and the graffiti . . .

'The thing is. What I wanted to tell you is that I wish I could go back in time,' I say suddenly. 'I was wrong to phone the police over Ned. That's what I needed to say to you. To your face.' I am thinking that she lost Isabella because she was bad to her core. But Ned? 'I should have phoned *you* and Ruby, not the police. I'm sorry I did that.' Again, I'm speaking faster and faster. Babbling. 'But I was afraid, for Ruby, and I did the wrong thing.'

She doesn't answer at first. Looks away to the garden and then finally back at me.

'Do you remember when we bumped into each other in that coffee shop?' she says.

'Of course.'

'I really did hate you back then. Blamed you utterly.' She pauses. 'This will sound terrible but it sort of helped me to hate you. I'm ashamed to say that I enjoyed the rage.' Her voice breaks. A pause. 'But so much has happened. I don't have the energy for hate anymore. And I don't blame you now.'

She sips again at her water. 'The fact is, Ned got unlucky. Fell in too young with the wrong crowd. He was actually in rehab three times. Did you know that?'

'No. I didn't realise it was more than once.'

'Three . . . times. And it never worked. So the truth is I blamed you because I didn't want to blame him.' She has tears brimming now and I again feel so very sorry for upsetting her. In that coffee shop. And now too. 'I think I knew deep down that he was never going to get clean. Stay clean. That the drugs were always going to find him. Finish him in the end. I was just shocked it happened so soon. So *young*.' A pause. 'I thought I had more time. To keep trying to *save* him.'

I reach across the counter and put my hand on hers. I expect her to pull away. But to my surprise, she doesn't.

'You're the first person, other than journalists, to ask to see me,' she says. 'Most people cross the road.'

I again take in the exhaustion in her eyes. 'Listen,' I say. 'Joe quit his job in sales.'

'Right. I'm sorry about that—'

'No, no. It's not a bad thing. It's a good thing. I had no idea he hated it so much. His job,' I add. 'But he had this sort of epiphany when he got better, after the coma. Seize the day and all that. He decided he wanted to change his whole life. Follow his dream. And he's like a different person. So much happier.'

I think of the time Joe and I sat up talking, really talking into the early hours. Incredulous. How Isabella was the woman in the nightclub. Tried to target him too and was furious when he wouldn't pay. He told me how sorry he was about all our conflict. How afraid he had been to tell me the truth about his work. How much he had grown to hate it.

'So what's he doing now?'

'Well, I have to admit that's why you're here.'

She looks confused and I find that I'm nervous to say it. Spit it out in case it sounds ridiculous.

'Joe has set up a landscape gardening business. I've honestly never seen him so happy. It's early days but it's going well. And Ned was always telling Ruby – and us too – how brilliant you are at gardening. Particularly good with design. And greenhouses.'

Still she's frowning.

'And I wondered, *we* wondered, if we might check in with you occasionally? For advice. Like a consultant. We would pay you, of course—'

'I don't want money. Don't need money. So what are you saying? That you'd like me to be involved in Joe's new *business*?' Her tone is incredulous.

'Yes. We would. We're doing a project for a new client with a garden very like yours. Huge. And we wondered if we could bounce Joe's plan past you. See what you think. They want a greenhouse and we're not entirely sure where to position it. We know you have a lot of experience and we wondered if we might pick your brains. Maybe over lunch?' I pause, my face flushed now. Cards on the table.

'The truth is we find it very quiet at home with the girls gone. And there aren't many people who understand what we've all been through. Why Joe needs this change. And so do I. And I wondered if maybe a change might be the thing for you too?'

I don't add that Joe and I lie in bed some nights talking about her now. How dreadful to be alone with what Isabella did.

Ned gone forever too.

Again she looks away to the window, to our own garden, which is thriving under Joe's new eye. A large vegetable patch and polytunnel at the far end beyond the lawn. I think of how animated

Joe is these days. Talking about design *as a series of rooms*, sketching his ideas at the breakfast bar. Muddy boots in the hall.

'I couldn't. I wouldn't want to intrude. I go mad, thinking about what Isabella did to your family. To all of you. I would find it—'

'*Please*,' I say, suddenly gripping her hand, maybe a little too tightly. Meeting her eyes. 'We would genuinely like you to be involved. Maybe a lunch together to at least talk it over?'

'And your girls would be OK with that?' Still she sounds incredulous. 'After everything that—'

'It was actually Ruby who suggested it.'

I think of the year when we did not talk at all. Me and Ruby. And now the *love you* WhatsApp from her at the end of every single day.

Barbara with no messages at all.

'I suppose I could think about it,' she says.

I continue to stare into her face, still holding on to her hand, thinking of all the other mothers. Of the bad and the broken. The smashed windows and graffiti. The skin and the bones.

Serving sentences for crimes they did not commit.

I sip my coffee. *Blow. Sip.* Still too hot.

I think of my own shell shock. That moment I discovered meeting Isabella in Paris was never an accident. That she wheedled my schedule out of an unsuspecting Clara and *stalked* me. Couldn't believe her luck when I offered the room share. Stole my hairbrush and some business cards from my bag. Took an imprint of my house keys.

'I'm going to take that as a yes,' I say finally, lifting my chin. *Enough now.*

Barbara doesn't answer, but after a long pause, she squeezes my hand and mouths *Thank you*. We sit very still. And only in this moment do I realise that she has started to cry. Silently.

As have I.

ACKNOWLEDGEMENTS

I am often asked where I get ideas for my thrillers and so I have a confession. And a big thank-you.

The seed for this story grew from a genuine anecdote told at a lovely girly lunch by one of the nicest people you could meet.

Yes. One of my friends really did once share her twin hotel room near an airport with a stranded young woman. And my friend really did have a moment, wondering – *Is this OK/safe?*

In real life, it all ended very happily. A genuine Good Samaritan act. But this author brain was immediately doing a fictional somersault, thinking . . . *Hang on; that could have gone horribly wrong.*

What if? What if?

The anecdote stayed with me. And so Laura, my fictional Good Samaritan (and nothing like my friend, by the way), was eventually born. And the rest, as we writers are prone to say, is history.

I can only apologise for my dark imagination turning such an entirely innocent happening into this twisty story.

Mea culpa!

I am also often asked if Matthew, the lovely Amelie and Mel Sanders are in other stories. So I'm very happy to report that the magnificent Matthew Hill is in *all* my psychological thrillers. They're all standalones and don't have to be read in a set order.

Sometimes Matthew has a big part. Sometimes just a cameo. But I do hope you'll enjoy meeting him, Melanie Sanders and the younger Amelie in other books.

And now to my other thank-yous. First, huge gratitude to my editors Maisie Lawrence and Ian Pindar, who have so skilfully helped me to polish this story into its best possible shape.

Next a herogram to my superstar agent Madeleine Milburn, whose enthusiastic cheerleading and expert guidance have been so critical to my author career.

Big hugs to my gorgeous family, who have always been the biggest fans of my writing, even in the long and difficult years when I was struggling to get my first book deal.

And finally, as always, my sincere thanks to *you* – my readers. I would be nowhere without you. Your support, reviews and messages mean the world to me. So, if you have enjoyed *What Have I Done?*, I would be so grateful if you would leave a rating or review on Amazon as these really do help other readers to find my books.

Also – feel free to say hello. You can find my website at www.teresadriscoll.com and can also say hi on X @TeresaDriscoll or www.facebook.com/teresadriscollauthor and Instagram @ tkdriscoll_author.

I will be delighted to hear from you.

Warm wishes to you all,

Teresa

If you couldn't stop turning the pages as Laura tried to keep her family safe, then you'll absolutely love *I Am Watching You* by Teresa Driscoll.

What would it take to make you intervene?

When Ella overhears two attractive young men flirting with teenage girls on a train, she thinks nothing of it – until she realises they are fresh out of prison and her maternal instinct is put on high alert. But just as she's decided to call for help, something stops her. The next day, she wakes up to the news that one of the girls – beautiful, green-eyed Anna – has disappeared. And now someone is watching Ella too . . .

An utterly gripping and incredibly addictive psychological thriller packed with twists! Available now or keep reading for an exclusive extract!

JULY 2015

CHAPTER 1

THE WITNESS

I made a mistake. I know that now.

The only reason I did what I did was what I heard on that train. And I ask you, in all truthfulness – how would you have felt?

Until that moment, I had never considered myself prudish. Or naive. OK, OK, so I had a pretty conventional – some might say sheltered – upbringing but . . . Heavens. Look at me now. I've lived a bit. Learned a lot. Pretty average, I would argue, on the Richter scale of moral behaviour, which is why what I heard so shook me.

I thought they were nice girls, you see.

Of course, I really shouldn't listen in on other people's conversations. But it's impossible not to on public transport, don't you find? So many barking into their mobile phones while everyone else ramps up the volume to compete. To be heard.

On reflection, I would probably not have become so sucked in had my book been better, but to my eternal regret I bought the book for the same reason I bought the magazine with wind turbines on the cover.

I read somewhere that by your forties you are supposed to care more about what you think of others than what they think of you – so why is it I am still waiting for this to kick in?

If you want to buy Hello! *magazine, just buy it, Ella.* What does it matter what the bored student on the cash desk thinks?

But no. I pick the obscure environmental magazine and the worthy biography, so that by the time the two young men get on with their black plastic bin bags at Exeter, I am bored to my very bones.

A question for you now.

What would you think if you saw two men board a train, each holding a black bin bag – contents unknown? For myself, the mother of a teenage son whose bedroom is subject to a health and safety order, I merely think, *Typical. Couldn't even find a holdall, lads?*

They are loud and boisterous, skylarking in the way that so many men in their twenties do – only just making the train, with the plumped-up platform guard blowing his whistle in furious disapproval.

After messing about with the automatic door – *open, shut, open, shut* – which they inevitably find hilarious beyond the facts, they settle into the seats nearest the luggage racks. But then, apparently spotting the two girls from Cornwall, they glance knowingly at each other and head further down the carriage to the seats directly behind them.

I smile to myself. See, I'm no killjoy. I was young once.

I watch the girls go all quiet and shy, one widening her eyes at her friend – and yes, one of the men is especially striking, like a model or a member of a boy band. And it all reminds me of that very particular feeling in your tummy.

You know.

So I am not at all surprised or in the least bit disapproving when the men stand up and the good-looking one then leans over the top of the dividing seats, wondering if he might fetch the girls something from the buffet, '. . . seeing as I'm going?'

Next there are name swaps and quite a bit of giggling, and the dance begins.

Two coffees and four lagers later, the young men have joined the girls – all seated near enough for me to follow the full conversation.

I know, I know. I really shouldn't be listening, but we've been over this. I'm bored, remember. They're loud.

So then. The girls repeat what I have already gleaned from their earlier gossiping. This trip to London is their first solo visit to the capital – a gift from their parents to celebrate the end of GCSEs. They are booked into a budget hotel, have tickets for *Les Misérables* and have never been this excited.

'You kidding me? You really never been to London on your own before?' Karl, the boy-band lookalike, is amazed. 'Can be a tricky place, you know, girls. London. You need to watch yourselves. Taxi not tube when you get out of the theatre. You hear me?'

I am liking Karl now. He is recommending shops and market stalls – also a club where he says they will be safe if they fancy some decent music and dancing after the show. He is writing down the name on a piece of paper for them. Knows the bouncer. 'Mention my name, OK?'

And then Anna, the taller of the two friends from Cornwall, is wondering about the black bags and I am secretly delighted that she has asked, for I am curious also, smiling in anticipation of the teasing. *Boys. So disorganised. What are you like, eh?*

But no.

The two young men have just got out of prison. The black bags contain their personal effects.

I can actually hear myself swallowing then – a rush of fluid suddenly filling the back of my throat and my pulse now unwelcome percussion in my ear.

The pause button is pressed, but not for long enough. Much too quickly, the girls are regrouping. 'You having us on?'

No. The boys are not having them on. They have decided to be straight with people. Have made their mistakes and paid their dues but refuse to be ashamed.

Cards on the table, girls? Karl has served a sentence at Exeter prison for assault; Antony for theft. Karl was merely sticking up for a friend, you understand, and – hand on heart – would do the same again. His friend was being picked on in a bar and he hates bullying.

Me, I am struggling with the paradox – bullying versus assault, and do we really lock people up for minor altercations? – but the girls seem fascinated, and in their sweet and liberal naivety are saying that loyalty is a good thing and they had a bloke from prison who came into their school once and told them how he had completely turned his life around after serving time over drugs. Covered in tattoos, he was. *Covered.*

'Wow. Jail. So what was that really like?'

It is at this point I consider my role.

Privately I am picturing Anna's mother toasting her bottom by her Aga, worrying with her husband if their little girl will be all right, and he is telling her not to fuss so. *They are growing up fast. Sensible girls. They will be fine, love.*

And I am thinking that they are not fine at all. For Karl is now thinking that the safest thing for the girls would be to have someone who knows London well chaperoning them during their visit.

Karl and Antony are going to stay with friends in Vauxhall and fancy a big night to celebrate their release. How about they meet the girls after the theatre and try the club together?

This is when I decide that I need to phone the girls' parents. They have named their hamlet. Anna lives on a farm. It's not rocket science. I can phone the post office or local pub; how many farms can there be?

But now Anna isn't sure at all. No. They should probably have an early night so they can hit the shops tomorrow morning. They have this plan, see, to go to Liberty's first thing because Sarah is determined to try on something by Stella McCartney and get a picture on her phone.

Good girl, I am thinking. Sensible girl. *Spare me the intervention, Anna.* But there is a complication, for Sarah seems suddenly to have taken a shine to Antony. There is a second trip to the buffet and they swap seats on their return – Anna now sitting with Karl and Sarah with Antony, who is telling her about his regrets at stuffing up his life. He only turned to crime out of desperation, he says, because he couldn't get a job. Couldn't support his son.

Son?

It sweeps over me, then. The shadow from the thatched canopy of my chocolate-box life – me shrinking smaller and smaller into the shade as Antony explains that he is fighting his ex for access, telling Sarah that there is no way he is going to have his son growing up not knowing his dad. 'Don't you think that would be just terrible, Sarah? For him to grow up not knowing his dad?'

Sarah is the one who is surprising me now – there's a catch in her throat as she says she thinks it's really cool that he cares so very much, because many young men wouldn't, would just walk away from the responsibility. 'I feel really awful now. Us banging on about Stella McCartney.'

And the truth? At this point I have absolutely no idea about any of it anymore. What do I know? A woman whose son's only access battle involved an 18-certificate film at the local cinema.

An hour of whispering follows and I try very hard to read again, to take in the pluses of the quieter generation of wind turbines, but then Antony and Sarah are off to the buffet again. *More lager*, I am thinking. *Big mistake, Sarah*. And this is when I decide.

Yes. I will head to the buffet myself on the pretext of needing coffee, and in the queue or passing in the corridor will feign trouble with my phone. I will ask Sarah for help – hoping to separate her from Antony for a quiet word – and give a little warning that she needs to step away from this nonsense or I will be phoning her parents. *Immediately, you understand me, Sarah? I can find out their number.*

Our carriage is three away from the buffet. I stumble into seats passing through the second, bump-bump-bumping my thighs, and then feel for my phone in the pocket of my jacket as I pass through the automatic doors into the connecting space.

And that's when I hear them.

No shame. No attempt even to keep themselves quiet about it. Making out, loud and proud, in the train toilet. Rutting in the cubicle like a pair of animals.

I know it's them from what he's saying. How long it's been. How grateful he is. 'Sarah, oh Sarah . . .'

And yes, I admit it. I am completely shocked to the core of my very being. Hot with humiliation. Furious. Winded and desperate, more than anything on this planet, to escape the noise.

Also the shame of my naivety. My ridiculous assumptions.

I stumble across the corridor to the next set of automatic doors and into the carriage, breathless and flustered in the scramble to put distance between myself and the evidence of my miscalculation.

Nice girls?

In the buffet queue, I am listening again to the pulse in my ear as I wonder if someone else will have heard them by now. Even reported them?

And then I am thinking, *Report them? Report them to whom, Ella? Will you just listen to yourself? Other people will do precisely what you should have done from the off. They will mind their own.*

At which point my emotions begin to change and I am wondering instead how I came to be this out of touch, this buttoned up. This woman who evidently has not the first clue about young people. Or anything much.

Into my head now – a kaleidoscope of memories. Pictures torn around the edges. The magazines we found in our son's room. That night after the cinema when we came home early to find Luke trying to override the Sky security to watch porn.

So that on this wretched train, I find that I need very urgently to speak to my husband. To my Tony. To reset my compass.

I need to ask him if the whole problem here is not with them but with me. *Am I altogether ridiculous, Tony? No, really – I need you to be honest with me. When we had that row over the Sky channels and Luke's magazines.*

Am I the most terrible prude? Am I?

I do try to ring him, actually – that night from the hotel after the conference session. I want to tell him how I did the sensible thing and moved to the other end of the train. Minded my own. The girls clearly quite streetwise enough.

But he is out and hasn't taken his mobile, being one of the few who still thinks they give you brain cancer, and so I speak instead to Luke and find that it calms me to hear him describe supper – a tagine from a recipe he downloaded on a new app. He loves to cook, my Luke, and I am teasing him about the state of the kitchen, betting he has used every appliance and pan on the property.

Then it is the morning in the hotel.

I so hate this sensation – that out-of-body numbness born of air conditioning, a foreign bed and lack of discipline over the minibar. My hotel treat – a brandy or two after a long day.

It is barely six thirty and I long for more sleep. Ten futile minutes and I give up, eyeing the sachets of sadness in the little bowl alongside the kettle. I always do this in hotel rooms. Kid myself that I will drink instant coffee just this once, only to pour it down the bathroom sink.

I stare at the line of empty miniatures, wincing as a terrible thought flutters into the room. I glance at the phone by the bed and feel a punch of dread, the familiar frisson of fear that I have done something embarrassing, something I am going to regret.

I turn back to the row of bottles and remember that after the second brandy last night, I decided to phone directory enquiries to track down the girls' parents. I go cold momentarily at the thought of this, my memory still hazy. *Did you actually ring? Think, Ella, think.*

I stare again at the phone and concentrate hard. Ah, yes. I am remembering now, my shoulders relaxing as I finally see it. I was holding the phone and then at the *very* point of dialling, I realised that I wasn't thinking straight, and not just because of the brandy. My motivation was skewed. I wanted to phone not because I was worried for the girls, but as a punishment, because I was angry at how Sarah had made me feel.

And so I did the sensible thing. I put the phone back down, I turned out the light and I went to sleep.

Good. This is very good. The relief now so overwhelming that I decide by way of celebration that I will try the instant coffee after all.

I flick on the kettle first and then the television. And that is when it comes. The single moment – suspended at first and then stretching, stretching, beyond this room, beyond this city. The moment in time in which I realise my life is never going to be the same again.

Not ever.

The sound is muted from the late-night film I watched with the subtitles on to spare disturbing the guests next door.

But the picture is unmistakable. Beautiful. A photograph from her Facebook page. Her green eyes glowing and her blonde hair cascading down her back. She is at the beach; I recognise St Michael's Mount behind her.

And somehow my body has zoomed backwards – through the pillow and the bedstead and the wall – until I am watching the screen from much further away. This screen that is scrolling putrid, awful words: *Missing . . . Anna . . . Missing . . . Anna . . .* The kettle screaming angry clouds onto the mirror while I am planning the calls in my head all at once.

A black and terrible jumble of excuses. None of them good enough. To the police. To Tony.

You have to understand that I was going to phone . . .

ABOUT THE AUTHOR

Photo © 2015 Claire Tregaskis

For more than twenty-five years as a journalist – including fifteen years as a BBC TV news presenter – Teresa Driscoll followed stories into the shadows of life. Covering crime for so long, she watched and was deeply moved by all the ripples each case caused, and the haunting impact on the families, friends and witnesses involved. It is those ripples that she explores in her darker fiction.

Teresa's novels have sold more than two million copies and have been published in twenty languages. She lives in beautiful Devon with her family. You can find out more about her books on her website (www.teresadriscoll.com) or by following her on X (@TeresaDriscoll), Facebook (www.facebook.com/teresadriscollauthor) or Instagram (@tkdriscoll_author).

Follow the Author on Amazon

If you enjoyed this book, follow Teresa Driscoll on Amazon to be notified when the author releases a new book!

To do this, please follow these instructions:

Desktop:

1) Search for the author's name on Amazon or in the Amazon App.
2) Click on the author's name to arrive on their Amazon page.
3) Click the 'Follow' button.

Mobile and Tablet:

1) Search for the author's name on Amazon or in the Amazon App.
2) Click on one of the author's books.
3) Click on the author's name to arrive on their Amazon page.
4) Click the 'Follow' button.

Kindle eReader and Kindle App:

If you enjoyed this book on a Kindle eReader or in the Kindle App, you will find the author 'Follow' button after the last page.

Printed in Dunstable, United Kingdom